Mary H. Villars

Stories of Home and Home Folks or Leaves from a Parsonage

Portfolio

Volume I

Mary H. Villars

Stories of Home and Home Folks or Leaves from a Parsonage Portfolio
Volume I

ISBN/EAN: 9783744750585

Printed in Europe, USA, Canada, Australia, Japan

Cover: Foto ©Andreas Hilbeck / pixelio.de

More available books at **www.hansebooks.com**

STORIES

OF

HOME AND HOME FOLKS;

OR,

Leaves from a Parsonage Portfolio.

BY

MRS. MARY H. VILLARS.

VOLUME I.

EACH VOLUME COMPLETE IN ITSELF.

CINCINNATI:

PRINTED BY WALDEN & STOWE,

FOR THE AUTHOR.

1882.

DEDICATION.

PREFACE.

IN placing before the public this little volume, I do not presume that it will attract so much by its merit as a literary production as from the fact that almost every story has its origin in some real incident, and that it has for its characters real and not ideal heroes and heroines. It is in *fact* what it is in *name*, Stories of Home and Home Folks.

I have not found it necessary to go outside the bounds of my native land for material for my pen pictures, but have culled from the experiences and acquaintances of sixteen years in the itinerancy of the Methodist Episcopal Church.

My readers may possibly recognize here and there a character, the original of which was either a friend or an acquaintance, and perchance some who read these pages will recognize, if not themselves, at least sentiments to which they have at some time given utterance; and while these stories may not interest all, yet I trust there is enough of real home life and heart sympathy to touch an answering chord in the hearts of those to whom it is dedicated, and that the effort to instruct as well as to please will not prove an entire failure.

It has not been my aim to have my pictures overdrawn, nor to take any but home pictures of the common every-day life of the common every-day folk, who make up the larger portion of this busy world of ours. It is not the stories of the rich and great that I record, but as a rule only "The short and simple annals of the poor," from the little perplexities of the child to the trials and victories of maturer years; from Maggie's trials or Bennie's simple faith, to the struggle of the man or woman over the temptation to distrust the watchful oversight of a loving Father, I have tried to be faithful to the real life of the people with whom I have come in contact; and if in my efforts to "point a moral or adorn a tale" I shall have been the means of lifting up some burdened one,—if I shall have succeeded in pointing some troubled sister to the Source of all consolation, if I shall have been so fortunate as to trace some steps of the life of those who have gained victories over self or over outside hindrances, footsteps that another similarly situated,

"Seeing, may take heart again,"

I shall be content, feeling that the mission for which these pages were written is being accomplished. Firm in the belief that

"Whate'er may die and be forgot,
Work done for God, it dieth not,"

this little volume is thus sent out upon its mission by the

AUTHOR.

CONTENTS.

8 CONTENTS.

STORIES

OF

HOME AND HOME FOLKS.

THE MORGAN FAMILY.

A Christmas Story.

CHRISTMAS eve has come once more—that evening so filled with joyful anticipation to the young, and memories both of joys and sorrows to the middle-aged and the gray haired. In mansion or cottage it would be remembered and observed in ways as various as the tastes and ability of the occupants.

In the home of Henry Morgan there had been such preparation as their circumstances would allow, and the children, four in number, were full of excitement over the prospect of extra puddings and pies, and the presents which they hoped to receive on the morrow; for the mother, firm in the opinion that there is as much happiness in the anticipation as in the possession of a treasure, had led them to expect gifts of some kind, and each had in turn wished and guessed as to the gifts they would receive. The Christmas preparations in the home of the Morgans would have seemed meager indeed to their wealthy neighbors; but here it was a rare treat, such as the eldest child, a girl of eleven years, could not remember having enjoyed in her short life.

A little less than one year previous Henry Morgan had signed the pledge of total abstinence, and, contrary to the prophecies of those who had no faith in "temperance excitement," he had thus far faithfully kept it. From the bright promise of his early manhood and marriage, he had gone down, through drink, step by step, until at the end of twelve years his little home had been taken for drink-bills, and his family reduced to such poverty and wretchedness as only the family of the inebriate can know; for there is a certain pride about a poverty which comes through sickness or misfortune which enables the poor to hold up their heads, even though they may have only rags and a crust. But the poverty which comes through dissipation, and consequent degradation of a loved one, brings with it a sense of shame and heartache that must be buried out of sight, and which only gnaws the deeper because it is covered up from the world.

Those of Morgan's friends who had seen his fall and sincerely lamented it, had rejoiced when he signed the pledge, and made an effort to regain his own self-respect and his former position in society. A printer, and thorough master of his trade, he was not long in obtaining employment when once it was known that he had given up drink; and while some shook their heads and doubted, there were others who had faith in the man and his strength of purpose,

and who gave him a word of cheer and a "God
bless you!" when they saw his struggle with appetite.
Christian friends had gathered around him, and Mrs.
Morgan's pastor, a man who could thoroughly sympathize with the unfortunate in their effort to reform,
had gently and lovingly pointed him to the true
Source of strength, and the man had accepted it
humbly, yet confidently, and walked in that strength
from day to day.

Little by little their circumstances had improved.
He had rented a more comfortable house, and had
added little comforts to the rooms. His family were
decently clothed and his children attended the public
schools, while his wife's careworn face was gradually
taking on a more hopeful look.

On this particular evening, as Mrs. Morgan sits at
her work, completing a pair of mittens which are to
occupy the stockings of one of the sleepers to-night,
and to do service in a merry game of snow-ball on
the morrow, she is busy with other thoughts than of
the work in her hands. Her husband is sitting at
the table near by, looking over a memorandum of
the year's receipts and expenditures. His face is
partially turned from her, but she casts an occasional
glance toward him as she works, while her face seems
half-way between smiles and tears. She is thinking
of one year ago, when, with scarcely fuel enough to
keep her half-clad children from freezing, and with
but a crust of bread and a few potatoes for their
evening meal, she had waited, with weary limbs and
with aching heart, the steps of him she called husband. She remembers how he came at a late hour

reeling under the effects of liquor bought with the
money which should have given her children food
and fire. As the picture rises before her in all its
sickening realities, the tears gather in her eyes and
course the way down her cheeks. But as she brushes
them hastily away, lest he should look up, and, seeing
her tears, divine the cause, there comes to her heart
a sense of thankfulness as she looks on her husband
as he sits opposite her, clothed in his right mind, and
her tears flow afresh ; but they are tears of joy and
gratitude to God for the restoration of him she loves.
With a silent thanksgiving for the present happiness,
and a prayer for the future of her family, she takes
up the work which had fallen from her hands.

Presently Morgan closes his memorandum, and,
laying it on the table, turns toward his wife. The
movement is a very quiet one; but Mary Morgan
feels that his gaze is fastened on her, and she does
not look up, for she knows there are traces of
tears still on her face, and she does not want him
to see them to-night; for she says, "He will not
understand fully, and it will only pain him." But he
sees, nevertheless, and *thinks* he understands. He
thinks it is because he had so little surplus funds
from which to purchase the supplies for the children's
treat; and then their house is so small and poor compared with one they once had; and the same picture
rises before his memory that had come to Mary a
few moments before, only it looks far worse to the
man than it did to the woman, because through it
all she had not been to blame, while in his heart
there are pangs of self-reproach.

"Mary." The word is spoken so suddenly and with such earnestness that Mary starts like a detected culprit. She looks up without speaking, and Morgan says, a little huskily, and with evident hesitation— for he can not readily speak his own heart, even to his best friend—"I wish I could have furnished you with a better house and something more for the children; but you said we were not to go in debt. I hope you will not feel disappointed too much. If I can only have a little time you shall see better days"—and, with a bitter sense of the time and money wasted in former years, he stops abruptly, crumbling his paper in his hands with a nervous motion, striving to hide the feelings that are choking his utterance.

"This will be a very happy Christmas to me," she says, earnestly. "O Henry, so much happier"—then, conscious of what she was about to say, stops short, affrighted lest she has given offense. But Morgan is not offended, although his quickened conscience has caught her meaning. In a moment he is standing at her side, his hand laid caressingly upon her shoulder as he looks into her upturned face and completes the sentence:

"So much happier than the last. Is that it?"

Mary only puts up both her hands, and, drawing his from her shoulder, holds it against her cheek, while her tears fall upon it. "Hush!" she says, almost in a whisper. "I did not intend to hurt you, but my heart is so full that I said more than I ought. I was contrasting to-night with last year, but I was not complaining. My heart is full of gratitude to our heavenly Father because he has dispersed the clouds and let the sun shine upon us once more. Let us forget the past, and only think of a brighter future for ourselves and our children." And, with her face beaming with a peace that can only come from a sure hope in Him who is strength to the weak, she looks the assurance and trust which she feels in her husband's steadfastness to his pledge and to his consecration vows.

For reply, he stoops and kisses her upturned face, and with a sigh, which is half relief and half regret, he drops into his chair, from which he has risen, and, leaning his elbows on the table, covers his face with his hands.

Mary resumes her knitting, which has made but slow progress during the last few minutes, and for a little while there is nothing heard in the room but the click of the needles and the tick, tick of the little clock as it measures off the passing minutes.

These two had not been in the habit of expressing their thoughts to each other very freely. Of late years Mary had grown accustomed to hiding her grief in her own bosom, thinking it better to hide in silence a wound that would only grow worse by exhibiting; and her husband, conscious of his wrong course, yet without sufficient courage or resolution to free himself from the chain that bound him, had shrunk within himself more and more, and the almost year of sobriety and pure living had only partially restored the confidence and confiding of former years.

Presently Morgan looks up with an earnest inquiry on his face: "Don't you sometimes feel as if the present was only a sort of pleasant dream? Or do you really have faith enough in me to believe that it will last?"

"I have faith in God, on whose arm you are leaning, and I have faith enough in *you*, because you are leaning on that arm, to believe that you will keep the vows made to God and to me."

"And you say this, knowing where I have been in the past? Knowing my weakness, you still believe in me and trust me?"

The question is asked in a voice deep and passionate in its earnestness, and Morgan waits with breathless anxiety to hear her words of faith in himself reiterated; as if the very hearing of them gave him strength.

The answer comes firm and decided, while her eyes meet his with a perfect confidence: "Knowing all the past, I still believe in you and trust you; for your strength is not your own, but God's."

Morgan draws a deep breath of relief, but bows his head upon the table as if in silent prayer. When he again looks up there is a new light beaming from his eyes, that are moist with unshed tears.

"Mary, I think I can endure almost any thing now. During the past year I have felt that I had so forfeited your confidence by my past life that you could never trust me again. But you have lifted the last burden from my heart; and, by God's help, I will never shame you again."

With what a sense of peace and rest did they kneel in silent prayer that Christmas eve, as, contemplating the advent of God's greatest and best gift to men, they also gave thanks for the gift of restored faith and confidence in each other. There was a dark past that must be covered up, and if not forgotten, then remembered as a warning by the one, and with tender charity by the other, while their future would only seem brighter by the contrast.

A Little Gossip.

WELL, that duty is performed, and I am glad it is over with." And as Mrs. Webb picked up an unfinished garment from the work-table, and seated herself preparatory to work, she did not look as if the call which she had just been making, although it may have been considered a duty, had been a very beneficial one.

"Was not your visit a pleasant one?" asked Mrs. Routh, the lady addressed.

"O, I don't know; perhaps I ought not to say it, but really, mother, that woman always makes me tired when I listen to her talk."

"What does she say, or what did she say on this particular occasion, that seems to have wearied you so?" asked the mother, quietly.

"Why, it was one continual gossip about her neighbors and her neighbors' affairs," responded Mrs. Webb, a little impatiently.

"I did not take her to be an ill-natured person when I have met her in your house."

"No, not particularly ill-natured, but she doesn't seem to be interested in any thing that I would call interesting. She talked about such trifles: the number of visitors Mrs. Morris has, the new dresses of Mrs. Hall and her daughter, the new parlor set which

2

Mrs. Newman has purchased, and wondered if her daughter Nellie wasn't going to marry soon; and— O dear, I'm glad to be home again."

"And I am sorry I urged you to go, if your visit was not a pleasant one," replied the mother; "but Mrs. Burton was so kind when you and the children were ill that I felt anxious that you should show a disposition to be neighborly. Did she seem disposed to criticise their actions—to find fault with them?"

"No, I can not say that she did. She did not seem to think they were extravagant or wicked, or any thing of that kind; only her mind seemed so taken up with other people's affairs, and I hate gossip."

Mrs. Routh did not reply, though an amused smile lurked about her mouth.

"What is there so very funny about what I have said?" asked Mrs. Webb, as she noticed the amused look.

"I was only wondering if there was much difference between Mrs. Burton's 'gossip' and our present conversation."

Mrs. Webb laughed, and colored at the implied rebuke. "O, well, you know I never give free reins to my tongue, except with you, and in this case I was provoked to it. But I thought you condemned gossip as much as I."

"And so I do, of the harmful kind; but we must not condemn too hastily, or speak too severely of the faults of others, or we shall find ourselves committing the very sin which we condemn. Gossip may be harmless in its intent, and yet lead to evil results; and it may be really ill-natured calumny, and intended to do injury; but very often it is mere idle chitchat, that does no harm except as it worries those who are compelled to listen; and you women who have the time and means for improving yourselves mentally are not half charitable enough toward those who must work and talk, or else not talk at all. From what I have seen of Mrs. Burton, I think she makes up for whatever she may lack in mental culture by being sweet and motherly."

"I am sure she has rare opportunity for developing the latter accomplishment, and to test the strength of its sweetness, with ten children to care for," answered Mrs. Webb.

"Yes; and the fact that she has been mother and housekeeper in one during the greater part of her married life, is some excuse for her not being thoroughly conversant with the current topics of the day; and we have great reason very often to be thankful for these same domestic women, even though their conversation may tire some of their strong-minded sisters."

"O mother, don't insinuate that I am strong-minded; I am sure I have all the symptoms of a weak mind. Haven't I been 'ruffling' and 'tucking' for the last three days? I am almost sure that you insisted on my making that little visit this afternoon to get me away from the sewing-machine, as much as from neighborly feeling for Mrs. Burton."

"Perhaps so — killed two birds with one stone," laughingly responded Mrs. Routh. "But, seriously, I do not think you make allowance enough for Mrs. Burton, and others situated as she is. From your own statement, her talk about her neighbors was prompted by kindly feeling, and not through a desire to criticise. As there was nothing wrong in Mrs. Morris having many visitors, nor in the new dresses of Mrs. Hall and her daughter, nor in Mrs. Newman's parlor set, if they were able to afford these luxuries, I presume they would not feel offended at the discussion of them by their neighbor; and as to every one being engaged in intellectual pursuits, I think if Hettie was as fond of books and magazines as her mistress is, our dinners would be rather scant at times."

"No doubt of it; I acknowledge that I do not want a book-worm or politician in my kitchen. I am glad Hettie likes her business, and sticks to it."

"Your neighbors and others, like her, have not time for much else besides their household and family affairs, and while they may not improve all their opportunities, yet there is excuse for the mother who is overwhelmed with such cares, and if she can make her hours of toil pass a little more pleasantly by a little harmless light talk, I do not see that she is any more censurable than those so-called great minds who insist that light reading is necessary for their mental rest and recreation."

Martha's Talent.

—◦—◦—◦—

OU are surely not done practicing already? Why, I am certain, Martha, that you have not been in the parlor three-quarters of an hour, and I have not heard the piano for half that length of time," said Mrs. Grey, as her daughter, a rosy-cheeked girl of fifteen, came into the sitting-room with a shiver, and held out her blue fingers to the glowing grate.

"I can't help that; I practiced as long as I could sit still; seems to *me* that it was nearer three hours than three-quarters, and I do n't see that I play one bit better than I did yesterday," said the daughter, despairingly.

"I am sorry you do not take more pains in learning your lessons. If you do not practice more, Miss Williams will certainly insist on your taking the lesson over again," said her mother, with a sigh.

"Over again," repeated Martha, impatiently. "Why, mamma, I have taken that lesson 'over again' for three whole weeks, and I played it more this afternoon than I ever did."

"Well, I do n't see, for *my* part, why you can not take more pains with your music. Your sister Nettie has no such trouble; her teacher says *she* always has good lessons," complained Mrs. Grey.

"O, well, Nettie *likes* it, and I do n't; and then,

as Miss Williams says, *she* has a talent.   Who wants
to sit two long hours drumming at the piano, only to
make a senseless racket, and annoy other people?   I
would rather help Mrs. Maloney wash *any* day," replied Martha, with a shrug of her shoulders.

"Martha, I am surprised that you are so ungrateful, after all that your father and I have done
for you."

"Well, I know you are very kind, but I have n't
patience to practice; and I don't see the good of it,
any way;" and Martha Grey ran out of the room, shut-
ting the door with a bang, and was soon in the kitch-
en, teasing the cook to let her make the waffles for tea.

"Sure, now, Miss Marthy, and had n't ye better
be 'tendin' to yer music, or finishin' the tidy ye begun for the rocker, instead of bothering here, and
soilin' yer nice dress wid the cookin'?" asked Hannah, good-naturedly.

"O, bother the music, and the tidy, too," answered Martha; "if I am in your *way*, I'll leave the
kitchen, but I am not going to practice any more to-
night, or knit either."

"I am sure y're never in *my* way, but ye know
yer mother do n't want ye to have great rough hands
that are niver fit to be seen in the parlor at all; and
they'll be rough enough, sure, if ye wurruk much in
the kitchen."

"O, fiddlesticks on the white hands; where's the
flour? I 'll make them white enough."

And Martha went dancing off to the pantry, with
a tin pan in one hand and shaking a big iron spoon
at Hannah, in mock defiance, with the other.

Martha Grey was a sore trial to her ladylike mother. Mrs. Grey was very anxious that her daughters should create a stir, if not in the world at large, at least in their own immediate circle, by their proficiency in music.

Nettie, the elder, a young lady of twenty years, bid fair to fulfill all her fond mother's expectations. Having considerable talent, a naturally musical voice, combined with almost indefatigable perseverance in practicing, she promised to become a musician of rather more than ordinary attainments; but Martha, alas, gave no such promise. With a fair talent for almost every other study, she entirely failed in this, although she had been compelled to sit at the piano, practicing scales and finger exercises for a part of every day for the past four years. To be sure, she had not practiced very diligently, for when shut up in the parlor to practice she invariably managed to spend the greater part of the time in rearranging the chairs, or the ornaments on the parlor table, and finally slipping out to the kitchen and coaxing Hannah to let her help cook, as in the commencement of our story, even at the risk of a reprimand from her mother for coming to the table with a face "as red as Mrs. Maloney's," and "such a contrast to Nettie's ladylike appearance."

On the evening after the above little incident, while Nettie was practicing a new piece, and Martha was curled up on the divan, deeply engrossed in Mungo Park, Mrs. Grey laid in her complaint to her husband for the one-hundredth time. " I wish you could persuade Martha to pay a little more attention

to her music. Really, I am quite discouraged. Only
yesterday, when Mrs. Fitzgerald was here to tea, I
asked Martha to play, and she broke down in the middle of the first piece. I was *so* mortified. I should not
have asked *her* to play, but Nettie had gone out
riding. I thought perhaps her failure would make
her more careful to-day, but she has been more neg-
ligent than usual." And Mrs. Grey sighed wearily.

Martha fidgeted uneasily; she was not, however,
much afraid of her father's reproofs. Not having
what his wife called "a talent for music" himself, he
generally tried to make excuses for his "stupid"
daughter. He looked from Mrs. Grey to Martha,
who was trying to look unconscious.

"Well, daughter, what have you to say?" asked
her father, kindly; "guilty, or not guilty?"

"Guilty, papa;" and then, looking up, added
archly, "but I made the cake for tea, and you know
Mrs. Fitzgerald thought it splendid, and congratu-
lated mamma on having such an excellent cook as
Hannah. But please, papa," more earnestly, "I can
not play on the piano worth a cent, and I am afraid I
never shall; but I *can* cook a little, and I like it too,"
glancing at her mother's shocked face. "I made the
waffles for tea, and you said yourself they were very
nice. And *I* made the toast this morning," triumphantly.

"Martha," said her mother, severely, "am I to
understand that you are in the *habit* of doing Hannah's work? I certainly can not afford to pay her for
work she does not do."

"O mamma, it isn't her fault," pleaded Martha,

frightened lest the blame of her disobedience should fall on Hannah. "She only let me because I teased her so; and indeed, mamma, she was so busy yesterday that she did not have time to make cake, and so I helped her."

"Martha," said Mr. Grey, kindly yet seriously, "I would be better pleased if you would attend to your music, too. I don't object to your cooking, though your mother says it soils your clothes and makes your hands rough; but your music lessons cost money, and I should like you to profit by them."

"But, papa, I just hate the piano. I would rather scour knives or churn, any day. I shall never play nicely, like Nettie; and what's the use trying?"

Mr. Grey smiled at his daughter's vigorous mode of expression, and turned to look into the fire. Mrs. Grey resumed her knitting, while Martha, muttering, "I guess my name spoiled me," turned to her book again.

After a few moments Mr. Grey said to his wife: "Suppose we let Martha give up her music, and let her do what she likes. It seems to me that it is no use to punish her by making her do what she says she *hates;* and you know it will be a great saving to my purse," he added, looking slyly toward his daughter.

"O, papa, do you really mean it? May I put away all my music, and do something I like?" asked the girl, breathlessly, as, throwing her book on the table, she danced across the room to slip one arm about her father's neck.

"There, there, wait a moment; I have not said

3

so yet," laughed Mr. Grey. "I only suggested it to your mother."

"But we have spent so much money giving her lessons that it seems too bad to have it all thrown away," objected her mother.

"Better throw that away, and then stop, than to keep throwing away. And if she wants to be Bridget, give her the chance, if it will make her any happier."

"O, *do* say yes," pleaded Martha, eagerly. "I can keep accounts and look after the expenses splendidly—better than you can, I expect, mamma; for *I* like it, and *you* don't."

Martha's eager voice had attracted Nettie's attention, and she came in to know what had happened. She contented herself with expressing her surprise at some "people's tastes." Mr. Grey drew his second daughter down on his knee, telling her to throw away her music if she wanted to, and declaring that one genius in the family was enough, any way.

The mother shed a few tears over her disappointment; but finally comforted herself with the thought that she had one daughter that she need not be ashamed of.

Martha was delighted with the idea of being allowed to "keep house instead of torturing that horrid piano;" and years after, when her mother's health failed and the whole responsibility of managing the household affairs fell upon her, both Mr. and Mrs. Grey were very thankful that they had a daughter who understood housekeeping and cookery, even though she could not appreciate Mozart or Mendelssohn.

Be Just as Well as Generous.

—◦—◦—◦—

RS. HARPER had just finished her afternoon toilet, and taken up her basket of
patchwork, when the door bell rang, and
Mrs. Wells, a neighbor, a sister in the Church,
came in to chat an hour or two. They were
both earnest workers, and the conversation soon
turned on Church interests.

"How much have you concluded to give
toward the new organ, Sister Harper?" asked
the visitor.

"I have not really decided yet; probably
twenty dollars."

"O Sister Harper, you surely will not stop at
twenty dollars, or twice twenty! Brother Brown
asked me to-day what I thought you would give,
and I told him *not less* than one hundred dollars,
any way."

"But, Sister Wells, I can not afford to give so
much. I am obliged to pay Ann three and a half
per week, and my husband's income is not large."

"O, but you don't know how to manage your
girls as well as *I* do. I was determined that Sister
Hill should not give more than *I*, so I subscribed
one hundred, though I could not see at the time
where the money was to come from. So I concluded
to pay out less for kitchen work, and now I only pay

Susan two and a half a week, and that saves fifty-two dollars during the year. The other forty-eight shall be got in some way. Susan objected at first, but I told her I could not pay a cent more, so she gave in at last. My work is heavier than yours too. Could n't you manage to save some in that way?"

"Perhaps I *might*, but really I do not feel like asking Ann to work for any less. She has an invalid mother who has to be helped."

"That is just what Susan said; but you can't believe the half they say. They always have some such story ready in case of an emergency."

"That may be true, but I feel that we are paying more for an organ than we can well afford, and more than is really necessary."

"Why, Sister Harper! you would n't have us buy a cheap instrument when the Presbyterians have such a nice one?"

"Of course I would, if we can not afford a better."

"Well I shall not be satisfied until we can have as good as any body else, and I shall do all *I* can do to get it. I am sorry you will not give more toward it."

"If I find that I can afford it I certainly shall, but I must pay my debts first," said Mrs. Harper pleasantly, and so the subject dropped.

The organ was purchased and placed in the church. Every body was pleased, for it was a fine affair, even surpassing the one in the neighboring church. Mrs. Wells gave her one hundred, and Mrs. Harper her twenty dollars, and others accordingly, some less than they were able to afford, others more. The Autumn passed away and Winter set in. Mrs. Wells, in the mean time, took frequent occasion to laugh at her friend for what she called her loose financiering. However, Mrs. Harper still insisted that she believed she had done her duty, and felt conscience clear, although she acknowledged that she would have been glad to have given more.

One cold bright day in the latter part of January Mrs. Harper called upon Mrs. Wells, and asked her to go with her to make a few calls on some sick people in the poor part of town. The two ladies were soon in the little sleigh, snugly wrapped in their robes and mufflers, and as the pony drew them along at a steady pace the bells made pleasant music. As they were tucking themselves in Mrs. Wells discovered a basket crowded into the corner of the sleigh, and exclaimed laughingly, "Well, Sister Harper, have you been to market? or, are you just going?"

"Neither, Sister Wells, that is what my husband calls my 'Commissary Department.' I only have a few goodies that Ann put in for a couple of bed-ridden old women that I expect to visit before we get home."

"Do you take goodies to your poor friends *every* time you go out?" asked Mrs. Wells in a slightly surprised tone.

"Not *always*, but frequently. It does them so much good to think you care for them. Somebody says, 'The nearest way to a man's heart is by way of his stomach,' and I guess it is equally true of women. They seem to appreciate your efforts to

benefit their souls if they find you care for their
bodies as well."

"Now I call that real selfish, do n't you?"

"Well, it may be, but we have to take people as
they are, not as we would like them to be. But
here we are at Widow Smith's."   •

Tying the pony to a dilapidated fence the two
ladies were soon in the low room which served as
kitchen, parlor, and bedroom, Mrs. Harper carrying
several little packages taken from the basket in the
sleigh. The furniture of the room was scant, but
the bed upon which the woman lay was clean and
comfortable looking.

"Well, Mrs. Smith, how are you feeling to-day?"
asked Mrs. Harper cheerily.

"Much better, thank you; the medicine you sent
me last week has done me a world of good. I have
slept pretty good at night for three or four nights.
And the blanket you sent has been a real blessing. My old bones need more cover than when I
was young, and since Jennie died there has been no
one to provide such things for the old woman. To
be sure, Maggie is a good girl, but it is as much as
she can do to buy what we eat and pay house rent,"
and the invalid wiped away a tear.

"Here are some cookies that I have brought
you," Mrs. Harper said kindly, "and a quarter of
tea—*my* mother always loved her tea; and here is a
glass of jelly, real grape, that Ann bought from a
neighbor on purpose for you. If you dissolve a
spoonful in a glass of cold water it will make a very
pleasant drink. And here is a shoulder shawl from

Ann too; she said it would be so nice for you to throw over your shoulders when you feel like sitting up a bit. O, yes, she can spare it very well," as the woman seemed loath to take it. "I made Ann a present of a new one at Christmas, and she said she would spare this for you. "So," she added brightly, "my little gift has benefited three persons already: you, Ann, and myself. But we must go now," and they departed amid a shower of thanks from the sick woman.

As soon as they were seated in the sleigh Mrs. Wells said, "Now, Sister Harper, I never want you to plead poverty to *me again*. Why by that old woman's own story you have already spent as much as one-half of your subscription for our organ. And then it seems you make your hired girl presents besides. More than *I* can do, I am sure. Besides, it is only money thrown away."

"I don't think so, Sister Wells; I am sure Ann deserves all she gets, and then by helping her a little, by way of an occasional present, she has a little money to spend on others, and so she has the opportunity to enjoy the luxury of giving as well as myself." ·

Mrs. Wells laughed merrily: "What funny ideas you do have about giving! Now *I* never thought about the *luxury of giving* as you call it. But every one to their notion."

"Yes, that is *my* way, you know," Mrs. Harper answered good humoredly. "This is our last stopping place," as she reined up the horse in front of a rickety old house on a back street.

Up an outside stairway, that trembled and creaked beneath their feet, the two women slowly climbed, each with her arms full; for Mrs. Wells, out of sympathy to her friend, had volunteered to carry a part of her bundles. Mrs. Harper knocked at a door at the head of the stairs; a faint voice said, "Come in," and the two entered. Every thing in the room betokened extreme poverty. On a low bed lay a woman of about forty-five, pale, and emaciated, while by her side lay a child of perhaps ten years, but very small, with hollow eyes and sunken cheeks, that told of suffering and want.

"Is that you, Mrs. Harper?" asked the woman, as that lady bid her a good afternoon.

"Yes, Mrs. Maloney, it is me; but can't you see me?"

"No ma'am, my eyes are a deal worse than when you were here last. And that ain't all, either. I'm afeard I shall niver see again," said the sick woman sadly. "I can just tell daylight from dark, and that is all."

"But I thought your eyes were so much better in the Fall; you told me your medicine was helping them!"

"Indeed, it did, ma'am; but, ye see, I've had none for a long time. Norah has been sick and had to have medicine, and Susan's wages are not so good as they were. The lady she works for said she couldn't pay so much this year, and so Susan had to take what was offered her, for she couldn't afford to be idle. Mebbe we shouldn't be so bad off and weak like, but we have had to live saving, and don't get

many nice things to eat, and Norah and me have no
taste for dry bread and p'taties now. Susan only
gets two and a half a week, and it don't go very far
in buyin' clothes for four and food for three. Neddie
earns enough mostly to pay the rint, and *sometimes* a
few cents over. If I could get somethin' nice for
Norah to eat I shouldn't care for myself," laying her
thin hand on the child's head. "She's been longin'
for an orange all day, poor child. But who is that
with you?" as Mrs. Wells moved uneasily in her
chair.

"It is Mrs. Wells, a friend of mine; and here is
an orange for Norah," and she placed it in the child's
hand.

"O, thank you, ma'am," Mrs. Maloney answered,
gratefully. "Wells—Wells," she repeated, slowly;
"why, that's the name of the lady that Susan wur-
ruks for."

Mrs. Wells got up hastily, and came to the bedside.

"Yes, Mrs. Maloney, Susan lives with me; but,
really, I didn't know you were so bad off as this,"
she said, earnestly.

"Susan is not the one to bother other people
with her throubles without the asking," the sick
woman answered, a little proudly; "and if I was
well enough to care for Norah, ye'd never hear ov
the likes ov me complainin' to any one."

Mrs. Harper glanced at the face of her friend,
and saw the tears of sorrow and wounded pride trick-
ling down her cheeks, and hastily interrupted Mrs.
Maloney, saying: "We have brought a nice basket

of dainties, that will be good for you as well as
Norah," and she began to undo the parcels. "I
knew you were not able to bake, so I have brought
you a loaf and some cakes of Ann's baking; I'll
warrant them nice. Here are some dried peaches,
and a can of plums; and here is a paper full of
crullers for Neddie—not for you nor Norah, remember; they are too rich for you, but if Neddie is like
my boys, I am sure he will appreciate them."

Mrs. Maloney murmured a "God bless you," as
she covered her face with the corner of the ragged
quilt, to hide her tears.

As the ladies turned to go, Mrs. Wells only said,
"I will see you again soon, Mrs. Maloney," and
hurriedly left the room.

When they were once more in their sleigh, Mrs.
Wells turned to her companion and said, excitedly,
while the tears were streaming down her face, "Sister Harper, why did you not tell me of this, instead
of bringing me here in this way? You certainly
know me too well to suppose that I would willingly
be the cause of such suffering and privation!"

"Indeed, my dear sister, I had not the slightest
idea that the woman was Susan's mother; I have
not been there since the Autumn until to-day, and I
did n't even know that Susan's name was Maloney. I
heard yesterday, through our pastor, that the woman
was in great need, and only came to see what I could
do for her."

"O, what a blunder I have made," sobbed Mrs.
Wells; "I did n't suppose that I was robbing any one
when I reduced Susan's wages. If that child dies,

or her mother loses her sight, I shall never forgive myself."

"We are all liable to make mistakes," said Mrs. Harper, soothingly, "and that is one reason that I am so slow to promise, unless I am sure I can afford it."

When Mrs. Wells reached home, her first work was to send for Susan to come to the sitting-room. The girl came, and as her mistress looked at her she wondered she had never noticed before how tired and anxious she looked. Bidding her be seated, she said, "I have just been to visit your mother, Susan." The girl started uneasily. "Why did you not tell me how needy you were at home?"

Susan hesitated a moment, and then said, "I was afraid you would think I just told it to get my wages raised, ma'am."

"Well, next time I want you to tell me all about such things, and not wait for me to find it out when it is, perhaps, too late to do any good."

"O Mrs. Wells, is Norah worse?" cried the girl, with whitening cheeks.

"No, I *guess* not, Susan; but I am afraid that it is too late to cure your mother's eyes. I think you had better go to your mother to-night, as she needs you badly; or, perhaps you had better wait until to-morrow, and then stay awhile with her."

"Please, Mrs. Wells, interrupted Susan, eagerly, "I think mother needs my wages worse than she does me; if I stop work, there will be nothing for them to live on."

"Never mind that, Susan; your wages may go on, just the same; and here is five dollars—it is all I have just now—take it, and get some medicine and nourishing food for your mother and sister; and from this on your wages will be the same that they were last year—three dollars and a half per week.".

"You are very kind, indeed," sobbed Susan, completely overcome by this unexpected kindness; "and I'll work my fingers off to please you, when I come back."

"That would be rather too much," said Mrs. Wells, smiling through her tears. "Now, you had better go to your work; I would like you to do up some extra baking, so that I can do without you a week, if possible."

"Indeed, and I will, ma'am," and Susan left the room, with the smiles and tears struggling for the mastery.

The next day there was a bed comforter and blankets, a pair of sheets, and several pairs of woolen stockings and skirts for the sick girl, left at Mrs. Maloney's door by the expressman; and in the evening Susan came, with a market-basket well filled with such things as the poor like, and yet so seldom are permitted to enjoy, and with the extra five dollars from Mrs. Wells, besides her wages for two weeks in advance, in her pocket.

Through the providence of God, Norah recovered, and Mrs. Maloney's eyes were partially cured, but she continued an invalid.

Mrs. Wells always took pains to send some little

dainty to the sick woman when Susan made her
weekly visit, and she never again undertook to re-
duce the wages of the poor in order that she
might increase her own subscription to benevolent
enterprises, or to foster Church pride; but in all
her giving she was careful to be just as well as
generous.

THE PREACHER'S WIFE AT CONFERENCE.

PRESUME there is no one who more thoroughly enjoys an annual conference than the preacher's wife, the preacher not excepted. She has had a year of earnest work among her husband's people, and she has looked forward to this annual gathering as the one bright spot in what would otherwise, perhaps, have proved a dull year. The best talent of the Church is to be gathered there; the best speakers are to occupy pulpit and platform; and to this she looks forward as a season of solid enjoyment and profit; for, no matter how eloquent her husband may be, she is, if a true wife, too much interested in his success to enjoy his sermons as she would those of a stranger. But here she can sit and enjoy the sermons, even though the speaker should make a few grammatical blunders, or should occasionally fail to make a point as "clear as sunshine." Or, if one of the numerous agents, usually present, should chance to be prosy or occupy too much time, she can even endure that, in the hope that a certain particular friend of hers may profit by the infliction, and not "go and do likewise."

Here is a preacher's wife who comes to conference for the first time in many years. Her hair, like that of her husband, has grown gray while she has been toiling in the Master's vineyard. She feels that for her there are only a few more years of toil, and then comes eternal rest; and she comes up to this annual gathering, this Feast of the Harvest, as to a sort of reunion, the last, perhaps, for her, until the great " Harvest Home."

Here is one who could not be with us last year. A little home treasure required all her care then—but now the little one is laid away among strangers in the village graveyard, and the mother is with us to-day, clad in the habiliments of woe. Gladly would she have denied herself indulgence if she could have kept her treasure; but it could not be.

There sits another, who has come from a poor circuit, from a salary of five hundred dollars, with two hundred of it unpaid. But, by dint of economy and a few music-scholars, or by teaching the village school, she has managed to keep even; and at her husband's earnest entreaty, she decided to come to conference, even at the risk of hearing some of the brethren hint, in no very polite terms, that preachers' wives are very much in the way, "taking up some of the best places, which would otherwise have been reserved for traveling agents and visiting brethren."

And here is a young wife, as yet but slightly acquainted with the pleasantness and unpleasantness of the itinerancy, and she looks on with curiosity and surprise at the amount of business done and the number of speeches made in so short a time.

But, of whatever age or circumstances, she comes to reap the benefits and enjoy the privileges which may there offer themselves. And enjoy them she

does; in a measure, too, which her husband, who
goes "up to Jerusalem" yearly, fails to appreciate.
I remember sitting in the same pew, for several suc-
cessive sessions of our annual conferences, with a
preacher's wife whom I had never met at such .a
gathering before. She told me it was her first visit
for ten years. She was a sweet-faced, patient-looking
woman, just such a one as you would expect to see
deny herself all the pleasures that others might enjoy
them; and the way she literally feasted on the intellectual bounties placed before her added greatly to
my own enjoyment of the same.

The words of our conference hymn, "And are
we yet alive?" seem peculiarly appropriate to the
preachers themselves after the year's battle, but it is
none the less so to the preacher's wife. Her husband's troubles have been hers, and she has probably
felt them in even a greater degree than he; for in
his case he has had the satisfaction of taking an act-
ive part in the contest, and putting to rights whatever
it was in his power to right. But the wife, in most
cases, must simply endure; and all know that endur-
ing is much more trying than doing. When hinderances come in our pathway, it is a real satisfaction
to be able to take hold and lift them out of our
way, even though it requires an effort to do so; but
to see our pathway obstructed, and not be able to
lift a finger—to sit in silence (in patience, if possible,)
until another removes the obstacle, no matter how
tardy their motions may be—requires a full supply
of grace; how much, no one knows better than the
preacher's wife. And now, as they sing, her memory

carries her back to this or that dark hour when
troubles came so thick and fast that it seemed almost
impossible to bear them.

> " But out of all the Lord
> Hath brought us by his love."

And our hearts grow thankful as we remember his
great mercy.   How solemn the moment when we
bow around the sacramental board; and, as we com-
memorate the death and sufferings of our Redeemer,
we feel that it is a blessed privilege to help bear the
Gospel to a sin-stricken world.   Where the preacher's wife goes to conference to be benefited by what
she sees and hears (and I trust there are few who go
for any other purpose), the time and money she
spends is a good investment, both for herself and the
people among whom her lot may be cast.

The better people understand the working of our
Church machinery, the more interest will they feel in
the Church; and the preacher's wife who goes to
conference and watches carefully the transaction of
the business, who hears the reports of our benevolent
institutions, the calls that are made upon our Church
funds, will better understand the needs of the Church,
and will know better how to work for her interest in
the future; and I often wish the entire membership
of the Methodist Episcopal Church could attend an
. annual conference at least once in two years.   They
would, perhaps, be enabled to see what some have
failed hitherto to see; namely, how small their sacri-
fices are, both in gifts and work, compared with the
real needs of the Church.

4

—◦—◦—◦—

"I SUPPOSE the probationers will be received into full membership next Sabbath, will they not?" asked Lulu Rayburn of her friend, Helen Wynne, as they sat in Helen's cozy room, busy at some fancy work as they talked familiarly together.

"Yes," answered Helen, looking up from counting threads. "Of course you are going to be received?"

"My name was read as one of the 'elect,' I believe; but I hardly think I will go any further," said Lulu, with an effort to appear careless.

"You surely are not in earnest!" and Helen dropped her work in surprise.

"Yes, I am, though. Are *you* going to be received?"

"Yes, I expect to be; though I scarcely feel myself worthy of a place in the Church," Helen answered in a low tone. "But why are you not?"

"O, well," laughing a little uneasily, "I am not 'worthy,' as you say; and, then, I only gave my name to the Church because I was over-persuaded, and I guess I will have it dropped."

"But you were in earnest, surely, last Winter," and Helen's face showed the surprise she felt.

"Yes, I was in earnest then, I suppose; but I

do n't feel like going any further now, and I do n't like the idea of being coaxed to be a Christian. I am going to have my name dropped, and some time when there is no religious excitement, if I feel like it, I will unite with the Church again."

"Better not depend too much on feeling, Lulu, but be a Christian from principle. If you wait for some time when there is no religious excitement, you will very likely not 'feel like it.' As to being 'coaxed,' I am sure it took a great deal of coaxing to get me to take the first step, and you were among the most earnest pleaders that I had; and I have been glad every day since that I allowed you to influence me to give my heart to the Savior's keeping."

"Well, Helen, I am glad you enjoy yourself in that way; but it has never been much pleasure to me; and, as I do not believe in doing penance, I have concluded not to punish the flesh by trying to obey Church rules. If the Church was not so strict, I would like to remain in it; for it is more respectable nowadays to belong to the Church than to be an 'outsider,' but I am not willing to give up every thing," and Lulu gave her shoulder an impatient shrug.

"But the Church only asks you to give up the things which it considers hurtful to your religious prosperity," said Helen.

"I prefer being my own judge in such matters, and my 'religious' prosperity is not enhanced by keeping me from harmless amusements."

"Not harmless amusements, of course. But what do you call harmless amusements, Lulu?"

"Well, dancing is one. I'm sure I don't see any harm in it; and I would go without my supper any day for the sake of a dance. Why, only three weeks ago I dressed in fifteen minutes, to catch the evening train, so as to reach M—— in time for that big dancing party."

"O Lou, you surely have not been dancing!" and Helen's voice and face were full of pain.

"Of course I have — more than once, too. I would have told you before, but I knew you would look so horrified. I suppose if the leaders had known it they would not have placed my name among the 'recommended.'"

"No, I presume not," answered Helen, slowly. "But were you really happy in such amusement?"

"May be not quite as happy as I could wish; but we had a good time, and you know the preacher tells us not to expect perfect happiness here below."

"O Lulu!" and Helen's voice was full of tender reproach, "how can you talk so lightly? I am sure you do not feel as careless as you would make me believe. I can not say whether dancing is wrong in itself or not; but you know a dancing Church member is never ready to pray or talk for Christ."

"I know that. But what is the use of being so particular? Why can't we have a good time without being thought wicked and sinful?"

"And what do you call having a good time, my dear?" asked a pleasant voice, that caused the two young ladies to look toward the door, in which stood Mrs. Wynne, Helen's mother. "I have not been eavesdropping," she said, pleasantly, "and can not be sure of the subject, but just as I was about to pass your open door I heard Lulu's question, and, Yankee-like, will answer it by asking another. So, Lulu, give us your ideas;" and Mrs. Wynne took the chair her daughter had brought forward, and waited for the answer.

"O, you know what I mean," answered the young lady, hesitatingly. "Going to parties, boat excursions, picnics, and such places where we can have a little fun."

"And you call that having a good time, I suppose," said Mrs. Wynne, gently.

"Why, yes. Do n't every body—at least young folks?"

"I suppose they do, generally; and we all need recreation of some sort; but the danger is, that in seeking for pleasure we may pass by it. People who *seek* for pleasure usually have a very erroneous conception of what constitutes a good time."

"Why, Mrs. Wynne, I thought it was natural to seek for pleasure."

"I presume that it is, to the unconverted heart; but happiness is seldom found for the seeking. It is only when we forget ourselves in striving to make others happy that we find our greatest and most unalloyed pleasure."

Lulu Rayburn made no reply to her friend's words for some time. At last she said, with a sigh:

"Well, Mrs. Wynne, I should like to be a Christian, but it costs so much. The Church wants us to give up *every thing*."

"No, my dear, not every thing. The Church only asks you to forego what it considers hurtful."

"And the Church wants to judge for me."

"Is it not wise to allow those who are older and more experienced than yourself to judge or decide for you? The rules and regulations of each Protestant Church organization have been drawn up by persons of established piety and good judgment; and these rules are not as a penance, but as a safeguard to keep you from harm. If all who take on themselves the name of Christ would strive earnestly to please God; if, when about to engage in amusements or any thing of a worldly nature, they would ask themselves the question, Will this be pleasing to God? can I ask his blessing upon me in doing this?—they would have but little difficulty in living up to the requirements of the Church."

"And so you think I do not try to please God?" Lulu said, a little nervously.

"I do not presume to judge you; for your own conscience will answer, if you will listen. But persons who have the fear of God, in its right sense, before their eyes, are a law unto themselves, and they scarcely think whether the rules of Church government allow or forbid; for God is in all their thoughts. My dear Lulu, the remedy for your perplexity is very simple. Get near to God, and you will soon lose all desire for those amusements which do not honor God. Your question reminds me of an anecdote of Bishop M'Ilvaine. A young lady who, like you, was worrying over Church restraints, asked him the question, 'Is it wrong for Christians to dance?' The bishop's answer was given gently but firmly: 'My dear, Christians do not *want* to dance.' And to you, if you will strive to love God with all your heart, dancing and card-playing, with other questionable forms of amusement, will soon lose all their sweetness to you. The only sure remedy for these difficulties is a continued hiding behind the cross. Clinging to Christ will take away your desire for those things which are not for your good, either temporally or spiritually."

BERTIE'S TEMPTATION.

HE day had been dull and gloomy. Just such a day as November can give—rainy and dark; not a regular pour-down, but a continual drizzle, drizzle, such as takes all the buoyancy out of every one, except it be a fun-loving boy.

The village school was out, and the boys and girls turned their steps homeward. The girls, wrapped in their water-proofs, walked slowly along, talking in subdued tones, as if their spirits had settled down to a level with the weather. The boys dashed out, regardless of the falling rain or of the mud beneath their feet, rushing past the girls, apparently forgetful that they were splashing dirty water upon them, or that the teacher had said: "Go home quietly."

After a race of about four blocks, Albert Forbes, a boy of some sixteen years, left his companions to continue their race, while he opened the gate in front of a respectable-looking residence, and ran up the walk, whistling merrily as he went. With a bound he landed on the upper step, utterly ignoring the fact that there were two below it, and swinging the door open with rather a positive motion, stopped his whistling to call out, eagerly: "O mother!"

A fretful voice from the sitting-room answered

him with, "O Bertie, I wish you would come home
more quietly. My head aches, and you shake my
nerves until I feel as if I should fly; your brother
never comes into the house in that way. There,
now!" as he entered the room and threw his hat on
the lounge, instead of hanging it in its proper place;
"do pick up your hat; you know that is not the
place for it;" adding, in a despairing tone, "O dear!
I wonder if you will ever learn to be orderly."

By this time the light was all gone from the boy's
face, and, muttering that he could n't "always be
thinking," he turned and went to the parlor, where
he found his elder sister, a young lady of twenty,
poring over the pages of a new book.

She looked up as her brother entered the room,
and said, a little impatiently, "Close the door."

Bertie closed the door, and, walking slowly across
the room to a front window, stood looking out.

His sister's eyes followed him, and, catching a
glimpse of his not over-clean boots, she exclaimed:
"O Bert, look at your feet! How can you come
into the parlor so? the carpet will be spoiled. There!
your toes are touching the curtain."

Bertie looked down at his feet, and then, slowly
drawing them away from the curtain, he began whistling a tune, at the same time drumming an accompaniment with his knuckles on the casement.

His sister turned her eyes again to her book, but
her brother's noise seemed to annoy her, and at last
she said, in no very amiable tone, "Do, Bert, stop
that noise. I do n't see why you can 't be more gen-
teel; Fred never does so."

5

"I wonder when I shall hear the last of my brother's perfections?" asked Bertie, scornfully.   "Of
course, he never does wrong, and I ought to take
him as my model.   It's nothing but 'Bert, don't do
this,' or 'Don't do that,' and 'Why can't you be polite, like Fred?' from one week to the next.   I only
hope that when I am twenty-five I shall be capable
of doing something else besides oiling my hair and
talking soft talk to the ladies.   Where's Nellie?"

"Gone on an errand for me," replied his sister,
without looking up.

"O dear! I wish I had gone nutting with Ed
Cole and Frank Howell.   They teased me to go, but
mother always frets so when I go with them," and,
with a restless, dissatisfied air, Bertie left the parlor,
and went to his own room.

You must not imagine, dear reader, that Mrs.
Forbes was lacking in love for this noisy, restless
boy of hers; far from it.   She loved him dearly; but,
being in delicate health herself, she preferred quiet,
and did not consider that a healthy boy of sixteen
could not sit down and keep quiet as easily as a
woman of forty-five.   Her eldest son was what is
called a "ladies' man," in the better sense of that
word—polite, soft-voiced, and always ready to do the
agreeable, provided there was no hard work in it.
To his mother and sister Fred was perfection, and
they had sounded his praise in the ears of his brother
until he had become tired of the unpleasant contrast,
and so prejudiced him against Fred that he could not
appreciate the good qualities he did possess.

Mr. Forbes, like too many husbands and fathers,

in this fast age, was too busy trying to meet the family expenses to pay much attention to the wants of his youngest boy, except to see that he was properly clothed and sent to school.

Allie, the sister mentioned before, was kind and ladylike, in her way, but she had not the patience to bear with her younger brother's romping, boisterous ways.

However, Bertie had one warm friend, who thought him "the nicest brother in the world," and that was Nellie, the youngest of the family, a girl of fourteen. Nellie was never so busy but she could leave book or work for a game of ball or croquet, often in secret preferring the former, although she had not the courage to say so in the presence of her elder brother and sister.

Bertie's room failed to offer any attraction this evening, and finally he left it, saying to himself, "I believe I will go over to Ed Cole's, and see if they have gone nutting. They'll be glad to see me, any way. I wish Allie would do her own errands, and let Nell stay at home when I want her; I like her best of all. I do n't care if she is n't ladylike, she is jolly good company, anyhow."

Bertie found Ed Cole had not gone nutting, but he and two or three other boys were going up town to "look around," and they begged him to go with them. Bertie knew that his parents did not approve of his loafing the streets at any time, and especially in such company; but the temptation was strong, and when the boys hinted that he was afraid to go down town without his mother, this decided him. He determined to show them that he was old enough to go down town once without asking leave; but it was with a dissatisfied feeling that he locked arms with a rough boy, two years his senior, and went through a back street, to avoid passing his own door.

In the mean time sister Nellie had returned home and missed her favorite brother. Allie had not seen him since he left the parlor, and his mother presumed he was in his room. But no Bertie came to tea, and Mr. Forbes was too hurried to inquire after him. Eight o'clock came, and he had not returned. The mother grew uneasy and went to the window every few minutes, trying to pierce into the darkness, or listening for his footsteps on the gravel. Allie took up a book and tried to read, but her sisterly anxiety was too strong for her to enjoy that favorite pastime. Nellie sat crocheting, but her face was very anxious, and twice she asked Fred in a whisper if he wouldn't go and look for him. But Fred only laughed lightly, and said Bert was able to take care of himself. When, however, the clock struck and the boy had not returned they were all thoroughly alarmed.

In the mean time, Mr. Forbes had locked his office and was walking briskly toward home. As he turned a corner of the street he saw a crowd in front of him and heard loud, taunting words mingled with oaths, and as he came nearer he saw two boys grappling each other, while the crowd cheered them on. It was only for a moment, however, when the larger of the two dealt his antagonist a blow that sent him reeling backward, and he fell heavily to the pavement, his head striking the curbstone. Mr. Forbes pressed through the crowd to see if the boy was hurt, the idlers giving way when they saw who it was. He held his lantern so that the light could fall on the upturned face. He started back with an exclamation of surprise and terror as he recognized the face of his youngest boy, pale as death, and unconscious. Two bystanders volunteered to carry him home, while the father hastened home to prepare his family for the shock. Mrs. Forbes met them at the door with a terror-stricken face and led the way to Bertie's room, while the sisters clung to each other and sobbed in affright as they saw the pale face and limp form.

By the aid of proper restoratives Albert was, in a short time, restored to consciousness, as he had only been stunned and not seriously hurt. Then Mr. Forbes insisted on Fred and the girls retiring to rest, while he and the mother stayed to watch until about midnight, when Bertie sank into a quiet sleep, and then father and mother went to rest with heavy hearts. It was evident to them that their son had not only been in bad company, but that he had also been drinking.

Bertie awoke next morning with a pain in his head and a ringing in his ears; and when he tried to rise the room seemed to spin round with him, and he sank back on his pillow and covered his face with his hands as the remembrance of all that had passed the night before came rushing upon him. As he lay and thought of it all he began to wonder if the family would come to ask after him; and, though he longed to see them, yet he almost wished they would not come. Presently there was a rap, and then the door opened softly and Nellie came in, with an anxious look on her face. He looked at her, his own face flushing scarlet, and then turning away his head he put out a hand as if to motion her away, and finally sobbed out,

"O Nellie, dear."

And Nellie came and laid her face close upon his pillow and sobbed with him.

At last he found voice to ask, "Nell, do you know how it happened?"

"Not all," Nellie answered, tearfully, though her face showed that she suspected more than she knew. And then, with his face turned toward the wall, that he might not see her tears, Bertie told her all. She proved a poor comforter, so far as words were concerned, but the kiss she imprinted on his forehead was more to Bertie than words. She sat by the bed for some moments in silence, and then looking up, Bertie asked doubtfully,

"Do you think mother will come?"

Nellie nodded assent.

"Do you think she will forgive me for disgracing you all? Mother always seemed afraid I would do something bad; but, indeed, Nellie, I didn't mean to do wrong at first."

"Mother loves you, any way," said his sister, ready to sob again. And Bertie said, with a sigh of relief, "Now, sister, leave me alone a little while."

Nellie went softly out and left her brother to his thoughts. They were not of the pleasantest kind,

but they helped him to make some very earnest
resolves for the future.

Nellie brought his breakfast, but he only tasted
it; his head was aching sadly, and his heart worse.
About ten o'clock, as he lay wondering if his mother
was not coming at all, he heard a well-known step,
and then his door opened. He looked up, although
he had intended not to do so. The face he saw
was very pale and the eyes were red with weeping.
Involuntarily he reached out both hands and whispered under his breath, "Mother!" and in a moment
more he was sobbing on her shoulder. In a few
minutes he found voice to tell her all about it, — how
the boys had dared him to drink, and how at first
he thought he would just put it to his lips; and then
he drank a glass the same as the others; how they
called him proud, and "baby," because he would
not stand a treat: and finally they had provoked him
till they came to blows.

"O mother, can you forgive me?" he fairly
sobbed out, as he finished; "I did n't intend to go,
but Allie found fault with me, and Nellie was gone,
and you had the headache—and there was nothing
for me to do."

Mrs. Forbes winced as Bertie gave his reasons
for going, and she remembered her impatience at his
noise; and her heart told her she had not tried as
she might to make her home attractive to her restless but affectionate boy, and she answered more
lovingly than was her wont, "Yes, dear, mother
forgives all, and you and I will try to be more to
each other than we have been. And, O, my son,

mother did not know that she was sending you into temptation when she complained of your noisy ways."

In the evening Bertie was able to go down to supper, although he would much rather have taken it in his own room than to face the rest of the family; but he felt that he must do it some time, and the sooner it was over the better. Fred and Allie spoke kindly to him, but no reference was made to the events or preceding night. His father laid his hand upon his head with a caressing motion, and as their eyes met Bertie felt that all was forgiven, and though the tears would come there was joy in his .heart in spite of his feeling of shame at his wrong-doing.

From that time there was a better understanding between the family and their "irrepressible" boy. There seemed to be a feeling on their part that by their system of repression they had driven him into bad company; while Bertie felt that so long as they were so kind to him and so thoughtful for his happiness, no self-denial would be too hard to endure as an atonement for the sorrow he had caused them.

Mothers-in-Law.

A ND so you are really going to be married,
Hildreth?"

The young man addressed was lounging in
an arm-chair in the hotel bar-room, reading
the morning journal. He looked up at his
questioner and laughed a little lightly.

"Well, yes, provided all things go on
smoothly. You know the old adage, 'There's
many a slip,' etc."

"Yes, I know, but I guess you are in for
it. By the way, where are you going to reside?
I understand that your mother-in-law elect
is a widow, and your prospective wife an only daughter. But of course you will not think of taking the
old lady into your family," replied his companion.

"We shall live on the old homestead. Mrs.
Warren is not willing to leave the old home, and of
course she could not live there alone."

"Whew! Well, you must be love-sick with a
vengeance, if you are willing to live with the old lady.
The idea of your doing such a thing. For my part
I would rather eat boarding-house hash and sew on
my own buttons all my life than run the risk of being
bored by having a mother-in-law about every day."
And the speaker looked thoroughly disgusted as he
reached for a match to light his second cigar.

"O, I don't apprehend any serious trouble," replied Hildreth, coldly. "I think I know how to manage my own affairs, and hardly think a mother-in-law will be likely to take the reins out of my hands."

"You may boast now," answered his companion knowingly, "but just wait till she has had you under her thumb for a year and see if you dare say your soul's your own."

The young men had been talking, apparently oblivious of the presence of a third party, a man of some forty-five or fifty years, a stranger who was stopping at the hotel, and who had been writing busily at the desk near by during their conversation. Turning around from his desk he said, pleasantly, "Young gentlemen, may I say a word, too?"

The young men laughed, and Hildreth colored as he saw they had had a listener, but both readily assented to hear what the stranger had to say, and he continued: "I have, unintentionally, been a listener to your conversation, and I find that you have imbibed notions that may do you an injury, and others also. There is too much of a disposition to find fault with these who are often our best friends. A woman who has raised a daughter who is worthy to be the wife of an honest, respectable, young man, is not likely to be a very bad person herself, though she may be far from perfect. My own experience is so different from the popularly conceived notion of mothers-in-law that I can never hear a word spoken of them lightly, or in condemnation, without entering my protest against it. When I married, some twenty

years ago, my wife's mother, being a widow, came
to make her home with us, and I confess that I had
some little fear that it might mar our domestic peace,
but prepared myself with something of the feeling
of a martyr to endure it all patiently for my wife's
sake. But I was very agreeably disappointed. We
were both young and ignorant of business or housekeeping, and her oversight saved me many a dollar
that would otherwise have been spent foolishly or
wasted. And her loving watchfulness often smoothed
over little misunderstandings between us that might
have ended in heartache or alienation. Once, when
envy and calumny were doing their utmost to rob
me of my good name, she stood by me and up-
held me by her encouragement and confidence, for
if she ever doubted me for a moment she never permitted me to see that she did. Sometimes I have
thought that if it had not been for her faith in my
uprightness, perhaps even my wife would have
doubted me; but she stood firmly by me, and her
faith buoyed us up till the trouble was over, and
when my good name was established without a stain
there was no one who rejoiced more than she."

"But didn't it seem a little like you were being
constantly watched and criticised to have her always
in your house?" asked Hildreth.

"I did feel a little that way at first, but the feeling left me in less than six months, and I came to
look upon her as a sort of guardian angel who was
watching over us and ministering to our welfare.
No, young gentlemen, I have had reason many times
to thank God for giving me such a friend, and when

she was laid in her last earthly resting place there
was no truer mourner than myself. There is no
class of people who are more liable to be misunder-
stood than step-mothers or mothers-in-law, and
though I have had no experience with the first I
have with the second, and I can say that while
mothers-in-law may have their faults, so have sons-in-
law, and there is as much need for reform on their
part as on their mothers-in-law. I beg pardon for my
intrusion upon your conversation, but the memory
of that mother is like a sweet incense to me to-day,
and I could not let this opportunity pass without
giving my testimony to the goodness and disin-
terested affection of at least one mother-in-law. I
am not much in favor of 'post-mortem laudation,'
but I had inscribed upon the marble that marks her
resting place, 'Servant of God, well done,' and I feel
that no higher encomium could be pronounced on
any one."

A Story for Little Girls.

——◦◦◦——

IT was a very sober face that Lula Norton held up for her mother's evening kiss as she came in from school, and the mother's watchful eye quickly detected the cloud on her daughter's usually happy face. She said nothing then, but waited until the little girl's bed-time.

When Lula was nicely tucked in between the fleecy blankets, ready for her good-night talk with mamma, Mrs. Norton seated herself on the side of the little bed, and waited for her daughter to commence the conversation. But Lula's busy tongue was, for once, still. At last her mother said kindly: "What is it, Lula?"

"O mamma, I know it is n't right, but I felt so angry and disappointed to-day. You know I have had such a time blotting my copy-book this Winter; and teacher told me if I made any blots this week she would have to keep me in from recess; and I did try so hard to be neat; and to-day Jenny Groves let her pen fall on my book, and it rolled over and over and blotted my book so badly; and Miss Brown was displeased and reproved me when she saw it, and then kept me in from recess.

"But why did n't you tell her how it happened?" asked Mrs. Norton.

"She never asked me, mamma; and you know she does not allow us to tell on each other. I would n't have minded so much, but Jennie never appeared as if she knew any thing about it; and when recess came she walked out of the school-room without even looking toward me. And now Miss Brown is displeased with me, and thinks I do n't try to please her. She *always* kisses me good-bye, mamma; but to-night she only said, 'Good-bye, Lula,' O *so* coldly; and it 's all Jennie's fault, and I never will forgive her as long as I live!" and Lula gave vent to her pent-up grief in a good cry, with her face buried in her pillow.

"My daughter must not say that," said her mother, sadly. "If we would have forgiveness, we must also forgive."

"But, mamma, it is so hard to be blamed for what you did n't do."

"If your teacher does n't know, *God* does," said Mrs. Norton, softly.

"I suppose so; but that does n't seem to make it any easier. I did want to be marked perfect *this* week. I suppose God does know; but I would like for teacher to know, and the scholars, too;" and Lula gave way to a fresh burst of tears.

"Lula," said her mother, presently, "I think our heavenly Father will make it all right some day, and your teacher will find out in some way that you are not in fault. I hope my little girl will try not to feel angry at her school-mate, even though Jennie did not do quite right on her part. Shall we ask Jesus to make it all right with your teacher if he thinks

best; and, if not, to give you grace to bear it patiently?"

"If you please, mamma," Lula replied, in a low
tone; and then Mrs. Norton kneeled and prayed God
to help her daughter to bear reproach without murmuring—to try to do right, even though others might
not understand her.

As she kissed her mother good-night, Lula whispered: "I 'll *try* to think it is all right, mamma; but
it *is* hard to be blamed for what you did n't do."

The next morning Lula took her seat in school
with a face still clouded with the remembrance of
yesterday's disgrace, and with a feeling very near
akin to anger toward Jennie Groves still lingering in
her heart. But she applied herself diligently to her
studies, and had the satisfaction of hearing her teacher's words of approval. As the girls were taking
their seats at the close of the afternoon recess, Jennie
drew Lula's face down to hers, and whispered peni-
tently, "Lula, I told teacher all about it, and she is
so glad." Lula did not need to ask her seat-mate
what she meant by "it;" for the affair of yesterday
had been in her mind all day, and she only gave one
glance toward her teacher, whose eyes met hers with
a look of sympathy, and then she laid her head
down on her desk and cried for very joy.

After the scholars had finished their recitations,
Miss Brown told them to put away their books, as
she had something to say to them. Lula's heart
gave a great throb, and she looked toward her seat-
mate; but Jennie turned away with a very pale face
as if she would avoid Lula's inquiring eyes.

"Children," said Miss Brown, "I wish to say that I punished Lula Norton wrongfully yesterday. Jennie Groves wishes me to say that it was she who blotted Lula's book, and that she is sorry she was not brave enough to acknowledge it yesterday. And *I* wish to say that *I* am sorry that I did not inquire more particularly before punishing Lula for a fault of which she was not guilty. By Jennie's request the mark for carelessness is erased from Lula's record and placed on *hers.*"

After a few more words to her pupils about the necessity of being perfectly honest, Miss Brown proceeded to close the school. But neither Lula nor Jennie joined their voices with that of their schoolmates in singing the evening hymn. Jennie laid her head upon her desk, and sobbed bitterly. It had cost her a hard struggle to tell her teacher that she had blotted Lula's book, and had then permitted her to be punished wrongfully. Lula was so glad that the blame had been lifted from herself that she could no longer feel any anger in her heart toward Jennie, and she put her arm gently about her neck and cried with her.

After school was dismissed the two little girls lingered for a few moments to say good-bye to their teacher. Miss Brown had imposed no penalty upon Jennie, for she saw she had already suffered enough; and so, as she bid her good-bye, she drew the little, tear-stained face to hers, and kissed it so tenderly that Jennie knew the past was forgiven. Lula's joy for her own vindication was so mingled with pity for her school-mate that she hardly knew whether she ought to be glad or not. As she lifted her face to her teacher for her accustomed kiss, and Miss Brown encircled her with her arms and said, "I am very glad my little Lula was brave enough to bear her trouble so patiently," Lula thought, "If my teacher knew how wickedly I felt last night, she would not call me patient or brave."

A glance at Lula's face told Mrs. Norton that the cloud had been dispelled from her daughter's heart, and she took her in her arms lovingly, and then held her from her a moment as she looked inquiringly into the bright, happy eyes. Lula understood the look, and answered:

"It is all right now, mamma, and I am so sorry I was so wicked and ugly last night. Jennie told the teacher all about it, and *she* told the scholars; and I am glad, only I feel so sorry for Jennie;" and again. the little girl's eyes were filled with tears.

"Jennie has gained a great victory over herself by confessing her fault," said Mrs. Norton, kindly, "and she will, no doubt, next time be braver than to let another suffer for her fault. I hope my little girl will only be the better for this trial."

"O mamma, I *know* I shall be more patient next time, and I feel as if I could never be so angry with any one again;" and Lula once more twined her arms about her mother's neck.

Mrs. Norton replied tenderly as she returned her daughter's caress:

"We must not trust too much in our own strength, Lula, but we must ask God's help. And there is a verse of Scripture that I would like for you to commit to memory. It is this : 'For what glory is it if, when ye be buffeted for your *faults*, ye shall take it patiently? But if when ye do *well* and suffer for it, ye take it patiently, this is acceptable to God.' "

Fashionable Calls.

—◆◇◆—

"O DEAR, I do wonder if it pays, after all!" and Mrs. Harris threw her gloves and parasol on the sofa and sank into a chair, at the same time fanning herself vigorously. Her husband, who had just come home to tea, looked up in surprise at the complaining words and disconsolate tones of his wife, and asked, "Wonder if *what* pays? Have you been making investments in railroad bonds and become frightened for fear the company is shaky?"

"No, hush, do; men are such teases! But I really feel as if it was all a waste of time."

"As you have n't told me yet what you are talking about, I shall have to wait until you enlighten me a little before giving my opinion; though, come to think of it,' you have n't asked me for it yet," said Mr. Harris laughingly.

"Well, then, if you must know, I mean fashionable calls. I have been walking and talking all the afternoon, and am nearly roasted and quite tired out, and I do not believe that we have said a dozen sensible things in the whole afternoon. If it was not for seeming selfish and unsociable I would rather stay at home and patch."

"Well, I did n't suppose that *any thing* could put *you* out so. What has happened any way? It is half an hour before tea will be ready, suppose you give me a sketch of the 'leading events,' as the reporters say," and Mr. Harris laid down his paper and leaned back in his chair with mock dignity by way of signifying his readiness to listen. His wife loosened the ties of her bonnet and laid it on her knee, stroking the plume caressingly.

"The first place at which we called was Mrs. Jones's. She had just been having trouble with her cook, and we had to listen while she told us of all the trouble she has had with hired help for the last ten years. One always burnt the bread, one fried the steak too hard, one had too many beaux, another wasted the tea and sugar, another had such a temper, and still another was too slow, and so on, winding up with a rousing benediction on the present queen of the kitchen. Neither Mrs. Armstrong nor myself succeeded in putting in a half dozen sentences during our stay, and that was a full half hour, and as there was only one side to the story we might have come to the conclusion that the whole line of hired help was a sad failure, and the sooner it was wiped out the better."

"Why didn't you tell her what a treasure our Mollie is?"

"Tell her! why she didn't give me a chance. We were obliged to leave her at the door with an unfinished sentence on her lips, though we had prolonged our call fifteen minutes beyond the time allotted. From there we went to Mrs. Newton's. She looked surprised, and I thought a little sorry, to see us, though I have been owing her a call for four months. She showed us into the parlor, raised one of the blinds about six inches, letting in barely enough light for us to see each other's faces. As soon as we were seated she took occasion to say she hoped we would excuse the appearance of the house, she knew it wasn't fit to invite any body into, but she expected to clean house next week. I ventured to say that the house did n't look as if it needed cleaning, which was true, from the fact that the room was so dark that I could not tell whether it was clean or dirty. But she insisted that it was shocking dirty—ashamed to have company—but she had been waiting for a new carpet, and Mr. Newton was *so* slow, never got a new piece of furniture until the old fell to pieces. Wished she had a husband like Mr. Harris; *he* always seemed to anticipate his wife's wants, and so on to the end."

"Her remarks were very flattering to me, I am sure, though not so much so to Newton if he had heard it," laughed Mr. Harris.

"I presume he hears *enough* of it, for any woman who will scold *about* her husband will scold *at* him."

"And what next?"

"O, it was all in the same strain as long as we stayed. I tried to apologize for Mr. Newton, but she would n't listen to any apology, and so we hurried away, and drew a long sigh of relief when we found ourselves again in the street; and then—are you tired?"

"Tired! no, not I. I have been dying, as the girls say, to know what women talked about when they went 'calling,' and I want to hear all about it.

But *I* thought they talked about their neighbors more than *themselves*."

"Wait a moment; I haven't come to that yet. The next place we called was at Mrs. Fitzgerald's. She had been shopping this morning, and wanted me to tell her how to have her little girl's dresses made. Wanted to know if I couldn't cut her some patterns. 'It did cost so much to buy new patterns every Spring.' I felt provoked. Wanted me to turn dress-maker for her little cherubs, and pay me in, Thank you, when Fitzgerald gets a third larger salary than you! I told her I didn't understand pleasing other people, and suggested that she go to the dress-maker and get some newer styles. No, indeed, she couldn't afford that. 'Fitzgerald only gave me so much to buy material and to pay the seamstress, but Mrs. Graves was showing me her little girls' dresses, so nice! and I am bound her children shall not dress better than mine if Graves does have a share in the corner store; and so I spent all my money for the material, and now I will have to work my fingers off to get them made up.' And I thought, Well; if you are so silly as to kill yourself trying to dress like your rich neighbors, it isn't much difference if you do work your fingers off."

"Which was not a very charitable thought," said Mr. Harris, dryly.

"Of course not. But it did sound so foolish that I could not help thinking, though I dare not speak. Mrs. Hickman was brimful of gossip about Mr. Bloomfield's failure. She knew it would be so; had told James over and over, and wanted him to talk with Bloomfield about his extravagant ways, but he said Bloomfield knew his own business, and he should not bother about what was no concern of his. And then she told us how she had called there one evening when the family were at tea: '*Miss* Bloomfield came into the sitting-room and left the door partly open. I just looked in, careless like, you know, and as true as I live the table was all rigged out in china, and they had two kinds of cake on the table, and no company, either! I told James when I came home that I would n't be surprised if they should see the day when they would be glad to get one kind of cake. He said it was none of my business, he guessed. But I told him it *was* some of my business when my neighbors were going to destruction right before my eyes. Says he, "Why didn't you tell Miss Bloomfield yourself?" "Tell Miss Bloomfield!" says I, "why she would a' ordered me out of doors in a minute." "And served you right," says James, snappishly. I told him I wished he would n't take Miss Bloomfield's part and find fault with me, and he looked kind a surprised, and asked, "Who's finding fault?" But I ain't a bit sorry they failed. May be they won't think themselves better than their neighbors.' And I really believe the woman is glad they failed."

"Why didn't you tell her that Bloomfield did not fail through extravagance?"   •

"Mrs. Armstrong did as soon as she stopped long enough for us to put in a word. You would have laughed to see how blank she looked when

Mrs. Armstrong told her that Mr. Bloomfield failed because the bank where his money was deposited had suspended payment, and not because of his wife's extravagance. But she insisted that it was good enough for them; they need n't be so stuck up."

"Was that the last call you made?"

"O, no, we made three others, a little shorter, and just about as profitable, and I feel that the time has been wasted. I have been wanting to go and see old Mrs. Moore for some time; she always rests me so when I spend an hour with her, and she gives me such good advice about the children, that my work seems lighter for a week after I have been there. I felt that it would be better for me to go there to-day, but I have been owing these calls for so long that I felt it a duty to make them; but I feel as if I had wasted precious time in talking with and about people for whom I cared but little, and who cared still less for me, and I have a great mind to say that I will never make another fashionable call," and Mrs. Harris leaned back in her chair as if perplexed.

"Well, if this is a specimen of fashionable calls, I do not wonder that you are disgusted with them," said her husband, half-jokingly, half-seriously.

"O, it is not always so bad as to-day. Sometimes I call on entire strangers and find the visit very profitable. You remember Mrs. Adams, who united with our Church in the Winter? Well, the first time I called on her I expected to stay just ten minutes, and I stayed an hour. I was positively ashamed when I looked at my watch, but her conversation was so pleasant and instructive that I forgot about her being a stranger, and she did me ever so much good; but usually these fashionable calls are so insipid, and the conversation either so trifling or so gossipy, that I always feel condemned after making them."

"Then I should n't make them."

"O yes, that is all you men know about it. We should have half our neighbors offended if we only returned the pleasant calls."

"Well, then, I suppose what can't be cured must be endured; but it seems to me with a little perseverance and tact the sensible women might inaugurate a reform in the matter of calls, or at least in the conversation at such times."

" Yes, and suffer the fate of other lady reformers, be laughed at by one-half the world and make the other half afraid of you. But there goes the tea bell. I guess I must have been gossiping, too, for tea is later than usual and I am not through with my complaints yet."

7

"O DEAR, I have about come to the conclusion that it is wicked to be poor!"
exclaimed Minnie Ray, a girl of some
sixteen Summers, as she entered her mother's
sitting-room and threw herself, with a gesture
of impatience, into the little rocker by the
window.

Her mother looked up with a surprised,
pained expression, and then said, kindly, "My
daughter forgets that she is finding fault with
a wise Providence when she talks in that
way."

"Now, mother, you know I do n't mean that;
but I do get tired of being poor. It has always been
'economize' and 'save' ever since"—she was going
to say, "ever since papa died," but she stopped
short, as she glanced at her mother and saw the tears
stealing down her cheeks, and the next moment her
arms were about her mother's neck, and Minnie was
kissing away the tears.

"O mother, I did n't mean to hurt your feelings;
I know you do all you can for me, and I do n't want
to seem ungrateful; but it is hard to want to go, and
can not, because you have nothing fit to wear," and
then, as she saw by her mother's face that she did
not understand this sudden outbreak, she added, "I

forgot that I had not told you, but I got this from the post-office, only a little while ago," and she laid a note in her mother's hand, and then seated herself on a stool at her feet, and watched her as she read.

It was a note from one of her young friends, with an invitation for herself and her brother Henry to attend a small party at her house, the following week. The note mentioned one or two of her particular friends who were expected to be present, and closed with the injunction, "Don't fail to come."

Mrs. Ray sat holding the note in her hand for some minutes, without speaking; at last she said, "Perhaps we can manage some way; could you not make over your blue merino, and wear that?"

"O no, mother! I wore that to almost every party I attended last Winter; and I heard Fannie Miller ask Jane Rivers, the evening of her party, if that 'old blue' was all I had. No, mother, I would rather stay at home than wear that shabby dress." And, gathering up the invitation and note, she left the room.

Mrs. Ray looked after her daughter, and the tears gathered in her eyes. She was a widow, and had seen better days, but Mr. Ray had been unfortunate in business, losing all that he had laid up, and, dying shortly after his failure, had left his wife and two children penniless, with the exception of a small cottage, in the suburbs of the town. For two years they had contrived, with Minnie's help, to take in sewing enough to keep them above actual want, and to keep Henry, who was two years older than Minnie, in school, in order that he might fit himself for a clerkship, and thus support his mother and sister; but it had only been by doing as Minnie had said— by economizing and saving.

At the tea-table nothing was said upon the sub-ject of the party, but Minnie's face bore the traces of tears, and she carried the subject to her bedroom, and revolved it over and over in her mind, as her head rested on the pillow, deciding a half-dozen times to wear last Winter's dress, and as often deciding to stay at home in preference, and finally ended by fall-ing asleep with the matter still unsettled.

At breakfast Mrs. Ray said: ''I have about fif-teen dollars in the drawer, Minnie, which I do not particularly need just now; if you like, you can take that and buy you a dress to wear to the party. I am anxious you should go, and your brother does not wish to go without you, so you had better accept the invitation."

Minnie's face brightened perceptibly while her mother was speaking, but she hesitated a moment before answering; at last she said: ''I do want to go so much, mother, but I feel as if it was hardly right to take your money; I am afraid that you will need it."

But Mrs. Ray insisted that she did not need the money just then; and by the next Winter Henry would probably be in a position to earn something. So, thanking her mother, Minnie took the money, and prepared to go out to make the desired purchase, begging her brother to go with her, to help se-lect it.

Yielding to her persuasions, Henry put on his hat, and they were soon in the street.

As they walked along, Minnie tried to entertain her brother, by telling him who were to be present at the coming party.

"But what is the matter with you? you do n't seem half so interested as you did before breakfast."

"Minnie," said Henry, suddenly, speaking as if he had not heard a word of what his sister had been saying, "do you know what mother was saving that money for?"

"No," and Minnie's blue eyes opened wide at the suddenness of the question, "what was it?"

"She told me last week that she had almost money enough saved to buy herself a new cloak for this Winter, and that her old one was getting so thin that she was not comfortable in it, now that the days were growing colder."

Minnie's eyes sought the ground, and her step seemed to have suddenly lost its elasticity. At last she said, in a very low tone, "Did mother really say that?"

"Of course, she did! And you did n't know it? I thought as much when you took the money this morning."

Minnie's rosy lips quivered, and her eyes looked very misty as her brother stopped talking; but she looked up at him with sudden resolution in her voice. "I am not going down town this morning."

Henry looked at her in surprise. "Why? what new notion have you taken now?"

"O nothing, only I do n't believe I will get the dress to-day; come."

And almost before her brother was aware of it, their faces were turned homeward.

At the gate he left her, and went to his school. Minnie walked slowly up the path, and entered the house. Mrs. Ray was busy, at the center-table, arranging the books and papers that had been misplaced the previous evening, and humming a tune in a low, contented tone.

Minnie stood looking at her mother's sweet, patient face, for a moment, and then, quickly gliding to her side, putting her arm around her waist, and speaking in a trembling voice, she said: "Mother, how could you give me all your money, when you were needing it yourself?"

"Why, Minnie, what brought you back so soon? And who told you I needed the money? did I not say I could do without it?"

"I came back because I am not going to buy a dress, when you need the money for something else. Henry said you were intending to buy a cloak for yourself, as soon as you could save enough. No," as her mother drew back her hand as Minnie tried to put the money in it, "you must take it back; indeed, I could not wear the dress if I should get it, knowing that you were needing a cloak to keep you warm; no, mother dear, I am not so selfish as that, if I am a little vain sometimes."

Thus entreated, Mrs. Ray took the money from her daughter's hand, and then, folding her lovingly in her arms, imprinted a kiss upon the upturned face.

Minnie slipped quietly from her mother's arms, and went to her own room, feeling far happier than when she started out to buy the coveted dress.

She took down the blue merino, and looked it over. It did not look half so "shabby" as it did the evening before.

"I do believe that I can fix it so that it will do to wear," Minnie said aloud; and then, in a lower tone, "How selfish mother and Henry must have thought me; but," as if in apology for herself, "mother never complains, and how could I know that her cloak was not warm enough?"

Minnie remodeled the merino, and the bright, glad look with which her brother greeted her as she entered the little sitting-room with it on, ready to accompany him to her friend's house, on the evening of the party, was reward enough for all her self-denial. And when, outside the gate, her brother drew her arm within his own, and said, in a low, loving tone, "My little sister is dearer to me in what she calls her shabby merino than if she had purchased a new dress at the cost of mother's comfort and health," her cup of happiness was full.

The evening passed off pleasantly, even though some of the company were better dressed than she; and as she hung the dress in its accustomed place that night, she made up her mind that, after all, real happiness did not consist in dressing better than her companions, but in doing right, and thinking of others' comfort more than her own gratification.

Mrs. Clayton's Experiment.

HAT have you been doing to-day that you are so tired?" asked Frank Clayton one evening, as he glanced at his wife's flushed face and heard the little, tired sigh. "It seems to me that, with only our two selves in family, you do not need to work so hard or seem so tired as you do every evening lately."

"O, the house-work is not much, but the sewing thrown in with it makes it rather heavy sometimes; and just now my Spring dresses are to make, and last year's ones to make over, making extra work at present. But I will soon be through, and then I shall have a little rest."

"But, Mary, why not put your dresses out, and have them made up, and so get rid of the worry? I would rather pay for having them made than to see you looking so worn and tired every night."

"O dear, that is all *you know* about it! With your salary, if I should hire my dresses made, there would be nothing left to buy the next ones; for it costs almost as much to get a dress made in the present style as it does to buy the material; and when I hire them made up, it takes almost as much time running back and forth every day as it would if I did the work myself."

"Well, then, why not make them plainer, and so

save time? How long have you been at work on your Spring and Summer dresses?"

"Two weeks."

"And how long before you will be through?"

"About three weeks."

"Two and three are five. Five weeks of hard work over patterns and sewing-machines—and all in order that you may be fashionably dressed! Fie, fie, wife! I thought you had a stronger head than that." And Frank Clayton leaned back in his easy-chair, and laughed heartily at the foolishness of women.

"But, Frank," pleaded his wife when his mirth had subsided a little, "you like to see me well dressed, I am sure; and I dress more to please you than any one else."

"But why can't you be well dressed, as you call it, without so many furbelows and frizzes? Why, you must have spent an hour in getting your hair into that wonderful state of confusion. Very becoming, I admit; but where is the use of it? I shall like you just as well in a plain dress and smoothly combed hair as I do in flounces and frizzes. And, then, there is the extra amount of cooking you women do. It seems to me that it is a sort of strife to see who can do the most unnecessary work. If you women would dress plainer, and could be content to put plain food on your tables, we husbands would hear less about tired and overworked wives?"

Having delivered himself of this wise little speech, Mr. Clayton drew up a hassock, and placed his slippered feet upon it, and was soon deep in the "latest

from Washington." Mrs. Clayton gave a little sigh,
as if his argument was unanswerable, and then took
up her basting, so that she might have a little work
"ready for the machine" on the morrow.

Frank Clayton had been married two years, and
was living very comfortably on a salary of twelve
hundred a year. Mrs. Clayton, with a desire to help
her husband, kept no "girl," but did all her work,
except the washing and ironing. It was hard work,
for she had not been accustomed to the care of a
house; but when she compared her little home with
that of her neighbors and friends, she had the satisfaction of knowing that, although her furniture was
not so costly or her house so large, it was just as
neat and tasty.

The next morning after Frank's little lecture, just
as he had said good-bye and started for the office, he
stopped, with his hand on the gate, and called out
pleasantly: "I forgot to tell you I saw Will Hartley
yesterday, and invited him to dine with us to-day.
Of course you will be glad to see him." And, with
a light laugh, he closed the gate, and went down
street.

Now, Will Hartley was an old friend of Mary's;
in fact, Frank had felt very much inclined to be jealous of him during courting days. Mary turned from
the door with an impatient gesture. "I declare it is
too bad, when I am so busy! I wonder if Frank
ever thinks it is any work for me to have company to
dinner two or three days out of a week?" Then,
with a mischievous smile: "I know what I will do.
I will dress plainly and cook a plain dinner. That

was his own advice. I will try it once, and see how he will like it."

As her dinner progressed, Mary felt strongly tempted to make a pudding, or some extra dish that she had been accustomed to make for her husband's dinner. Mr. Hartley had praised the puddings and pies at her mother's table; and now, if those things were missing from hers, he would think she did not know how to make them. However, she put the temptation aside, and provided a plain dinner, without pudding or pies. When all was ready, she went to her room to "dress for dinner." Selecting one of her school dresses, that had been laid by because it was out of style, she dressed herself in it, and smiled as she saw how old-fashioned she looked without flounce or overskirt. Then, instead of the usual dainty ruche and bright ribbon, she pinned on a plain linen collar. Her hair she twisted, not in a magnificent coil about her classic head—for there was not enough of it for that—but in a little knot at the back of her head, or, more correctly speaking, at the back of her neck, and then took a glance into her mirror to see the effect. It must be confessed it was rather a sickly smile that greeted the plain little figure in the glass; but she determined to carry out her programme, "even if Mr. Hartley does think me a guy."

Just then she heard a voice in the hall, and in a moment she was shaking hands with Will Hartley, and watching her husband to see if he noticed the change in her dress. He did notice it, and gave a little start, and his cheeks flushed for an instant; for he had pictured to himself how he would quietly triumph over his bachelor friend, as Mary, daintily attired, should do the honors of mistress of his little establishment. As for Hartley, he looked a little surprised at first, and the glance he bestowed on Mrs. Clayton said plainer than he was aware, "What a change!"

After a few moments' chat Mary led the way to the dining-room. The meal passed off pleasantly, only after Frank had made a very good dinner he shoved back his plate and sat as if waiting for something more. But Mary was, apparently, too much engaged in relating some incident of school days to notice the silent hint. At last he said in a low tone, "Ready for the pudding, Mary." But Mary only replied indifferently, as if it were not a matter of any consequence,

"There is no pudding to-day," and continued her story, utterly regardless of her husband's blank look.

As they left the table and repaired to the sitting-room Frank thought, "Now she will change her dress and show Hartley that she is just as pretty as she was three years ago." But he was disappointed in this, for Mrs. Clayton soon appeared in the same dress she had worn at dinner. Hartley asked for music, and she seated herself at the piano and sang and played as merrily as if she were dressed in the extreme of fashion. Mr. Hartley soon took leave of his hostess, and Clayton accompanied him down town, promising to be home early.

On his return he found her reading a new book, and dressed in the identical garb she had worn at dinner.

"Are you sick to-day?" asked Frank in an anxious tone, as he seated himself by her side.

Mary answered pleasantly, "No, I never felt better in my life."

"Then what in the name of goodness is the matter?" asked Frank in an injured tone; "I expected you would take extra pains to look well when you knew Hartley was coming, but instead of that I never saw you look so dowdyish."

"O no, not dowdyish; I am sure I was neat and clean."

"O yes, neat and clean enough, I suppose, but your hair looks just like Biddy Malone's, only not quite so frowsy."

"Mary drew half a sigh, and said innocently, "I am sure I thought you would be pleased."

"Pleased!" echoed Clayton. "What do you mean?"

"Why, only last night you lectured me on the vanity of dress, and said you would like me just as well dressed plainly as in flounces and frizzes."

"O!" fairly gasped Frank, as the truth began to dawn upon him. "And so you thought you would try plain dressing and cooking, did you?". Then seeing he was cornered, he added humbly, "Well, I do think you women might do with less of such work, but you went to extremes, which was hardly fair, especially when an old friend was coming, and you must have known that I wanted you to do your best."

"How unreasonable you are! I never tried harder to be agreeable in my life."

"I know it, but I couldn't enjoy any thing for looking at your dress. And then that song, I suppose under other circumstances I should have enjoyed it; as it was I didn't understand three consecutive words for looking at that knot on the back of your neck," and looking up he caught the merry twinkle of his wife's eye, and laughed in spite of himself.

"So you don't want me to dress in this style, nor omit the pudding and pies at dinner any more?" asked Mary demurely.

"O, you can leave off the pies and pudding when we are alone, if you like, but I should not be willing to have you adopt your present style of dress even if no one saw you but myself," responded Clayton meekly.

"Then I suppose I may return to my flounces and frizzes; and for my part.I shall not be sorry, but I am afraid if all husbands are like you a woman's crusade against dress would not prove as successful as their crusade against whisky has proved." And so ended Mrs. Clayton's experiment in dress and cooking reform.

For Company's Sake.

RED MELTON had been in the village of S—— a little over a year, when his old friend and college chum, Clark Liston, passed through the place and called to see him. Liston's parents were well to do and had given their son the benefit of their means in educating and training him for business, and while they were doing this they had not neglected the more important part, the religious culture. Fred Melton had been trained with equal care, morally and intellectually, but at the close of his school days his father died, leaving but little of this world's goods, and Fred suddenly found himself thrown upon his own resources, with a mother and sister looking to him for support. He accordingly sought and obtained a situation in S—— as clerk for a dry-goods merchant, and there young Liston found him. Melton's joy was unbounded at the sight of his old friend, and as it was near the hour of closing up, he insisted on taking his friend with him to his own room, that he might enjoy his company undisturbed. Once inside his own room, he turned to his friend, as he gave him a chair, with, "Liston, old chum, it's good of you to remember a fellow this way. I have been thinking of you to-day, and wishing we could have an old-time chat, but I did n't know where you were, and then since father's death every thing is so different with us, that I did n't know but you had forgotten me," with a sigh.

"Our school-days were too pleasant to allow me to forget so soon, Fred," replied Liston, warmly; "but between business and 'society,' I have been too busy to visit you until now, and now we are together let's not waste time in regrets. Suppose we compare notes. How has time served you?"

"O, well enough," and Fred Melton turned his eyes on the blaze of the little grate as he leaned back in the chair he had drawn near his friend. Something in the voice more than the words caused Liston to look up into his friend's face inquiringly, but seeing he was not inclined to pursue the subject he changed the conversation from themselves to sketching some of their old associates, and so the evening passed away very pleasantly, although they were twice interrupted by raps at the door, which Melton answered by stepping into the hall and closing the door after him, conversing with the caller in low tones. Clark Liston said nothing, but the evening's intercourse showed him too plainly that his friend was not the Fred Melton of a year and a half ago. The next morning being Sabbath, Liston inquired where his friend attended Church.

"At the Methodist, when I go at all. Do n't attend very regularly; but of course you want to go."

And so they went. The bright, clear morning, the cool, bracing air, and the ringing of church bells, all tended to fill the minds of the two friends with thoughts of Him who had made the Sabbath for his children. The sermon was plain and practical, without effort at rhetoric or oratory. The services over, Melton turned to go, but Liston said,

"Wait a moment, I want to speak to the minister."

"Do you know him?" asked Melton, in a tone of surprise.

"No, but I mean to; I have enjoyed his sermon and I wish to tell him so."

"Well, you will have to introduce yourself, for I am not acquainted with him." And then, as he noticed his friend's surprised look, he laughed a little uneasily, and turned to watch the congregation as they passed out. After a few pleasant words with the pastor the two young men wended their way, almost silently, to the boarding-house. After dinner, when they were once more in Melton's room, Clark Liston turned to his friend and asked,

"Fred, how is this? What has changed you so?"

Melton laughed lighly. "Changed! How?"

"You know what I mean? You are not what you were eighteen months ago." . For some moments the two sat in silence. Then Melton said,

"Well, chum, you are just like you always were, reading a fellow whether he wants you to or not. It *is* true that I am not just what I was when you and I left school."

"But how did it happen? Why are you different?"

"Well, Clark, I may as well tell you first as last; may be I shall feel better if I do; and your coming

8

has brought back old times so fresh that I have been hearing home voices all day. But, I suppose, with your strict notions of Christian courage and manliness, you will despise me when you hear what I have to tell, and I have gone further back than you think. To-day is the first time in six months that I have been to Church, and if it hadn't been for you I shouldn't have gone to-day. I had arranged for a good time in a different way, but your coming put a stop to it. I am not sorry though, and Clark, I may as well make a clean breast of it, I have not been as strictly temperate as you and I were taught to be in the good old times."

Clark looked up at his friend, his face full of reproach, "O, Fred, how could you?"

"Now please, chum, don't scold, or I shall never get through. I didn't intend it, and the fact is, *you* don't know any thing about it. *You* never had to go among strangers, without money or position, and with nothing but your face to recommend you."

"Where was your Church letter?" asked Liston, without looking up.

"I carried it to Church for a few Sabbaths, but there was no opportunity offered to hand it in, and so I laid it away."

"But didn't you find friends?"

"Not such as could be called real friends, nor such as *you* would care to associate with. I went to Church and Sabbath-school for nearly three months, and was as much a stranger at the close as on the first Sabbath. Not a soul seemed interested in me, or seemed to care whether I was a Christian or a reprobate, and finally I left off going altogether, and took Sunday walks instead; and I found plenty of company, too."

"But, Fred Melton, you *knew* better than that," and Liston spoke impatiently.

"Of course I did. But, Liston, I tell you, you can't understand until you are in my place. You have never known what it is to be hungry for friends. Your money and your family have carried you right along. I was a stranger, and the church-going people only stared at me, and I doubt whether they even asked their neighbors who I was. I have to stay in the store until respectable people have closed their doors. After nine and ten at night one doesn't find very choice company on the streets or in the hotel bar-rooms. I didn't enjoy it at first, and I don't yet, but what can I do? I *must* have company of some kind. One can't always mope. I hear that my employer has a pleasant family, but he has never invited me to his house. I don't blame him *now*, for I am scarcely a suitable companion for either his sons or daughters. I have not been invited to a single *home* since I have been here, but I *have* been invited to brilliant halls and other places for gambling; and I have gone there, too, though I have never taken part except for amusement. I suppose if Mr. Wilson knew that I frequented such places, he would turn me off. If he should I am ruined, and sometimes I feel as if I didn't care how soon," he added desperately.

Clark Liston had risen from his chair, while his friend was talking, and, laying his hand upon

his shoulder, and with a voice in which pity and reproach were mingled, said: "Fred, I can not tell
you how sorry I am to hear this of you."

"And *I* intended to keep it from you, but I
could n't. We always told each other every thing,
you know; and I was so *hungry for a friend.* The
company I keep are not friends, Clark. I have not
seen a person to whom I would tell my heart-thoughts
since I left home. I have sometimes wished I could
drink like some of the rest, and forget all about it;
but I have n't got that far yet."

"No; and, by the grace of God, you never
shall," and Clark Liston's voice had a ring in it that
made Melton look up in surprise. "Fred Melton,
you are too good a man to sink for want of friends.
Do you remember the pledge we took when we entered college? We promised always to stand by
each other, no difference what happened."

"But what can you do?" and Melton's voice
sounded hopeless enough. "I can not afford to give
up my situation, for my mother and sister need my
wages; you can't stay here, to watch over me, and
I am too weak and miserable to overcome alone."

"And you need not be alone. You know where
you used to go for strength; go to Him again. Go
as you used to, Fred. and ask him to help you to *stand*,
even though you should be denied an earthly friend.
Come, let us ask him now."

For a moment, Melton hesitated, but at last
bowed with his friend, with a heart broken and con-
trite. Then Liston prayed. In a voice almost as
tender as a mother's, he talked with God, pleading

that his friend might have strength to overcome. When they rose from their knees, Melton was sobbing like a child. After he had grown calmer, Liston proposed visiting the pastor to whom they had listened in the morning. Fred objected, but his friend insisted.

"I can not leave you as lonely as I found you, Fred; I want you to have at least one earthly friend to whom you can go, and Mr. H. is a true Christian, or I am no judge of faces."

They found the minister in his study, and were warmly welcomed. Liston briefly stated his friend's case, and found in the pastor a ready listener and sympathizer.

And when the two young men returned to their lodgings, they talked long and earnestly of the past and future, and covenanted anew to pray for each other, that they might be strengthened to withstand temptation, in any form or from whatever source.

Before retiring, Melton said: "Clark, I feel that something is due Mr. Wilson; he has trusted me, and I have deceived him into thinking I keep regular hours; will you go with me, in the morning, while I tell him about it?"

"No, Fred; go alone. It will be better for you to go to him and make a full confession."

"Perhaps I shall lose my situation; he is very strict."

"I do not think you need fear; but, even then, you had better do it. Start fair and square, and you will stand a better chance for the future. Father says, 'Nothing is so heavy to carry as a secret.'"

"Well, chum, I'll try. And I want to thank you for your kindness; and I shall feel grateful to my heavenly Father for sending you to visit me. Yesterday I was desperate enough to do almost any thing; to night I am happier than I have been for months. I shall burn my Church-letter, for I am not worthy of it; but I shall unite with the Church, as I did at first. By and by, when I am stronger, I will write mother all about it."

In the morning the friends separated — Liston to continue his journey, while Melton took his place, as usual, in the store. When Mr. Wilson came to the store, about nine o'clock, Melton asked for a private interview, which was readily granted; and then, with burning cheeks, but with a firm will, he told his employer of his course in the past few months, keeping back nothing.

As he recounted his lonely hours, and his efforts to confine himself to books, in the absence of other company, his employer listened with surprise. It had never entered his mind that the young man who had been so faithful to his business, could be passing through such temptation, and sinking beneath it. He had recommended him to a respectable boarding-house, paid his wages regularly, and considered his duty toward his clerk at an end; and yet Mr. Wilson was rather above the average Christian in most things. But his clerk's confession made a deep impression, and he more readily forgave his wrong-doing, feeling that himself, with others of his Church, were in a great measure to blame for it.

The next Sabbath, Fred Melton again gave his

name to the Church, and reconsecrated himself to God, and, through the kindness of his pastor and employer, he had no reason to go in forbidden paths in search of friends.

Six months later, in a letter to his friend Liston, he wrote: "I thank God every day for your visit of last Winter. I wish Christians could realize how many young men are going to ruin for the same reason that came so near being my destruction. Of course, I ought to have been strong enough to withstand the temptation; but I was not. I have talked with several of my old associates, in the past few months, and they nearly all seem to have fallen into bad habits from the same reason—nowhere else to go. You have, through God's grace, been the means of saving me from ruin; and I am trying to repay you and him by trying to reclaim others. I spent last evening at Mr. Wilson's; his family are all Christians, and I feel very grateful to them for their kindness to me and their faith in me. May my heavenly Father keep me from betraying their confidence. One thing I have determined on: if ever I have a home of my own, I will not close it against the homeless."

RETURNING from a trip down town this morning after our Church festival, I met my neighbor and sister in the Church, Mrs. Jones; and after the first salutations I remarked with probably an interrogation point in my voice: "I didn't see you at our festival last night. I counted on you as one of the helpers."

"No, we were not there. No one said any thing to me about it, and I didn't propose to crowd my company or help where I was not wanted."

"Why," I said, stammering for very surprise, "I thought every body was solicited to bake or contribute something."

"Well, yes, I believe the girls did call on me to bake a cake, and I thought then that I would, but the Church just treated us as if we were not members at all. No one asked me to help or asked my advice, or even invited us to attend; and I told Mr. Jones, if the Church could get along without us, I guess we could get along without it, and we stayed at home."

"But, sister Jones, didn't you hear the announcement from the pulpit on Sabbath, when the minister invited all to attend?"

"O, yes," with a little toss of the head; "but we don't go on invitations that were made for every body — Tom, Dick, and Harry, and their families. If we were wanted, why didn't somebody say so?" And Mrs. Jones looked the picture of offended dignity.

"Well, I am sure, I don't know. I was not on the committee of arrangements, but if I had been I would have as soon thought of sending an invitation to myself as to you. This was a Church affair, and I thought you were a part of the Church, and of course you would not wait for a special invitation."

"If my services were worth having, they were worth asking for; and I don't crowd myself on people, as I said before."

"I am sure, sister Jones, no offense was intended," I pleaded. "I suppose the committee did not think."

"O it didn't matter at all; if they can live without our help it's all right." However, Mrs. Jones's look and tone indicated that it made a great deal of difference to her, and that it would require some coaxing to smooth her injured feelings.

I went home "blue" and out of sorts, for I had considered our festival a success, at least as much so as hard work, late supper, and late hours could make it. "Net receipts one hundred and ten dollars, and nobody offended either," I had said to my husband, triumphantly, only two short hours before. He, the wiseacre, had smiled a little increduously, and said with a patronizing air, "Wait a little, my dear, the returns are not all in yet." And now here was sister Jones, cross as it was possible for a Methodist of

9

twenty-five years' standing to be, and that we all
know is sufficiently cross to be interesting, to say
the least.   At any rate, she had spoiled my peace of
mind, as Bridget would say, "intirely."

How could I tell husband about it?   I knew he
would only smile as usual, and say, "Of course,
such affairs always offend somebody."   And, sure
enough, when I reported our conversation—for I had
to tell some one to relieve my own mind—he made
almost the very comment that I had framed for him.

"But," I remonstrated, "it is perfectly absurd
for sister Jones to expect me to coax her to take
part in our Church entertainments.   She has been in
the Church longer than any woman who worked there
all day, and nearly all night, to make the festival a
success.   I think it is too ridiculous."

"O yes, I know it; but she makes the fact of
her having been in the Church so long the very reason
why she should have received special attention.   She
and her sister, Mrs. Green, will not come to Sabbath-
school because the superintendent has not solicited
them to take a class."

"Perhaps that is the reason brother Jones does n't
come to class, because you did n't appoint him
leader," I said, a little spitefully.

"Precisely, my dear; and they make things
pretty close for me, because I do n't appreciate their
talents.   My salary will fall short, probably, on account of their influence against me.   Besides, they
are making themselves quite unhappy over the slights
they imagine they have received from some of the
Church members."

"O dear! what does ail them, any way? It's enough to provoke a saint!" and I groaned in desperation."

"O, there is nothing very particular the matter with them, only they imagine themselves of greater importance than they really are, and they also imagine there is a conspiracy on the part of the Church to depreciate their value; and so they feel called upon to stand guard over their rights and privileges. They are so afraid that others will not recognize their rights that they are on a continual watch for evidence of neglect or lack of appreciation, and so keep themselves in a fume and fret all the time. I have to call on *their* families about twice as often as any others, or they feel neglected."

"Yes, I know that; and sister Jones counts every call I make at Mrs. R.'s, just opposite the Jones's. Not more than two weeks ago she took occasion to hint that it was not good policy for the pastor's wife to visit outsiders oftener than she did the Church members. I can't see why people should be so fussy. It just provokes me." And I presume I looked just a little fussy, too, at that time.

Husband said soothingly: "I wouldn't let it provoke me, if I were you. It's just their nature, I guess. They are over-sensitive, and they are not over-sensible, and they let little things annoy them— or, rather, they magnify the motes until they look immense beams—and they are thoroughly unhappy themselves, and certain to make a goodly number of the community and Church uncomfortable, if not unhappy."

" But why do n't you tell them how foolishly they act, and try to mend their ways?"

" Because they would only take that as an additional proof that I was taking sides against them, and would only make matters worse for them and also for myself."

" How can you put up with them ?   Do n't they worry you ?" and then I laughed just a little at the absurdity of my questioning.

Of course it worried him. Did n't I remember how awfully solemn he always looked on his return from a visit to the Joneses or Greens ?   And did n't I know that sisters Jones and Green always made it a rule to talk of their grievances every time they called at the parsonage, until I felt, after each visit, as if I was just recovering from an attack of neuralgia.   " Why will such people worry themselves and every one else about such trifles ?"

" I think they started wrong in the first place," said husband, thoughtfully, as he took up his pen— a hint of passing time, I suppose.   "They seem to have come into the Church under the impression that they were conferring a great honor upon it; and, therefore, they expect special deference to be shown them.   They are sort of spiritual invalids, or infants, whom the Church is bound to humor and amuse. Instead of being independent, and taking care of themselves, and working for the advancement of the cause of Christ, they labor for their own advancement.   Instead of asking, ' What can I do to build up the temporal or spiritual interests of the Church?' they are watching to see if their own interests are considered sufficiently by their brothers and sisters. There is an old saying that the happiest people are those who live to make others happy; but the Jones and Green class seem not to appreciate the sentiment, if they ever heard of it. The question with them seems to be, Does the Church show a proper appreciation of me and my talents? And, according to their notion, the Church is very blind, and they are unhappy over it. But, if I were you, I would n't worry over it at all. Just let sister Jones alone, and go on your way, and ten years from now you will be just as happy as if sister Jones had been sweet and pleasant."

And, with this consoling speech, the pastor turned to his writing-desk, and the pastor's wife to her housekeeping; but she could not help saying, as a sort of last word: "Well, I wish there were more earnest workers in the Church, and fewer touch-me-nots."

THOSE PARLORS.

—◦—•—•—

HOME should be a refuge, a haven of rest, a sort of paradise for every member of the family; and in order that all may feel at home it should be the business of each member of the family—not of the housewife only—to assist in making home pleasant, a place to be desired and longed for.

Not only should there be suitable food provided in a proper manner—although that is very necessary—but the numerous little things that combine to make home pleasant should not be forgotten. There are families who have plenty of means, who build a comfortable house, who furnish a parlor and a spare bedroom or two, with elegant furniture and carpets, and then shut them up, to be opened only when visitors come, while the rest of the house is furnished but meanly, not at all in keeping with the "company rooms." The family spend their evenings in the dining-room, or too frequently the kitchen, while the parlor, with its costly furnishing, grows moldy or dusty for want of use.

While spending a few weeks with a friend once, we called in company upon a mutual friend, whom I had not met for some years, and, while waiting for the lady to make her appearance, the husband, who chanced to be slightly indisposed, and had stayed at

home that afternoon, came into the parlor to entertain us. The room was so dark that, for a few
minutes, we could scarcely distinguish each other's
features. The gentleman looked about the room at
the closed shutters and drawn blinds, and apologized
for the darkness; yet he apparently did not feel
enough at home to open the shutters or withdraw
the blinds.

After our eyes had become accustomed to the
gloom, so that we could distinguish objects a little
more clearly, we crossed the room to examine some
engravings on the wall, and remarked upon their
beauty. To which the gentleman replied, in an in-
different tone: "O yes, they are rather fine; but I
scarcely ever see them. In fact, I believe I have not
been in this room more than two or three times in
the past year. My wife receives calls here, and the
girls spend an evening here occasionally with some
of their friends; and I believe that is about all the
use we have for a parlor." And yet he was a man
past the middle age, who had toiled hard all his life
to acquire the means to live independently, and was
still toiling to keep up appearances and to purchase
luxuries that he never enjoyed.

I looked at his silvered hair and stooping form,
and thought: "Is it right for father and mother to
work hard all their lives, merely that they may build
a handsome house and furnish its parlors for the comfort of comparative strangers, while they shut themselves up in two or three gloomy back-rooms until
they are totally unfit to enjoy the comforts they have
worked for?"

It is probable that his wife and daughters received fashionable calls there ; fashionable young men, probably, spent their evenings lolling on the luxurious sofas, talking nonsense to his daughters, while a seat in the dining-room was all he *expected*, and no one seemed to think it worth while to open the parlor or piano for "father's" comfort or amusement. It was as much the fault of the father, perhaps, as of any one else, but a mistake nevertheless.

Who is it that can not call to remembrance a half hour spent in one of those gloomy, sepulchral "best rooms," where the husband, if he chanced to come in, would sit down on the cushioned chairs as gingerly as if he were afraid they would crumble beneath him ?—where the children would eye each article on the table and "what-not" as eagerly as if they saw them for the first, and where even the housewife herself felt ill at ease ?

If home comforts are worth any thing at all, they ought to be so to our own families. Public opinion would condemn the man who would furnish pleasant rooms for his neighbor's wife and children, for fashionable young men to lounge in, while his own family were not allowed to enjoy them ; and public opinion ought to disapprove of the course of the wife and mother, who, after her husband has provided her with a comfortable home, and even luxuries, should refuse, through pride or a mistaken economy, to use and enjoy them with her husband and children.

It is often, however, as much the fault of the husband as the wife, by insisting, after he has furnished the costly rooms, that he does n't "care for such privacy," or that he has "no time for luxuries." If we can not afford to have such luxuries, and *use* them, let us have the courage to do without them until we *can* afford them.

As we ought to love our own companion and our own children better than any one else, so we ought to strive more for their happiness. The family that settles down in the kitchen for the evening, or never tries to surround its every-day life with little comforts and works of requirement, will show it when its members mingle in society. If we want our children to be easy and graceful in our neighbor's parlor, we must help them to cultivate ease and grace at home.

It is not absolutely necessary to have elegant homes in order to the cultivation of elegant or pleasant manners. Some would fail to attain to them in any home. But let our leisure hours be spent in neat and orderly rooms—in our parlor, if we have one. If not, let us make our rooms as pleasant as we can, making it a rule that our own loved ones shall have the best rooms and the best comforts that we can afford to give them; teaching our children to be polite by being polite to them; and there will be an air of taste and refinement about our families that will amply repay us for any sacrifice we may make.

If homes were all that their names signify, if the time and money spent for the pleasures and entertainment of fashionable acquaintances were expended in cultivating a taste for home pleasures, and in making home attractive, there would be fewer young men spending their evenings at billiard-saloons, and fathers would find home more attractive than the club-room.

The First Sabbath.

WHAT preacher's wife has ever forgotten it? You go to Church in the morning with all the memories of last Sabbath and last conference year clinging to you in spite of yourself.

You enter God's house with a sort of vague feeling of utter loneliness, yet with an instinctive consciousness that all eyes are upon you.

You seat yourself and try to lift your thoughts heavenward. But you can not pray with that feeling of rest and contentment that you could in the old church which has grown familiar to you by two or three years of prayer, conflict, and faith.

While you are striving to collect your thoughts, which are "backward straying," your husband rises from his seat in the pulpit, and announces the hymn, a song of thanksgiving and praise. Ah, you can join in *that*, for God's praise is the same wherever his people are gathered together. And when the choir strike the verse—

> "God is our sun, he makes our day,
>   God is our shield, he guards our way."

you join in with a glad heart. Glad that in the world's darkest hour we may have the Sun of right-

eousness pouring his blessed rays of comfort into
our hearts.

The hymn, the prayer, and the second hymn are
ended. The text is announced, and you try to
listen. But every now and then comes the thought,
"Not one familiar face in the whole congregation."
The late comers seat themselves, and cast a glance
around the church; their eyes fall upon the stranger, and straightway they conclude it is the "new
preacher's wife," and lean their heads down to tell
their next neighbor their opinion, frequently in a
voice loud enough for you to hear.

The sermon is over, the benediction is pronounced, and your husband comes down out of the
pulpit, and shakes hands with those nearest the
altar; for Methodist ministers do not usually wait for
a formal introduction. He touches your arm and
signifies his wish to introduce you to some of the
"brethren and sisters." Instantly you feel that your
measure is being taken—not for a new dress, but to
see whether you will suit or not. Usually the
"brethren" are satisfied if you speak cordially and
seem at ease. But not so the sisters. With a
woman's eye they note down your dress, words, and
even gestures; not with any unkind motive, perhaps,
but because it is their habit. At any rate, you feel
that you are being measured, from your bonnet to
your shoes.

After you have been introduced to several, and
you are slowly passing down the aisle, a sweet-faced
woman lays her hand upon your arm, and says in a
pleasant voice: "You are our new pastor's wife, I

suppose. My name is Mrs. ——. I live on the corner of —— street, opposite Sister B's. I am .coming to, see you soon, and shall be glad to see you at my home." Something in her voice and manner, more than her words, impresses you favor-·ably, and, during the week, you often wonder when she will call. As you near the door, an aged wo-man, one of God's chosen ones, meets you, presses your hand, and whispers a "God bless you," with her quivering lips. You lift your heart to God in thankfulness that there are some already in your new field who are calling down his blessing on you and yours.

Well is it for us that the "new" wears off in the course of a few weeks. Well for us, and our people, too; for we would make but poor helpmates for our husbands if the people should always feel as far off as on that first Sabbath.

But it does wear away in a short time. There is a funeral. One of the "little ones" of the flock, may be. Your husband is called upon to preach the funeral sermon. He does the best he can under the circumstances. He speaks of God's promises, and points the stricken ones to him who bore our griefs and carried our sorrows. The little one is laid in the grave, but the pastor is bound to that family by a new and sacred tie, and they feel that they love their new pastor better than they did a week ago. The chain that binds them is not easily broken, for one link in their affection is on the heavenly shore.

Thus it is. Funerals and weddings, sorrows and

joys, unite the hearts of pastor and people, and at the end of the year we are as loath to part with the friends as we were at the close of the former year. But parting must come. Every earthly joy has an end; but we live on, comforted by the hope that,

> "When our earthly life is ended,
>   And our earthly mission done,
> We shall go across the river
>   At the setting of the sun;
> And in God's celestial mansions,
>   Clothed in garments strangely fair,
> We shall know the bliss of heaven,
>   We shall meet each other there."

YOUR old neighbors—not the nominal, but the genuine, orthodox sort—have moved away, and the "next house" is vacant. A small board, on which is painted, in rough script: "For rent. Apply to J. Smith, west side Public Square," is tacked up on the corner of the building.

You have enjoyed the society of the former occupants most "intensely." Mrs. M., with her years of experience, had taken you to her motherly heart, when you most needed her counsel and love, and ever since her presence has been a sort of benediction to you at all times. Now you miss her bright face and cheery voice, and you begin to wonder who will occupy the house and your heart next.

Each noon and night you report as to the various applicants who have looked at the premises. Finally you announce to your Isaac, as he sits at his breakfast, sipping his coffee and reading the morning paper, "The Smith property is rented at last; a load of household goods was moved-in yesterday." You were too sleepy to tell the news. the evening previous. Isaac looks up absently, says something so inaudibly that you can not quite make out whether it was meant for your ears or his own, and drops his

eyes again to the money markets.   He is too busy
with up-town affairs to feel much interest in the
people of the home neighborhood; but not so his
Rebekah.   It is a matter of great import to you,
and only the most conscientious politeness prevents
your taking a glance from behind the parlor blinds,
"just to see what they look like, and if I shall like
them."

But it is not fair to judge your neighbors on
"moving day"—that day of days, a day which defies
the pen of poet or painter's pencil to do it justice.
With what a woeful effort at tidiness does the mistress of ceremonies smooth back her natural frizzes,
and how carefully she arranges the clean collar and
bright bit of ribbon about her neck, in order that she
may make a favorable impression on the neighbors to
whom she is going; but in spite of such efforts, the
collar is soon soiled, the ribbon is untied by catching
on nail or hook, and, finally, in sheer desperation,
it is taken off and tucked into the pocket, out of the
way.   No matter how much we may want to make
a favorable impression, it requires an extra amount
of self possession and watchfulness if we maintain our
dignity or amiability while moving bedsteads, hanging window-blinds, or arranging kitchen furniture.

But your new neighbors are in at last, and you
"watch and wait and wonder" as to who they may
be: you watch to see how they appear, day by day,
and you form your estimate accordingly; you wait
to see if they have many callers, and if they seem
to be respectable or fashionable; you wonder what
Church they will attend; if they are likely to be

agreeable people; if the children will be troublesome, or otherwise. You make inquiries of your old neighbors across the street, and of your callers, and of your pastor, perhaps. After you have succeeded in satisfying yourself of their respectability, according to your ideas, whatever they may be, you don your best dress and bonnet, and, with card-case in hand and your politest smile where you can call it up on short notice, you march up to your new neighbor's door and ring the bell.

There is a sort of mutual introduction between you and Mrs. Blank, a ceremony absolutely necessary, according to custom, although you may have seen the lady a score of times while you listened — unintentionally, of course — to the admonitions to the little Blanks, and she has quietly taken your measure as you talked with the workman who repaired the front portico, or while you gave directions to the tramp who spaded up the bed for early lettuce and radishes.

The formal introduction over, you and your neighbor drift into easy conversation; little commonplaces at first, and then the baby is brought in, and though it may be very commonplace and ordinary to most eyes, to the mother it is especially interesting, and if you have two or three cherubs at home you are easily interested in your neighbor's little one, and before you are aware of it you are both talking as easily or as earnestly as if you had known each other for months instead of minutes.

Isaac is probably so hurried that he has scarcely time to speak with his family. He "bolts" his food

and then "bolts" off to his shop or office, and if he
notices your interest in your neighbors probably
laughs at you for being so much concerned about
strangers. It doesn't matter to him whether they
are agreeable or selfish; but to you, shut in doors
the greater part of the time, your little ones on your
heart and hands, with but scant opportunity for social
culture, your neighbors go a long way toward making up your social circle. A mother who is nurse-
maid and housekeeper at the same time hasn't much
time for formal calls, dress parties, or expensive lecture courses; but society, or at least companionship,
is a necessity to her, and an agreeable neighbor goes
a good way toward supplying that want.

The husband and father is crowded with business,
providing the daily bread for which somebody must
work as well as pray, and when he comes home feels
more like resting than talking, perhaps. The dailies
are not always brought home the day they are received, for busy people somehow "forget" occasionally; and even dailies and magazines need something
else than mere perusal to give real satisfaction. A
magazine article, the Woman's Kingdom, or House
and Home, need companionship to give real pleasure
and profit in their perusal. Suppose there are occasional crumbs of gossip in neighborly intercourse, it
isn't all confined to the mothers, nor to the "locals"
in the town paper. And while the husband laughs
at the chat about little details of domestic work, of
which he catches a stray word, or an occasional
glimpse as Rebekah talks with her neighbor, Mrs. B.
or C., he doesn't know that those daily conversations,

about what seem to him only trifles, have been the means of saving him a good many dollars in actual outlay.

He fancies himself a liberal man, and admires his wife's new suit and the children's Summer outfits, and thinks he deserves especial praise for providing so handsomely. He doesn't know that the "supply" ran out long before the Spring clothing was all purchased, and that Rebekah's handsome suit was made over from a portion of her wedding trousseau that had lain in the trunk so long he had forgotten it, and that Bessie's suit, so fresh and becoming, is a "made-over" organdie of her mother's girlhood days, the whole thing planned and completed by those two women, Rebekah and her next door neighbor.

Perhaps, if he knew, Isaac would object to Rebekah's telling her neighbor about their private affairs and scant purse; but Rebekah's neighbor was no better off, and the two women put their heads together, and as a result the two families are "as stylish as any body." He doesn't know it, however; neither does he know that it took several hours of lying awake at night, besides the numerous consultations, before the planning was complete and they succeeded in making "old clothes look 'most as well as the new." Isaac doesn't understand how his wife comes to have such a liking for the old-fashioned woman across the street; but it is to her encouraging words and her affectionate sympathy that he owes his wife's cheery face and buoyant spirits. The dear old soul hasn't time to study the fashion plates, but she has time to listen to the little perplexities of the young mother and the inexperienced housekeeper, and has taken her into her heart, and Rebekah finds her a "joy forever," if not a beauty. There may be more romantic friendships, but I doubt whether there are any more sincere and unselfish ones than those formed between wives and mothers, who, with their hands, heads, and hearts crowded with domestic affairs, are drawn toward each other by the strong bond of sisterly love and sympathy growing out of a common experience.

WHAT SOME LITTLE GIRLS DID.

A True Story.

OE BARNES had been trying for nearly six months to overcome his appetite for rum, and his friends thought he had succeeded, when suddenly he was overtaken by temptation, and fell; and, like all other drunkards, when he returned to his cup he sank deeper into sin than before. All the efforts of his friends seemed vain. The pastor visited him, and urged him to try again; but, while he was ready to acknowledge his wrong-doing, he did not seem to have the will to try to overcome. "It's no use, sir. I've tried it for six months, and just when I thought myself safe I fell; and here I am, worse than before. My wife has lost all confidence in me, and my children only look on me as a poor drunkard. No, sir; it's no use. You may just as well let me go down at once. The sooner it is over, the better." The class-leader and Sunday-school superintendent visited him with no better success. To all their pleading he returned the same hopeless answer: "It's no use, sir; I can't reform."

Some four months previous he had taken charge of a class in Sunday-school, composed of a half-dozen little girls, of about ten years of age. He had proved quite successful as a teacher, and had won their affection, and their little hearts were very much grieved at his fall One day, as they were together talking about it, one of their number proposed that they go and ask him to come back to their school and teach them. After some little hesitancy, they agreed to go.

Providence favored them, and they found Barnes in his carpenter-shop, and, in a measure, sober. He looked surprised when he saw his visitors; but he invited them in, and gave them seats on his work-bench. Annie Stevens, the girl who had first pro-posed the visit, had been chosen as chief speaker, and she began, with some little trembling, " Mr. Barnes, we came to see if you would n't please come and teach our class next Sabbath." And then, al-most frightened at the sound of her own voice, she stopped short, at a loss what to say next.

The poor inebriate's face flushed painfully, and he said, in surprise, " Me?"

" Yes, *you*."

Barnes shook his head.

"O no; you do n't want such a fellow as me to teach *you*. Do n't you know that I have n't been sober for nearly a month ?"

" Yes, sir, we know it ; but you are going to quit that now ;" and little Annie's voice grew steadier.

"Am I? How do you know that ?" and the man spoke with half a sneer.

"O, we just *know* you will ;" and the little voices were raised eagerly as the girls slid down from their seat on the work-bench, and gathered around him. "*Please* say you 'll come."

" But, children, I can not ;" and the man's voice

was very husky. "Just as like as not I shall be drunk as a beast before night."

But they would not take "No" for an answer; and finally he promised to "think about it," and they went away.

The little, heaven-sent messengers had touched a chord in his heart which others, by their reasonings and pleadings, had failed to reach; and when they were gone, Joe Barnes sat there thinking about their faith in himself, and wondering why they had come. Finally he got up, put on his coat, and, after locking his door, he went to his home. Silently he passed by his wife and children, and locked himself in his bedroom. There he wept and prayed for strength to overcome the demon appetite, and to make himself worthy of the confidence of those dear little girls, who had so eloquently pleaded for his reform.

For three days he resisted the temptation to drink. On the fourth, for want of stimulants and loss of appetite for food, he was confined to his bed. His physician urged him to take just a little brandy and water. He shook his head. No; he would rather die than take it. When Sabbath came, he was still too sick to sit up; but when the next came around, he presented himself, very pale and weak, at the superintendent's desk, and asked if he could again have his class, and it was again given him.

In the afternoon he was in the class-room; and when he rose to ask the forgiveness of the Church for his wanderings, he told the story of the little workers.

Said he: "It did n't trouble me much when the preacher came; for I thought that it was his business to look after such as I.   When the class-leader came, his words did n't touch my heart, though I knew he earnestly desired to see me a sober man.   But when those little girls came, and climbed upon my work-bench, and began to beg me to come back, and said they *knew* I would reform, I thought, ' Surely, God has sent them ;' and it just broke my heart, and I went home and on my knees promised God that, by his help, I *would* conquer, and would make myself fit to teach such blessed angels."

And, through God's grace, he did conquer ; and, when visiting the place three years after, I found him still sober, and an earnest worker in. the temperance cause as well as in the Church.

Little folks are apt to think they can not do any thing to make people better; but these little ones did do what older and wiser heads had failed to do ; they succeeded in getting this poor, tempted, enslaved man to forsake his sins and again turn to God.   Will not our girls and boys of the cold-water army do likewise ?

A MERRY group of young ladies, spending an evening at Mrs. Lake's, were discussing—or, rather, chatting over—the custom of sending out anonymous letters on Valentine's day.

"I think it a splendid time to pay up old scores, and shall avail myself of the opportunity in one instance, at any rate," said one young lady, laughing gayly, as she thought of the chagrin of a certain young gentleman of her acquaintance, when he should receive a highly colored valentine, representing an exquisitely gotten-up dandy, with the title "Yourself" written below.

"I think it's lots of fun," responded Maggie Snow; "but I don't know that I dare send any thing but a genuine friendly valentine; mother is so set against the comic ones; 'blows in the dark' she calls them, and says no lady or gentleman should ever send one."

"Why, what harm can there be in having a little fun?"

"Especially when we know they prove it," queried one and another of the girls, in apparent disapproval of the new notion.

"No harm at all."

"And it serves to take the starch out of some
people, and gives them a chance to see themselves
as others see them," were the responses from one and
another; while two or three were inclined to take
Mrs. Snow's view of the matter.

"Who will settle this weighty question?" asked
Mary Washburne.

"Appoint a judge," suggested Gertrude Warren,
a niece of Mrs. Lake's, visiting in the house, and for
whose pleasure the young ladies had been invited to
tea; "let's leave it for auntie to decide."

The assent of the company was readily gained,
and they turned to Mrs. Lake, who had sat quietly
listening, without taking any part in the conversation.

"Now, auntie, tell me what you think of it. Is
it wrong to send comic valentines? and, if it is, where
is the harm? We have decided to leave it to your
decision, and if you say it is wrong we will not send
out a single one of that class this year. Isn't that
the bargain?" appealing to her companions.

"Yes, certainly; let's have the decision," chorused the group, eagerly.

"It is wrong—decidedly wrong—my dears;" and
then, as she saw their look of disappointment, "but
you want to know why I think so. Draw the sofa
and rockers nearer the fire, and, when you are comfortably seated, I will tell you why I object to the
custom of sending comic, or caricature, valentines.
There, now you are all ready and anxious to hear,
I suppose," as they gathered about her, and Mrs.
Lake's face beamed with motherly kindness on the

bright young eyes that looked into hers. "The custom of sending anonymous love letters on Valentine's day is of comparatively recent origin, and that of sending comic pictures and caricatures is still more recent; and, while the first is not a commendable practice, by any means, the latter is far less so. But perhaps you will better understand why I condemn the practice, if I give you some incidents which have fallen under my observation :

"A young man — honest, but uncultivated and awkward — was, through this foolish custom, driven out of a college where he had gone to prepare himself for a profession. Some wild boys, who thought more of fun than of their lessons or the feelings of others, sent him an ugly caricature of an awkward, overgrown youth. At the bottom of the page, a few lines of very poor poetry designated the young man as the original of the picture. Like most awkward people, he was only too conscious of his lack of culture, and, stung with the insult offered him, he left the school, and could not be persuaded to return to it or any other outside of his own neighborhood."

"O, he ought not to have cared for their nonsense, or should have given them as good as they had sent," and Maggie Snow laughed at the idea of any one "caring about such a little thing as that."

"But it was not a little thing to him, and he could not retaliate, as *you* could have done, perhaps, nor throw it aside and forget it, as you or others, -with your independence of spirit, could do. It was a trifling act, but their desire for sport turned the whole course of their schoolmate's future life.

"A mischievous young lady sent a caricature to a lady, writing a few lines in imitation of the handwriting of another lady, an intimate friend of the one to whom it was sent. She inclosed it in another envelope and returned it, as she supposed, to the offending party. The result was, a coolness sprang up between them, and finally their friendship was broken off altogether.

· "Another instance: A young man sent a letter to a young lady. The letter was without signature, but so worded as to lead her to infer that it was from a gentleman whose attentions she had been receiving for a long time, and to whom, while there was no formal engagement, she had become very much attached, and the gentleman had taken no pains to conceal his preference for her. The letter accused her of fickleness and an inclination to flirt. She, acting under the impression that it was from her lover, and that he had taken this way to reprove her for an imaginary offense, returned his former letters and some small gifts bestowed by him without a word of explanation. The gentleman, perfectly unable to comprehend the cause, called upon her, intending to ask for an explanation. The lady refused to see him, and he, feeling that injustice had been done him, made no further effort at a reconciliation, and their friendship came to an end, and it was not until months afterward that they learned that they had been the victims of a foolish jest, and then pride prevented them from offering any indication of a desire to renew their former friendship. The cause of all their trouble was a foolish desire to tease, and the young man who wrote the letter had no idea that his thoughtless joke would alienate the hearts of his friends. Of course the young lady acted rashly, but the young man who wrote the anonymous letter did wrong in making such a misunderstanding possible."

"O, but I would never do any thing that would cause such trouble as that," protested one of the young ladies with emphasis.   .

"When we send such missives we do not know what may be the result, and it is better not to incur the risk, even though we may gratify our desire for sport.

"A young gentleman who has any thing to say, that is worth saying, need not be ashamed to say it in person if the opportunity offers; and if it does not, a gentlemanly letter, properly signed, will be much more satisfactory to himself and to the lady who receives it than an anonymous one containing sickly sentimentalism of which both ought to be heartily ashamed. As to caricatures, no thoughtful person will send one, even to an enemy, unless there is a willful desire to wound or offend. You asked for my opinion, and I have given it, very frankly, and as you have bound yourselves not to send a caricature or comic picture this year, I trust you will be so well satisfied with the decision that by next year you will be willing to vote it down aitogether."

For a full minute a rather sober smile with an audible sigh, as they thought of their demolished air castles, was all the reply given to Mrs. Lake's little lecture. At last one of the number said,

"Well, Mrs. Lake, you have given us some new ideas."

"And spoiled some old ones besides," added
Mary Washburne, laughing a little uneasily.

"But, auntie, can't we use Valentine's Day at
all?" asked Gertrude, with a sorely disappointed look
in her eyes. Mrs. Lake looked into their faces with
a smile.

"I did n't intend to read you such a sober lecture; but I have known so many troubles, small and
great, grow out of this foolish custom, that I want to
see it abolished and something better take its place;
and you know you insisted on hearing my opinion,
and that is my apology. But, answering your question, Gertrude: There is one way in which we might
be allowed to send anonymous packages, and, in my
opinion, it would be a great improvement on the
present custom, and that is, in bestowing gifts or
charities where they are deserved. The anonymous
method would relieve the person receiving the gift
from the embarrassment of feeling obligated to a
particular person, and the donor from the no less
embarrassing position of receiving thanks for the
same. It is well not to let the 'left hand know what
the right hand doeth,' when we bestow charities, but
if we have aught against our brother or sister, or
they have a fault that needs mending, *it is our duty to
reprove*. We had better go in the spirit of kindness,
and, avoiding all unfair concealment, deal with them
as we would wish others to do by us under like circumstances. But, there, my lecture is at a close,
'and thanking the audience for the respectful attention,' I would suggest that we turn to something more
cheerful, and have a song with piano accompaniment."

ALTER WILLOUGHBY did not come down to breakfast on the morning after New-Year's. The fact that he had been brought home the night before in a state of semi-unconscious intoxication, and that his father had met him and assisted him to his room, made him shrink from meeting the family at the breakfast table. At a late hour he arose, dressed, and prepared to go out. Just as he had laid his hand on the knob of the front door, Mr. Willoughby opened the door of the study and said, "Walter, will you come in here a moment? I wish to speak with you." Very reluctantly the young man replaced his hat on the rack and, with his overcoat still on, entered his father's library, and stood waiting to hear the expected reproof. "Sit down, Walter, I want to talk with you about last night;" and Mr. Willoughby spoke kindly, though sadly. "I suppose you know in what condition you were brought home?"

Walter nodded, while an angry flush overspread his face. "I do, sir."

"And, I suppose, I need not tell you how mortified your mother and I feel, that *our* son should so far forget himself as to disgrace us in this manner."

Unconsciously Mr. Willoughby's tone had become

harder as he proceeded, and the son's face, which had at first reddened, now paled under the rebuke which cut more by the tone than the words. The father waited for a moment, and then continued: "Your mother and I are very much hurt at your conduct, but as this is the first offense of the kind we are willing to forgive you, provided it is not to be repeated in future." Walter had not looked up once while his father was speaking, and now he did not answer, but sat with his eyes fixed on the blazing grate.

For some moments the father waited for a reply, but none came, and then he said sadly, his love and anxiety overcoming his anger at his son's fault: "Are you not willing to promise this, my son?"

The young man rose from his seat and stood before his father. "No, I am *not* willing to make any such promise, because I should not be likely to keep it if I did," he said bitterly. "Mother is ashamed of me and mortified at what I have done? I am glad of it—may be it will do her good, and"——

"Walter," and Mr. Willoughby's voice was stern enough now, "Do you dare to speak disrespectfully of your mother?"

"Well, I—I—before I make any promises I want to speak with mother about it."

He paused, and then added, "I thought at first I would say nothing to her about it, but, perhaps, it is as well to have it over. Will you please ask mother to come in?"

When the mother came a few minutes after, her eyes red with weeping, the son arose respectfully and gave her the easy-chair, while Mr. Willoughby again resumed his seat.

As soon as his mother was seated, Walter said, hastily, as if anxious to get over an unpleasant task, "Father has been lecturing me on last night's doings, and says that you are willing to forgive me because it is the first time, and provided I promise that it shall not occur again. ·I want to say that last night was *not* the first by at least a half dozen times."

"O Walter!" and there was a world of agony in the mother's voice.

"Of course you are shocked and very much ashamed of me, but—please father," as Mr. Willoughby was about to speak, "don't interrupt me, I *will* say it; I have kept this from you until, I am afraid, your son is in a fair way to become a confirmed drunkard, and, if I *am*, you have no one to blame but yourselves! *If I die a drunkard it is you who have made me such!*" and the words were fairly hissed into the ears of the father and mother. Mr. Willoughby arose to his feet, and laid a hand on his son's shoulder.

"Walter, sit down. You are yet half-crazed with the liquors you drank yesterday, and I will not permit you thus to insult your mother and myself."

The young man shook off the father's hand.

"No, father, I am not drunk, but in sober earnest. The first wine I ever tasted my mother made, and *you* asked me to drink it; *you* filled the glass with your own hand, and told me it was harmless; and for nearly ten years you have been feeding my appetite with what you call '*domes-*

tic' wine, until now I am not satisfied with that alone, but must have something stronger. You want me to promise to keep sober in the future. I shall make no such promise, unless you and mother will agree to remove the accursed stuff from your table and out of my sight; and God only knows whether I shall be able to overcome my appetite even then;" and, with a groan, the unhappy young man sank into a . chair, and buried his face in his hands.

The father sat like one stunned, while the mother sobbed hysterically. Presently Walter looked up, and said sadly:

"If I could have gone on in my own way, without your knowing it, I never should have said what I have; but if you can not help me, perhaps you may save my brothers from a like temptation. And O, mother!" as, overcome by his feeling, he kneeled by her, and laid his head on her shoulder, "will you not help me? Forgive me for what I have said; for I have said it more for Harry's and Willy's sake than for my own. For God's sake, remove the temptation from them before it is too late."

The mother's only reply to this petition was to twine her arms around the neck of her penitent boy, and sob on his shoulder. When each had grown calmer, Walter rose from his knees, and, reaching out his hand to his father, he said

"Forgive me for the past and for what I have .said this morning, and I am willing to *try* to overcome my appetite for strong drink; but I can make no *promises.* I have vowed more than a dozen times that I would never touch it again, and have as often broken these vows; and I have no confidence in my good resolutions for the future."

Mr. Willoughby grasped his son's hand as he arose, and the two men stood facing each other—the one in the bloom of manhood's first years, the other with the gray hairs creeping in among the brown.

" My boy," and the father's voice trembled with emotion, "if I had known this in the beginning I would rather have given my own life than thus to have marred yours. But perhaps it is *not* too late. Your mother and I will help you, and God's grace is sufficient for all our needs. May he help us to do our duty !" and Mr. Willoughby left the room.

Walter turned to his mother, who still sat, like one in a dream, and said, trying to smile through his tears :

" Mother, have you no word of forgiveness or encouragement for your boy ?"

For an answer the mother drew her son to her arms, and kissed his flushed and feverish brow, and said :

"Forgive *me*, my child ; I knew not what I did."

Walter Willoughby did not go down town that day, but, hanging his overcoat again on the rack, he spent the day in his own room.

It is needless to say that there was no more "*domestic*" wine used in that household. Mr. and Mrs. Willoughby had learned, by sad experience, that fermented wine, even though under the title *homemade*, may create a thirst for stronger drinks, and lead to ruin.

Young Willoughby had many a hard struggle before he overcame his evil habits, and more than once he came near falling ; but, by the kind words and encouragement of his conscience-stricken parents, who spared no pains to atone for the wrong they had done to their boy, he finally became a sober man, and, through God's Spirit, a Christian man.

Mr. and Mrs. Willoughby not only removed the tempter from their own home, but they also used their influence to induce other parents to shun the foolish and sinful practice that had come so near wrecking their son's life, and which still caused them regrets, heartaches, and anxiety.

A CHRISTMAS STORY.

IT was a pleasant fireside picture. A handsome looking man of fifty years, seated at a table reading the evening paper, and opposite, a woman, younger perhaps by five or ten years. Looking at her face you would say she was not yet forty; but glancing at her hair you see that the silver is creeping into it, and you leave her age undecided. She is busy crocheting a comforter of bright Berlin wool. Her fingers fly swiftly, but every few minutes she turns her eyes toward the door, as if half-expecting it to open.

At last the gentleman laid down his paper, shrugged his shoulders and drew his chair a little nearer the fire. Presently he turned to his companion with,

"Only two more days until Christmas, wife. I declare, how time flies; I hardly realize that it is so near. By the way, have you decided what the children are to have this year? Only two days, you know."

The wife "knew." For the past four weeks her hands and head had been busy planning little surprises for her family. But in her heart was an aching, restless feeling, as she compared the coming Christmas with the last, and remembered that there

was one less to buy presents for now than on last
Christmas. And as her husband's words recalled the
past, she wondered if it was not a good opportunity
to put in one more plea for her first-born, her prodigal son. She answered, while the tears trembled in
her voice,

"Yes, I know, but it will hardly seem like
Christmas without Willie."

A cloud gathered on Mr. Dustan's face; his
manner changed. and he answered almost angrily,

"I thought we were done talking on that subject.
William has made his own choice, and he must abide
by it. No word of mine shall bring him home."
And with a quick, impatient movement, that showed
how unpleasant the subject was to him, he arose and
left the room. Mrs. Dustan picked up her work
again with a sigh; but the gathering tears, one by
one, trickled down her cheeks and fell upon the
bright work in her hands. At last, overcome by her
feelings, she bowed her head on the table and sobbed
aloud; but in a little while became calm, folded up
her work, took the light and left the room.

It was the old story. A wild, impetuous boy,
impatient of home restraint, a failure on the part of
the father to understand his boy's impulses, and an
effort to break the "stubborn" will instead of trying
to direct it. Under the influence of passion the boy
had left home, and the father's wounded pride refused to ask his son to return. One letter only
had Willie written home, asking "mother" not to
forget him, and saying, "If father says for me to
come home, I will." But the father would not say

it, despite the mother's pleading. Nothing more was heard of him. Ten months had passed, and the parents knew not whether he was living or dead.

Nothing was said about Christmas at the break-fast table the next morning. The children saw that father and mother were unusually silent and seemed to feel the gloom, and so it was almost a silent breakfast. But all day long Mrs. Dustan's words kept ringing in her husband's ears, "It will not seem like Christmas without Willie," and he wished she had not said it. On his way home he called to mind their wedding day, and the delicate, girlish form of her who stood by his side, and promised to take him "for better or for worse." And then Willie's face rose up before him, and he saw him as when a child he used to run to meet him on his return from the labors of the day. And, although he was proud of his younger children, yet the memory of his eldest boy stirred his heart, and the kiss he imprinted on his wife's cheek was more loving than usual. At the table he noticed, as never before, that she looked thin and pale, with a sadness about her mouth even when she smiled.

All the evening he cast occasional glances at her from behind his evening paper, to see if he was not mistaken about those faded cheeks. Something suggested that perhaps if he would send for Willie to come home her step would be less weary and her eyes brighter; but he put it aside immediately. "Of course she looks older; one can not expect a woman to look as rosy at forty as she did at twenty," he says to himself, and then turns to his paper to shut out unpleasant thoughts.

Presently Eddy, the youngest, a boy of ten years, left the table and the book he had been reading to look for another. Those within his reach did not suit, and at last climbing upon a chair, to see what was on the higher shelves, his eyes caught sight of a bundle of picture papers and old school books, and he eagerly called out,

"Mother, may I look at these old papers?"

Busy with her own thoughts she answered "Yes," without looking up, and Eddy, delighted with the prospect, brought them to the table. They proved to be Willie's books and papers, which the mother had stored away from all eyes but her own. For a few moments the boy busied himself with the pictures, and then picked up a soiled and torn Reader, with the owner's name and a date, five years back, written on the outside. The name was written in a cramped, boyish hand, and Eddy read slowly and distinctly, "Willie Dustan." The father gave an involuntary start, as if even the name of his absent boy stung him. Mrs. Dustan half arose to remove the books, but on a second thought resumed her seat, and the children gathered around their brother, and were soon deeply interested in books and papers that were "brother Willie's;" but their words were only in whispers, for they had learned months ago not to talk of Willie in their father's presence.

At last the books were put away, the good-nights were said, and Mr. Dustan was left to finish his paper. But it failed to interest him, and at last he laid it

down with a sigh.   As he did so, his eye caught
sight of something on the carpet.   He picked it up,
and found it to be Willie's Album, a present from
himself on the last Christmas, and he remembered
with a sigh the pleasures of that last Christmas.   There
was something in the boy's hand written on the first
page, but the father laid the book down and commenced pacing the floor.   He wondered if his boy
was still alive, and whether he thought of home and
would like to be there.   Again his eyes fell upon
the album.   He picked it up and turned again to the
first page, and before he was aware of it he was
reading, "This book is a Christmas present.   Father
and mother never forget to have some pleasant surprise for me, even though father does say I am the
most troublesome of all his children.   I am sixteen
years old, yet I do not remember a Christmas when
they failed to think of me.   I wonder if there will ever
come a Christmas when they will forget me.   I wonder if next Christmas will be as pleasant as this."

Mr. Dustan laid down the book.   "Perhaps I
was too hard on him.   People used to say Willie
looked like me.   May be we are too much alike in
temperament; but," with a sigh, "it is too late.   I
do not know where he is, and could not send for him
if I would."

Christmas morning came, clear and cold.   But
with all their greetings there is a chord missing, and
they all feel it, even down to Eddy, who is the most
joyous and thoughtless of all.   One package is yet
untouched, and Mr. Dustan picks it up and opens it.
It is a neat, gilt-edged Bible, and on the fly-leaf is

written: "To Willie, from his mother." It is the mother's token that her absent darling be not forgotten. He lays it down, glances at his wife's pale cheeks and tearful eyes, and wishes for her sake that Willie were home once more.

When breakfast was over and they had gathered around the fire for their morning devotion the story of Bethlehem's babe was selected as appropriate to the day. When they came to the verse, "Glory to God in the highest, on earth peace, and good will to men!" the father seemed to read it for the first time. "On earth peace;" but there was very little real peace in his heart on that morning. They knelt in prayer, but when they came to, "Forgive us our trespasses as we forgive those who trespass against us," his voice faltered and he felt that he could not say it as he should.

All day long the angel's song, and "Forgive us, as we forgive," seem strangely blended in his mind; even the church bell seemed to say, "Forgive." It was a sad day for both husband and wife, yet neither mentioned the great load that was weighing them down.

Evening came at last; once more they bowed in prayer while their thoughts were running out after the absent one who made the house so lively only one year ago. After the children had said their good-nights, Mr. and Mrs. Dustan were left alone. All day long the mother's heart had yearned for her boy; she had been hoping that the thought of this day would bring the wanderer home. But the day is past and he has not come. The day that opened clear and calm has been followed by a snow-storm at night, the wind is moaning through the trees, and the shutters, jarred by the storm, make the evening doubly sad. For some time they sat in silence, and then Mrs. Dustan arose and left the room. How long she was gone her husband never knew. Busy with his own thoughts, he scarcely missed her from his side; and as he sat there surveying the past and trying to look into the future, all his pride forsook him, and he saw only his boy as he was years ago, with his sweet, willful, yet cunning ways, and the father's heart triumphed over the man. All his anger was gone and he longed to take his child in his arms, willful and disobedient as he had been.

Presently there is a hand laid upon his shoulder, and Mrs. Dustan speaks, a sense of joyousness struggling through her grief:

"Father, if Willie should come back to us to-night, could you not forgive him for the sake of him who came to save *us?*"

Without lifting his bowed head, the father sobs out: "Yes, yes; for his sake! and I, too, have been wrong. I see it all now"—and before he has time to finish the sentence, there is an arm around his neck, and Willie's face is laid close beside his father's. "Father, I have come back. I was wrong; I am sorry for the past; I was so lonely, and when the Christmas bells reminded me of home, I could not stay away. Only be patient with me, father, and I will *try* to be a better boy."

Until long after midnight, they talked of the past and the future, and when they separated for the night they understood each other better than they ever had done before. .

And during the years that Willie remained under his father's roof, Mr. Dustan never forgot those pleading words of his returning prodigal: "Only be patient with me, father;" and the remembrance of that Christmas night helped both father and son to be patient of each other's faults.

The brothers and sisters were surprised, in the morning, at the news of Willie's return, and Eddy wished he "had only come Christmas morning, instead of at night." But the mother felt that God had brought it all about in his own good time, and Willie's return had been at the very hour when his father's heart was best prepared to receive him.

Living Within One's Means.

RS. HUBBARD was spending the afternoon with her friend, Mrs. Miller, and the two ladies sat with their work in the cozy sitting-room of the little cottage. They had only known each other for a couple of years, but these two years had been sufficient time in which to form a very strong mutual attachment, and they were usually very free to express their thoughts and wishes. To-day Mrs. Miller was not in her happiest mood, and was glad of a friend to whom she could unburden her heart.

"I have been telling Mr. Miller to-day, that I am tired of living in this little house, and I must have a larger one," she said, by way of introducing the subject uppermost in her mind.

"Why, Mrs. Miller! I am sure your house is very cozy and comfortable. I enjoy your little rooms and surroundings so much."

"Seeing them occasionally is very different from living in them year in and year out," Mrs. Miller answered, a little fretfully.

"I suppose your husband is able to buy a larger house," Mrs. Hubbard answered, quietly.

"Of course, he is, or I should n't ask him," and

Mrs. Miller looked hurt at the insinuation. "He has five thousand loaned where he can get it at six weeks' notice. I called on Mrs. Heath yesterday, and she has just got settled in her new house—in splendid style, too. When I came home, every thing here looked so shabby, and my rooms so little and 'boxy' compared with hers, that I took a good cry."

"But, my dear, your family is so much smaller than Mrs. Heath's that you do not need as large a house as she does."

Mrs. Hubbard did not dare say that Mr. Miller's income was smaller, too.

"That is just what husband said to-day; but I told him I never should be satisfied until I have a larger house. The Williamses offer theirs for just five thousand dollars, and it is cheap at that, and if teasing will do any good, I'm sure to have it;" and Mrs. Miller smiled knowingly, as she picked up her work again, which had dropped from her hands while talking.

Mrs. Hubbard did not return her friend's smile, but knitted very busily for a few moments, in silence; presently she said: "Would you like to hear a little story about myself?"

"Of course, I would; tell all the stories you please, but don't lecture me," and Mrs. Miller laughed a little uneasily.

"I don't want to lecture you, my friend; but in all our confidences, I believe I have never told you that my husband was once a merchant, with a little capital of his own, instead of a clerk at a thousand a year?"

"No, you never told me that!" and Mrs. Miller looked very much surprised.

"Ten years ago," said Mrs. Hubbard, "I began to feel that my house was getting too small for my family, and too small and shabby when compared with the residences of my fashionable friends; and so I undertook to persuade my husband to sell our little home and buy another, better suited to my taste, and, as I made myself believe, to our circumstances. I had hard work, at first, as John insisted that he could not spare the amount from his business; however, he finally agreed to my wishes, and bought a house in a more fashionable street. It was not so large as I should have liked, but it was a great deal larger and more showy than the old home, and I felt that it would be quite an advance on our former style of living. My husband did not seem as enthusiastic as myself about the matter, but I flattered myself that when we were once in our new home he would be as pleased as I was. When the time came for moving, I found that I had not half enough furniture, and what I had would look very shabby in the new house, and so I made the tour of the furniture shops, to procure furniture that was suitable. The prices were higher than I anticipated; but, of course I must have furniture, and so I ordered what I needed. When the men came to put up the furniture, there were a good many things which I had forgotten, and which they insisted I must have or my house would not be half furnished. I felt that the expense was too great, but persuaded myself that, as I had a nice house, it would be foolish not to furnish it properly. I felt a little bit frightened, when the bill was sent in, and I found it was nearly twice as much as I supposed it would be; but, as John paid it without complaining, I thought perhaps it would all come out right.

"I soon found, however, that my large house required more work to keep it in order than the small one, and I was compelled to hire another girl. My next-door neighbor had a nurse, and I found that, if I kept up with the style of our neighborhood, I must do as others did; and so I procured a nurse-girl, although I had serious doubts as to her capacity or morals. We soon sold the old home, although at considerable discount on our original price, and it served to help make up the second payment on the new home. Things went pretty well for a couple of years, though I found that I had to work harder than I had ever done, and John stayed late at the store, and always looked tired and worried. When the time came for the third payment, we found that we had not been able to save any thing from the profits of the store, and my husband must borrow the amount from a friend. I noticed that our Spring stock of goods was not as large as he had been in the habit of having; and, to my question as to why, he merely said he could not command the means at present. I did not know then, as I afterward learned, that the stock on hand had been purchased on time; but I could see that something was wrong. My husband looked troubled and worried; and sometimes I felt that, perhaps, it was the debt that troubled him, but shook off the idea as a mere fancy, and said to myself: 'It's all nonsense; John is just working too hard, and that makes him look worried and tired.' But at the end of the fourth year he told me we must lessen our expenses in some way, or he would not be able to meet his liabilities.

"'But how are we to do it?' I asked. 'Our children must dress as other children do.'

"'Well, I do n't know about that. I shall leave it to you, Nellie; but you *must* manage to lessen our expenses, unless you wish to do worse,' my husband replied, despondently.

"His look and tone frightened me, and I set to planning how I might save a *little*, at least. I dismissed my nurse, and took charge of my children myself. Then I dismissed my cook, and, with the help of my remaining girl, who was very inefficient, I tried to get along and retrench a little. But it was no use. For two years we fought the battle, with failures, and were defeated. Our debts had accumulated to such an extent that all our efforts to extricate ourselves proved unavailing. The times were hard, and those who had purchased goods of us on time could not pay, and we feared at last that we must sell off our stock of goods and our home to meet the demand of our creditors. Our beautiful home was sold under the auctioneer's hammer for the third of what it cost us. By selling every thing we could possibly spare, my husband was enabled to pay all his debts in full, and his good name was safe, which was some comfort. It was very humiliating for my husband to be compelled to ask for a position as salesman of men with whom he had formerly competed in business; and, though he easily obtained a situation, yet it was not pleasant to stay where we would meet those who had been our Summer friends, and who either turned a cold shoulder to us, or, what was a great deal harder to bear, pitied us, and so we came here; and, though our salary is not large, we are living within our income, and hope to save a little to purchase a *home* by and by—not a house for show, but for shelter and comfort." As Mrs. Hubbard finished her recital, Mrs. Miller's tears were flowing in sympathy with her friend's troubles. After a few moments' silence, Mrs. Hubbard said, timidly:

"I never thought to tell this to any one here; but during our acquaintance you have grown very dear to us, and I could not see you taking the step that almost beggared us without a word of warning. If the house were the only expense, you might, perhaps, venture safely; but, my dear Mrs. Miller, it is only the beginning of expense, and every new one only paves the way for another. My new house required new furniture, and a great deal of it; my new furniture required us to dress in style to correspond with our surroundings; the extra dress required extra expense in making and caring for; my large house compelled me to hire more help; and so one expense brought another, until we were brought to financial ruin."

"But one dislikes to live shabbier than one's . neighbors," objected Mrs. Miller, faintly.

"You live a great deal better than *some* of your neighbors; and I am sure that those of your friends who are worthy of the name love and respect you as

much in your little home as they would if you lived in
a palace."

Mrs. Miller sighed. "Well, perhaps, I *have* been
foolish. I think, for the present, I will say no more
about it."

Her friend smiled pleasantly. "Yes, I think I
would say just a little more. I would tell him, if I
were you, that I had concluded that I did not need
a new house—for a while, at least."

"Well, I guess I will, then; and I do n't wonder
your husband listened to your persuasions; for you
have a faculty for making people think your way the
right one."

"I hope my 'persuasions,' as you call them, will
not cause *you* as much trouble as they did us," Mrs.
Hubbard answered, as she put on her hat and shawl
to go home.

Mrs. Miller followed her friend's advice; and
when her husband, five years later, was *able* to build
a large house and furnish it nicely, without incurring
debt, she felt that she had been repaid for her waiting.

"AUNTIE," exclaimed Ella Lewis, one evening as she came in on her way from school, "Miss Harrison is getting up a Cold Water Band, and Ida Moore wanted brother Will and me to join it. I told her I thought temperance societies were for those who were drunkards or getting to be, and may be for men who have to go sometimes where people drink; but I think it's silly for girls to join Cold Water Bands; don't you think so, auntie?"

"What did your brother say about it?" asked Mrs. Meyer, without answering Ella's question.

"He was half a mind to give his name; but I laughed at the idea, and he said 'he guessed he wasn't in any danger yet;' and I say so too," replied Ella, with emphasis.

Mrs. Meyer sat thinking for a few minutes, and then said, "Ella, dear, come sit here by me, and I will tell you a little story. It is not a very pleasant one, and I do not often speak of it, but it may do you good to see what a mistake I made once. My father and mother died when I was only twelve years old, and my brother Harry was about two years younger, and we were left in the care of an uncle. In those days it was nothing unusual for people to

take their morning dram, and there were no temperance societies for little children; but when I was
about sixteen years of age there was a temperance
society organized in our village, and we were urged
to join it.   I laughed at the idea, and uncle did not
persuade us.   'Let every one do as he likes,' was
his motto.   Brother Harry was anxious to join the
society, but I ridiculed the suggestion, and hinted
that perhaps he was afraid to trust himself without
a pledge; and as he was. accustomed to look up to
me for counsel, and not caring to belong to a
society if I would not go with him, he said no more
about it.

"Time passed on, and Harry was eighteen, and I
twenty years of age.   I noticed that my brother
always took his morning bitters with uncle, and one
morning when uncle was away from home I saw
Harry go to the cupboard and take a glass of liquor.
I could scarcely have told why, but what I had seen
gave me a strong feeling of anxiety, and I wondered if he was in the habit of drinking when uncle
was gone, but I could not summon courage to speak
about it.   A few weeks afterwards I overheard uncle
telling aunt that he feared Harry was keeping unsuit-
able company, and was getting into bad habits.   I
longed to ask what he meant, but was too proud to
let him know that I shared their anxiety, though it
caused me many a sleepless night.   One evening,
about three months afterward, I heard a confused
murmur of voices in the hall, and stepping to the
door of my room I saw my uncle and a stranger
supporting my brother between them.   I started

forward with a cry of alarm, but uncle motioned me away, and I shall never forget the shock with which my brother's silly, maudlin words fell on my ears as he staggered to his room, nor the disgust which I felt as I looked upon his face and blood-shot eyes. I knew too well their meaning. Harry was *drunk! my* brother, and with a cry of shame and mortified pride I rushed back to my room to sob out my grief alone. The next morning I tried to remonstrate with Harry and to get him to promise never to touch the poison again. O, how his reply startled and stung me: 'Now, Nell, see here, I *wanted* to sign the pledge once, and I might have been a sober boy to-day if you had n't made fun of me and wanted to know if I needed a temperance society to keep me from being a drunkard. You would n't sign it yourself, and you *hindered me;* now you can take the consequence,' and there was a reckless bravado in face and tone. 'Last night *was n't the beginning,* only those fellows were such fools as to bring me home instead of keeping me out until *I was sober* or *you* asleep.'

"It was no use to plead. I had lost my influence over my brother. He already craved the alcoholic poison, and he seemed to take a sort of pleasure in telling me it was my own fault whenever I tried to persuade him to give it up. At twenty-five he was killed in a drunken row, and I felt as if I had killed him," and Mrs. Meyer stopped, overcome by her emotions.

"He ought to have been man enough to have governed his appetite, and not to have been led by others," said Ella, wiping away her tears which flowed at her aunt's recital.

"Yes, it is true, he ought; but I was the oldest, and he looked up to me in many things, and I might have prevented his acquiring a taste for stimulants if I had only been wise enough to use my influence right. If I could have saved him after I saw the danger I would have given my right hand, but it was too late then. No, Ella, it isn't silly for girls and boys to sign a temperance pledge, and I advise you to not only give your name to the society, but to urge your brother to do so. *You* may not be in danger, but your brother is; and if you influence him to take a pledge to total abstinence before he learns to drink you will save him from ruin, and you will not have the cause for sorrow and regret that I have to-day. It seems like opening the wound afresh to talk of it, but I could not bear to see you falling into the same error without giving you my own sad experience as a warning to you."

Ella kissed her aunt's forehead tenderly as she rose to go home. "I thank you very much for telling me this story, auntie; I am sure Will would not sign the pledge if I didn't, and it all looks so different to me now."

A word from his sister was all that Will Lewis needed, and together the brother and sister signed the pledge that evening, but Ella did not tell Mrs. Meyer's sad experience.

———————

T was a very weary pair of feet that carried Maggie Barr's body up the hill
to the residence of Mrs. Tate, her mother's rich neighbor.   But the errand must be
done, and there was no one else home could do
it but Maggie, as brother Dan was at work for
a neighboring farmer, and all the other children (and there were five of them) were younger
than Maggie; and so this errand, as well as a
good many other things, seemed to fall, as a
matter of course, upon this elder sister.   To be
sure, ten-year-old Harry might have done a
good many errands; but his eyes and ears were
always on the alert to see and hear all the fun there
was going, and he did n't always remember to de-
liver his messages correctly, nor hurry as fast as he
ought on the way; and so the *important* messages and
errands—and Maggie thought they were very many—
were intrusted to "sister Maggie."   Besides all these,
there was baby to watch and to amuse, at the same
time keeping an oversight of two-year-old Ned, who
would keep poking his fingers into baby's blue eyes
·and pink ears, in his efforts to explore their mysterious depths.   Then, there was the table to set three
times a day, and dishes to wash.

Maggie was only twelve years old, and sometimes

these numerous and mixed duties were not particularly inviting; but she was not often cross, neither
was she always good-natured, over them; and now,
after an unusually busy day, a message must be
carried to their neighbor in regard to some sewing
which Maggie's mother was doing for Mrs. Tate.

"Do n't stay long, dear," cautioned Mrs. Barr;
"for baby will want you while I strain the milk and
put it away."

As the child climbed the hill, each step grew
more and more wearisome; and when at last she
knocked at the door, she felt as if she could never
climb another hill without a new pair of feet, her
own were so tired.

The message was soon delivered, and the messenger on her way home; but the feet did not move
very rapidly, even though going down hill; for were
they not going to other duties instead of rest?

"O dear! I wonder if I shall always be busy,
busy!" queried Maggie, with a sigh, as she thought
of the weary steps she must take with baby, whose
"fretful hour" was sure to be when mamma was
busiest. "I do wish I could have time to read pretty
stories and have a good time, like other girls. Susie
Tate's mamma keeps a nurse-girl; and O, it must
be so nice to do as you please, and not be bothered about *any thing!*" And as Maggie contrasted
Susie's "good times" with her own rather homely
duties, she felt, as many a one of maturer years has
felt when weary and overworked, that, in some way,
things were not exactly evenly adjusted. The more
she thought it over, the more weary grew her feet,

and there came a lump in her throat that grew bigger, until, by the time she reached home, she felt as if it would choke her.

The mother was waiting for her to take baby, who seemed more than usually restless. At any other time Maggie would have held out her arms gladly to receive the little one; for she was proud of and loved this rosy-cheeked baby sister very much; but just now she was thinking of what a nice time Susie Tate was having, and how she "never could have a minute to herself," and the face that looked into baby's was not very encouraging; but she reached out her hands mechanically, and, without replying to her mother's comment upon her lengthy stay, she carried baby into the sitting-room. Maggie's dissatisfied feelings seemed to communicate themselves to baby, and she had no power to soothe to rest the little one, who usually "was better with sister Maggie than with any one else," as she had boasted more than a score of times. To-night all her efforts were of no avail. Baby would not sleep, and its fretful whimper culminated in a vigorous cry; and when Mrs. Barr's task was completed, she found both children in tears; for Maggie's grieved feelings had gotten the mastery, and she was weeping just as earnestly, although in silence.

After a few moments of motherly soothing, baby was sleeping peacefully in its crib, and Mrs. Barr turned her attention to Maggie, who had thrown herself on the lounge, and was crying quietly to herself. Seating herself on the lounge, she lifted Maggie's head, and laid it on her lap. Stroking the short curls tenderly, she said, softly, "What has happened that my little girl is crying like this?" The tender tone, the caressing hand, was just the one thing that could touch Maggie's heart, and in her present mood it touched the fountain of her tears, and, covering her face with her hands, she sobbed harder than ever. Mrs. Barr was puzzled. This was a new freak of her daughter's, and she could not comprehend its cause or guess its meaning.

After two or three ineffectual efforts to quiet her or learn the cause of her tears, she waited in silence till this outburst should have spent itself. When her sobs had ceased, the mother said:

"Will you not tell me your trouble, Maggie?"

"O mother, I am so tired of work, work all the time! I have to hurry in the morning, and all day; I am busy always, except when in school. I scarcely get to look at a book; and baby must be cared for, and dishes must be washed, and nobody cares how tired I get; and I do n't have nice things nor nice times, and it 's just awful to be 'sister Maggie' to so many. I wish I was in baby's place instead of having to work all the time. Susie Tate's mother keeps a nurse girl, and Susie can do just as she pleases; and—I am so tired of it all." And Maggie's words ended in another sob.

"But, Maggie, dear, Mrs. Tate has plenty of money, and we have not. Your father has only this little farm, and we can not afford so many luxuries as they. Besides, I would rather trust baby and Ned to their sister than to a hired nurse, but I did not know I was burdening you. I do not want my daughter to grow tired of her home and her brothers and sisters," and Mrs. Barr's voice had a suspicious tremor in it that made Maggie look up with an inquiring glance. "I will try to give you more time to yourself, but when you are out of school I need your help, and I have come to look for it, I guess. The money Mrs. Tate pays me for sewing is to buy you some of the nice things you say you never have, and I trust some of the steps you take are for your comfort as well as for others."

"But mamma, I heard papa say, if you *would* do that work, it must be used on yourself, and I am sure you like nice things as much as I do."

"I can do nicely without a new dress for the Winter. My last Winter's dresses are respectable and very comfortable."

"But, mother, don't you ever get tired of this humdrum work? Don't you wish you could rest and have nice times, like other people?"

"There are other people who don't have even such nice times as I have, my dear child."

"I don't mean that kind of other people, mother; but don't you wish you could ride in a carriage, and have beautiful clothes, and a grand house, and lots of things?"

"I am glad I have my children well and strong, and that your father is a sober, Christian man. Would you be willing to exchange your father for Mr. Tate, Maggie?"

"O no, not for the world! Why, John M'Donald, their gardener, says Mr. Tate comes home real drunk sometimes, and I would rather be poor than have papa like that; but, mamma, it seems as if *we* ought to have *some* of the nice times and nice things, instead of some one else having them all."

"My daughter had better not puzzle her brain over questions that wiser heads have failed to solve. And now if you will go to bed and sleep, I think things will have a brighter look in the morning than they have now." And with a loving good-night kiss Mrs. Barr sent Maggie to her bed.

Maggie's heart was considerably lighter, but the visions her waking hours had conjured up still lingered with her, and as she fell asleep there floated before her beautiful children and gayly dressed ladies in carriages of such magnificence as her childish fancy had loved to picture for herself and her parents and the children.

Things did look brighter in the morning, and Maggie tried to make amends for her fretfulness of the previous evening. She watched her mother as she went to and fro about the duties and cares of the house, and she could but notice the patience with which she looked after all the little details of her home. "I know mamma is tired, and yet she is so patient with it all. I wonder if she is ashamed of me for my crossness. I wonder if I will ever be so cross again. Yes, I expect so; but I won't let mother know—even if I get so cross I must bite my fingers off, so there now!" and Maggie set her teeth together with a decision that meant a victory over self, if possible.

When the day's work was done and the little ones all asleep, Maggie drew her chair beside her mother's and laid her head on her knee. After a few moments of silence, she said:

"Mamma, I've been thinking it all out to-day, and would rather be Maggie Barr than any body else, even if we ain't rich, and have no servants. And I've watched you all day, and I'm sorry I was cross yesterday, when I knew you had worked so hard all day long; and then, mamma, you sat up to sew for Mrs. Tate last night—O, I know you did, for the ruffles that were not hemmed last night were all finished this morning, and there is no fairy about this house unless it is you."

"Well, you are content to live just our humdrum life, as you called it, are you?" questioned Mrs. Barr.

. "Yes; but mother, I'll never ask you to overwork yourself for me—not if I never have a nice dress or hat as long as I live, you dear mother," and Maggie kissed the hand she had imprisoned as if she meant to keep it.

"I am glad you are looking at things more cheerfully, and I know your work will seem lighter, and I shall not feel mine nearly so heavy if my daughter is content. You are but a child, Maggie, but I have come to look to you for so many things that I am afraid my work would be very heavy without your help, and especially if I thought you were dissatisfied with your home. Your father can not give you many accomplishments, but he can give you a good, substantial education if his life and health is spared. There are a good many burdens that will fall upon you as my eldest daughter, but I trust you will be repaid in the abundant opportunities you may have for helping your younger brothers and sisters in their efforts to be good and true men and women. You are very dear to me, dearer than you can now understand, and I have looked forward to the time when I could lean on you for support and take you into my cabinet as chief counselor. Perhaps I am selfish, but I want to do that which will be the best for all my children." .

"You can never be selfish, I am sure, and I am sorry I made you unhappy last night. I'll do my best, see if I don't; and if I get cross at any time just give me a hint, and I'll straighten out the wrinkles double quick," and Maggie laughed even while she brushed away the tears. As she said good-night she stole an arm about her mother's neck and whispered, "I shan't mind being tired now since I know you understand and care about it."

PERHAPS some of my readers would like to know something about how little children spent their Christmas in what was called the "West," thirty years ago.

The school I am going to tell you of was not in a village, but in the edge of the woods in one of the eastern counties of Illinois.

We did n't have "vacation" then, as you do now, but sometimes the "schoolmaster"— that is what we called our teacher—would give us a treat of some kind.

Some three or four weeks before Christmas, the scholars would gather in groups at dinner-time and talk over the prospect for a good time at Christmas. Some of the larger boys would be appointed to interview the teacher, and find out, if possible, whether he was going to "treat" or not. Sometimes the master "did n't know," and then there would be guessing and planning about the prospect in view.

Sometimes some of the larger and ruder boys would suggest the idea of "locking him out" until he should come to terms; and sometimes the suggestion was carried into effect, so far as the locking out was concerned, but the means employed did not always bring the "master" to terms.

On this particular occasion, however, the master

was disposed to be accommodating, and the scholars, big and little, were all on tiptoe with expectation, and in our noonday caucuses we all voted that the master was splendid. I guess we did n't use that word, exactly; but we meant the same thing that you mean when you say splendid, or when you call your teacher or a playmate a "brick."

The day before Christmas was a busy one for the schoolmaster's wife and daughters, in getting the "treat" ready. On Christmas morning, the master came in sight, followed by his two oldest boys, lads of about sixteen and fourteen years of age, each laden with a basket, holding almost a bushel and closely covered.

The boys and girls all gathered at the door, hoping to get a peep, or at least a smell, of the "goodies," but a wave of the teacher's hand made them fall back a little, and the mysterious baskets, with their precious loads, were soon deposited in the box-like pulpit—for the school-house was made to answer the purpose of a church on Sundays. Then the master went to the door and "rapped" on it with his "ruler," to let us know that it was school time.

When we were all seated on the long wooden, backless benches, the schoolmaster adjusted his spectacles very carefully—he looked very much like the pictures we see nowadays of the old-time schoolmaster—then he pushed them up on his forehead, and looked about the room. After a little pause, he announced to the school that, "as to-day is Christmas, we will not study our usual lessons; but, if the school wishes, we will have spelling-school."

Of course, the school "wished" it, and a big boy
and girl were appointed by the master to "choose
up." I suppose my readers attended some of the
many spelling-schools which were held over the
country last Winter, so I need not tell you about ·
this one. We had no recess in those days, and our
school commenced at eight o'clock, instead of nine, .
as it does now; but the morning hours soon passed
away, and noon came, and then each family of children sat down to their cold dinner with good appe-
tites, and tempers, too, for that matter.

At one o'clock, the master's ruler called us to
order again, and that reminds me that I have forgotten to tell you what a nice time we had, and what
merry games we played, but that must go now, or
my letter will be too long.

When we were all quiet—and we got quiet sooner
than usual on that day—two boys and two girls, the
steadiest and best-behaved in the school, were selected to "pass" the—not candies and nuts, but—
cakes, pies (mince, apple and pumpkin), and doughnuts. The doughnuts were cut in all sorts of fanci-
ful shapes, and some were cut with thimbles, and
when fried were about the size and shape of a filbert,
and were called "kisses" by the little ones. Was n't
there grand fun when the "kisses" were distributed!
and did n't the schoolmaster and all make the old
school-house ring with merry laughter, when a little
fat-faced, curly-haired girl, her eyes swimming in
tears, called out:

"Please, master, George Castle has taken all my
kisses! won't you make him give 'em back?"

14

When the pies and cakes—do n't read it "pizen cakes," as I have heard children say it—were all disposed of, then the master brought out a liberal supply of rosy-cheeked apples. What fun we had in tossing them back and forth! and how the big boys and girls pared theirs carefully, and then swung the paring round their heads and cast it on the floor, to see what letter it would form! and how delighted they were when the paring formed the initial letter of the name of some special favorite or sweetheart!

At about half-past three, we were again "called to order," and the "big spelling class" took its place, and the lesson assigned on the previous day was spelled, and the school was dismissed.

The tired, but happy, children put on their wraps, and, taking their empty dinner-baskets on their arms, were soon on their way home, laughing and shouting, as they threw their snow-balls back and forth in merry glee.

All this was thirty years ago, and "the master sleeps upon the hill," and many of his pupils rest in the same graveyard; but on this Christmas the boys and girls who read this will have as merry a time as we had then, no doubt, though in a different way.

Cui Bono?

—o—•—o—

EAR me, I wonder if there really is any sense in it any way!" and little Mrs. Webb sat down and began working hurriedly on the button-hole she had begun before being called to the parlor to receive a caller.

"Why, what's the matter now? Do you consider buttons and button-holes a nuisance, and propose to dispense with them in the future?" asked her sister as she looked up from her book, as she sat by the sitting-room window.

"Now, Nellie, don't tease; you know I am not so silly as that."

"Well, what is it then? something serious, I know by your looks."

"As you are a young lady with but few cares and responsibilities resting upon you, perhaps you may not think so; but with me it is a serious matter, and I really wish—"

"Now, sister, I object to your making a speech until there is a motion before the house. Before you present your arguments I should like to know what you are talking about."

"Very well, then, here it is," and Mrs. Webb laughed at her sister's teasing. "I move that the rules of etiquette be so far modified as to allow a

lady to use her hands in necessary work while entertaining callers."

Nellie laughed gleefully. "Well, I don't know
as I shall agree with you, but for the sake of getting
it in shape I second the motion."

"And now, Mr. Chairman," said Mrs. Webb to
her husband, who had come in during the conversation, "will you please state the question?"

"Certainly, any thing to oblige you. Let me
see; how is it? O, yes; Resolved, That Mrs. Grundy
be asked to give the ladies permission to work and
gossip at the same time. Really, ladies, according
to *my* ideas of woman's *work* and *talk*, that will be
an utter impossibility."   .

"If you please, sir, you have not stated the
question fairly; and beside, I deny your right to pass
judgment at this stage of the debate," objected Mrs.
Webb. "But, seriously, what is the use of my sitting with my hands folded when I could work and
talk just as well? For instance, this afternoon I have
had five calls, which altogether have taken up two
hours of my time and put me that much behind with
my work. I was very glad to see each one who
called to day, but Gracie and Jennie are needing
their dresses so much that I should have enjoyed
their company a great deal more if I could have
been working these button holes while I was talking."

"But, sister, it seems to me that it would look
rude, and as if you were in a hurry for them to go,
if you were to keep on with your work when you
had company," said Nellie.

"I don't feel so, though perhaps others may,

and that is just where I want the reform to begin. Every married lady knows, or ought to know, that every woman who has a family to look after has need to be busy nearly all the time, and that if she spends all her afternoons in the parlor with idle hands that there will be times when her work is neglected."

"Yes; but, wife, you owe something to society as well as to your family," suggested Mr. Webb.

"I know it, and that is just the reason I want a change in the rules of etiquette. Why can not I be just as polite and entertaining with my basting or knitting in my hands as without? The last lady who called to-day was Mrs. Clark, and I was really glad to see her, and always enjoy her calls so much; but I was hurried and forgot to take my thimble off before I went into the parlor, and, I suppose, she saw it, or else judged from my looks that I was hurried with my work, and so only stayed a few minutes. Now if fashion, or society, or whatever you may call it, would have allowed me to take my work into the parlor I could have spent an hour in conversation very profitably, for Mrs. Clark is not one of the gossiping ones; but as it is, I feel that I hurried her away and lost an opportunity for social enjoyment that I need not have lost if it had not been for this foolish custom."

"But, Lucy, the rich, who are able to hire their work done, are not hurried as you are; would you have them take their work into the parlor, too?" asked Nellie.

"Yes; and it because they *are* rich and influential that I would have them do it. Of course, they need not take their calico and gingham there unless they wish, but almost every lady has some light bit of needle work or fancy knitting that she could keep on hand to pick up while she is entertaining callers, and so help us who are busier and less influential.''

" But, wife, would not your work make you feel unsocial and hurried?''

"Not a bit. The most social gatherings we have are where the ladies bring their work; don't you know how you laugh about our sewing circles?''

"Yes, and if you propose to talk about your neighbors after the manner of orthodox sewing societies, I shall object," laughed Mr. Webb.

"I think, my dear, you are making too many speeches for the president of a meeting. I have no notion of making my parlor a place for idle gossip; and, by the way, I think our sewing societies are censured a great deal more than they deserve. But I was going to say, the pleasantest gatherings we have are where the ladies bring their work, and the driest one I ever attended was where each one wore her best dress, and her most dignified manners, and sat idly talking or watching her neighbor.''

"Well, sister," suggested Nellie, "you have about as much independence as any one, suppose you 'start the fashion' as the milliners say, and take John's socks into the parlor and darn them while you entertain your next caller. I fancy Mrs. Grundy would turn up her aristocratic nose and lift her hands in disgust if you were to dare to such a thing.''

"I presume so; but it is not necessary that John's socks should be taken to the parlor. I can mend

them of evenings while he reads to me. ' I love company, and enjoy the calls of my friends as much as
any one, but I owe a duty to my family as well as
to others, and I am sure there is plenty of work that
would not look out of place in the parlor, and I have
a great mind to begin to *try* at least, to inaugurate a
new era in parlor etiquette."

"Well, I shall want time to think about it before
I agree to vote 'aye' on this very important question," said Nellie; "so I move that the discussion be
continued at our next meeting."

"And ladies," said Mr. Webb, as he picked up
his hat and turned to the door, "business is waiting,
and I must go; but I hope, if you undertake this
reform, that you will let me know how it is received
by your fashionable friends."

The Foster Family:

BUT, mother, I am tired of just the same kind of carpet all the time. I will have to work hard for five or six weeks to make it, and then it will be nothing but a rag carpet, after all. Why can't father get a nice ingrain for the front room?"

"Your father is saving his money to buy that farm of Mr. Johnson's. He thinks he gets it very cheap; but it will take all the money he can raise this Fall to make the first payment."

"I thought father had enough land already. I am sure it isn't a week since I heard him complaining because he had so much care on his mind. I wonder," a little bitterly, "if he thinks another farm, with another debt for two or three years, will *lighten* his cares any!"

"Ella," said her mother, half reprovingly, half apologetically, "your father is working hard to lay by something for his children, and you ought not to speak so. It will be very nice to have a farm of your own when you come to get married."

"I suppose father thinks he is working for our good; but I would rather have a *part* of the money now than to wait until I am married, which is not likely to be very soon, unless some of the work-hands choose to fall in love with me, and take me off your hands; and that is not likely to happen, as they always see me in the worst possible plight. It is nothing but drudge, drudge, all the time; kitchen and dairy, washing and ironing, sweeping and making beds, making and mending, without time to even comb my hair decently. I suppose, if ever I do marry, it will be to some one who has fallen in love with father's acres instead of his daughter. O, I *wish* I could have something nice and pretty just *once!*" and Ella Foster closed her lips with a very decided compression, and went on vigorously rubbing the coarse linen towel that she was ironing with an iron which had grown cold while she was warming up with her subject.

Mrs. Foster sighed as she turned from the table, where she was paring a basket of apples for the Winter's mince-meat, and went to the stove and put in an extra stick of wood before she replied to her daughter's complaint. At last she said, in a weary, discouraged tone:

"Well, Ellen, you may ask your father for the money, but I am afraid it will be useless. I am sure I wish you could have more leisure and nicer furniture; but your father thinks he can not afford to hire a girl, and he says the furniture is good enough."

Nothing more was said about the carpet at that time; but Ella made up her mind that she would ask for it as soon as she found a favorable opportunity.

The home of the Fosters was very much like many other homes. The father had commenced life as a poor man, and had, by the strictest economy and industry, succeeded in purchasing a little home

and paying for it. But the habits acquired during
those years were not easily laid aside, and as his
property had increased so had his desire for more;
and his wife, who in their early married life had denied herself every luxury, and worked hard day and
night, almost, to save money to pay for their home,
had not yet come to the time when she felt that she
could sit down and take the rest she really needed.
Her husband had kept adding a few acres to his
farm every two or three years, keeping himself just
enough in debt to require constant saving in order to
meet his engagements. He had seldom hired help
for his wife, though she had often needed it sadly;
but knowing her husband's desire to save, she had
refrained from complaining, and as Ella grew up she
was obliged to call on her for help here and there,
until, at the age of eighteen, the daughter had become, like her mother, a constant drudge.

Ella had inherited from her mother a strong love
for the beautiful, which amounted almost to a passion—the more so, apparently, because she had but
little opportunity to exercise or gratify her taste,
which, in spite of its crushing back, would crop out
in little, tastefully arranged ornaments, which she
contrived for her own room when the rest of the
family were asleep.

Ella was the youngest of two children. Others
had come to brighten their home; but they had only
tarried for a little while. Tom was the only son, two
years older than Ella, and dear to his mother and
sister as the very apple of their eye. He had shared
his father's toil ever since he was old enough to pull

weeds or hold a plow-handle; but lately he had shown considerable quickness in mastering the studies assigned him in the district school, and his mother's brother, who lived in the city, having taken quite a fancy to him, had, after considerable coaxing, succeeded in persuading his father to let him spend the Winter at his house, and attend school with his cousins—on the condition, however, that his board should not cost him any thing.

The evening after the conversation recorded above, Ella received a letter from her brother, saying he expected to come home during holidays, and adding:

"I should like to ask Lew Merrell, a schoolmate of mine, home with me, Ella; but his home is so much nicer than mine that I do n't like to. Could n't you coax father to get something new for the front room? I know you could brighten it up nicely if you had the chance. If you could only coax father to give you fifty dollars when he sells the hogs, you could make the old house look splendid, Puss! It won't be hard work to persuade mother; she likes nice things almost as well as you do. I want Lew to come; but I shall not ask him unless you can coax father to fix up the house. He has every thing so pleasant at home—not fine, you know, but so cheerful and neat."

These few lines decided Ella, and when her father came in to supper, and said he had sold his hogs for one cent more on the pound than he had expected to receive, she thought the opportunity a good one, and while he sat by the fire after supper, looking over the city paper, she asked, a little timidly:

"Father, how much money will you receive for the hogs you sold to-day?"

"About nine hundred dollars;" and Mr. Foster looked up, wondering why his daughter should be interested in the subject.

"Well, then, father, don't you think you could afford a new carpet for the front room? I mean an ingrain, like Aunt Mary has in her sitting-room."

Mr. Foster looked at her a moment, as if to be certain that he had heard correctly, and then said: "What has put that into your head? Your mother and I have been married twenty-five years, and never had any thing better than a rag carpet. No: ingrain, as you call it, will do for city folks; if you want a carpet, make one—you 've nothing else to do."

"But, father, I am tired of rag carpets, and I am tired of *making* them, too," persisted Ella.

"Well, what do you *want* to do? spend your time in crocheting or in gadding to the village, I suppose! No; I have other use for my money than to buy ingrain carpets with it. I must make a payment of six hundred dollars on the Johnson farm next week, and I have bargained for a corn-crusher that will cost fifty dollars. Smith says he saves one-third the amount of feed by his. Then I must look up some more yearlings, to feed the roughness to this Winter, and that will take all my spare change," and with this, for him, rather lengthy explanation, Mr. Foster turned to his paper again.

Ella made no reply; her little castle in the air had suddenly fallen, and, gathering up her work, she went to her own room, and, sitting down on a stool by the low window, she laid her head on the sill and sobbed quietly to herself. At last, when her feelings had spent themselves a little, she rose, lit the lamp, and sat down to finish the garment she was making.

"Father thinks more of his stock than he does of his family," she said to herself, impatiently. "I wonder how he could spare Tom; I wish *I* could get away from the farm for a year or two! No, I do n't, either; for then mother would have *my* work and *hers* both to do; but—O dear! I am *so* tired of it *all*," and again the tears welled up in the blue eyes, but were resolutely dashed away, and the work which had fallen in her lap was again taken up, and finally finished. Then she sought her pillow, to dream of bright-colored carpets and lace curtains, oddly mixed up with crushed corn and yearling calves.

The next day Ella reported to her mother the result of her petition.

Mrs. Foster sighed and bid her daughter be patient.

"Your father means it for your good, and he does n't feel the need of such things, as we do; you know he is seldom in the house, except at meal-times."

"I would n't care so much for myself," said Ella, tearfully; "but Tom wants to bring Lew Merrill home with him, and he can 't when every thing looks so shabby; and *I* do n't want strangers here, either, unless we can have things like other folks. I suppose Tom will have to come home alone, or stay at uncle's during holidays," and then, as if affrighted at the thought, she exclaimed: "O, I hope he will not stay there over Christmas; he has been gone nearly two months, now!"

Tom came home during holidays, but he did not bring his friend with him; his pride would not grant his schoolmate the opportunity to draw unpleasant contrasts between the two homes.

There were no Christmas presents bestowed in the home of the Fosters. For the first two years after their marriage, Mrs. Foster had made her husband a present, but he had not remembered her in like manner, and even laughed at the dressing-gown which she had made for him when he was sleeping, declaring that he didn't want to wear "woman's clothes," and so she had abandoned what had been a standing custom in her girlhood's home. Ella would occasionally express a wish that *she* could have pleasant surprises, as her cousins had on Christmas mornings, but her father always said he could not afford it, and so Christmas was pretty much the same to them as any other day, except that the kind-hearted city uncle would occasionally send his nephew and niece some little tokens of remembrance.

During vacation, Tom took occasion to say to his sister: "I shall never come back to the farm again. Of course, I shall come back and see the home folks; but I am not going to drudge here any longer. I would not mind staying here if there was any rest, but father never takes any himself, nor

allows any one else to. Uncle has offered me a
place in the shop with him, and I am going to accept it; and O, Puss, it is so pleasant at uncle's!
The girls all *work*, but they do n't have to keep at it
all the time. We have *such* fun of evenings; and
uncle and aunt are the best company of all."

"But what will *I* do when you are gone, Tom?
I shall be all alone, then."

"I know it; but if I stay it will not make it any
easier for *you*. Father will manage to keep us all
busy; you and mother are just wearing yourselves
to death, to make money, and then to think he
would n't buy you a new carpet! I declare it 's too
bad! I wonder if he has any idea how much
you and mother *save* every year, besides what he
gets for the butter and poultry? You had better
be a hired girl, and done with it; you would get to
rest *some* time, and have the pleasure of spending
what you earned, besides."

And Tom whittled away desperately at the pine
stick which he held in his hand, forgetful that he
was making dirt on the clean floor for his sister to
sweep up.

Ella made no reply to his impatient words, and
Tom looked up to see the tears stealing, one by
one, down her cheeks, as she hastily brushed them
away with the back of her hand, and went on set-
ting the table for dinner.

He jumped up hastily, threw the stick into the
fire, and shut his knife, exclaiming, as he did so:
"There, I 'll never say another word about it; I
know it makes you feel worse; and I *do n't* want

you to leave mother; but there's no use talking—I *can't* stand it, and I *won't.*"

And he was as good as his word.

He went back to school. After the school closed, he took a situation in his uncle's shop, and for a time he did well; but the sudden change from the severest drudgery to the liberty to go and come as he pleased was too much, and Tom Foster, bewildered by the allurements of city life, thrust upon him so suddenly, yielded to temptation, and became a fast young man.

The mother and Ella shed many bitter tears over the wayward one, while the father was often heard to say he "couldn't see why Tom should be so idle and shiftless, when he never knew any thing else but work till he was twenty," apparently unconscious that it was his "all work and no play" system which had driven his son from what *might have been* a pleasant and safe occupation, into temptations of which he had never even heard, and which he had not the power to resist.

JOYFUL TIDINGS.

"High in the belfry the old sexton stands,
Clasping the rope in his thin, bony hands,"

ND all along the principal streets of Phila-
delphia stood the sentinels ready to send
the tidings of the signing of the Declaration of Independence; and as the first sentry
received the news it was repeated to his neighbor, and so it was borne along the street, and
the command, " Ring, ring the bells!" reached
the old sexton, and he, in joyful obedience,
rings out the peal that tells of a nation's birth.

How the hearts of the people must have
leaped for joy as they heard the merry bells
peal forth the sounds which told them the blow
for liberty had been struck.

But seventeen hundred years before that joyful
ringing came the news to earth of a far more important event.

When Christ was born not *men* but *angels* stood
as sentries, ready to tell the joyful news one to another. O, what joyful news! Not that a nation
was trying to break the fetters which bound her, but
that the world's Deliverer had come.

"Swift through the vast expanse it flew,
And loud the echo rolled;
The theme, the song, the joy was new,
'T was more than heaven could hold.

Down through the portals of the sky
The impetuous torrent ran,
And angels flew with eager joy
To bear the news to man !"

And to-day in every pulpit in the land stands a sentry ready to call out to the waiting people, "Ring, ring the bells!" and may we not hope that ere many more Christmas days shall roll around that the line of sentries shall encircle our earth, and the joy bells shall be rung, one after another, until they shall awake one grand jubilee of joy all around the world?

No wonder the shepherds "were sore afraid," for they were unaccustomed to such sights. Not often had they heard of the angel of the Lord appearing to men of such humble station as they. True, the angels had visited man, but not with such glory as this. The glory of God is not often manifested to mortal eyes.

But not long does the angel leave them in dread or suspense. "Fear not; for behold I bring you good tidings of great joy, which shall be to all people," and then, while they listen with bated breath, he proceeds, "for unto you is born this day in the city of David, a Savior, which is Christ the Lord!" How the announcement must have thrilled on the ears of these shepherds of Judea!

For ages the Israelites had been looking forward to the promised coming of the Messiah, and their hearts had many times cried out, "How long, O Lord, how long!"

These shepherds had heard of the promises given by the prophet Isaiah of the coming of Him who was to be called Wonderful, Counselor, the Mighty God, the Everlasting Father, the Prince of Peace, and now their hearts filled with rapture at the good news. And even while they were wondering and amazed at the strange tidings, "suddenly there was with the angel a multitude of the heavenly host," and there burst forth from the celestial choir one glad song, one grand anthem, one triumphal chorus! "Glory to God in the highest, on earth peace, good will to men!" And if the shepherds realized the meaning of the wonderful message they, too, said, "Glory to God!"

"Glory to God in the highest," sang the angel choir. "Glory to God" has been sung by myriads of happy voices, by vast numbers of redeemed souls since that eventful night; and "Glory to God in the highest, *amen and amen!*" echo our hearts to-day as we read the "sweet story of old!"

If Jesus, whose nativity was heralded by the heavenly messengers, had been born in a palace, man might, in his perverseness, have thought he was sent only to the rich. But while his advent was proclaimed by the angel of the Lord, his birth was lowly, and so was his whole life.

Perhaps on this Christmas day some of God's children may be tempted to feel that their lot is a hard one. But none need be without comfort. Jesus spent his whole earth-life in poverty, yet he was heir to a crown. And so is every child of God (no matter how poverty stricken) heir to a crown of eternal life, bought with the precious blood of him whose birth we celebrate.

Meet it is that we celebrate the anniversary of God's great gift to *us* by the bestowal of gifts upon his poor. Not to the rich, who will not value our offerings, but to those whose life has been robbed of many blessings which *we* enjoy. O, how poor would *we* be to-day if it were not for the blessed gift of God's dear Son!

Meet it is that we bow our heads in humble thankfulness while we read, "For unto us a child is born, unto us a Son is given, and the government shall be upon his shoulder; and his name shall be called Wonderful, Counselor, the Mighty God, the Everlasting Father, the Prince of Peace." And as we close the Book let us lift our hearts in prayer to God, that *we* who have received such a glorious gift may also receive more of his Holy Spirit, more of his grace in our hearts, that shall make us meek and lowly, more like our blessed Savior, our Elder Brother, and God's dear Son.

Ah, over and over will that sweet story be repeated on this festal day! Little faces will, be upturned to hear the oft repeated story; little lips will quiver and young eyes will grow moist, aye, *and old ones too*, as the touching story of the heavenly Babe is repeated in the costly temple or humble chapel, in palace or cot. And hearts will be made tenderer for others' sorrows by hearing of the loving sympathy of him who came to save us. How sweetly simple the story, and yet so freighted with the destiny of souls! "Behold, I bring *you* good tidings of great joy;" and not to *you* only, but "which shall be to all people." The whole world is to rejoice at the humble birth. All nations shall be glad because of his advent.

"Lying in a manger." Lowliest of the lowly, and yet the sharer of the Eternal Throne! were ever poverty and royalty so united! His mother the wife of a carpenter, himself laid in a manger! Yet the angel of the Lord commissioned to bear the news to *man.*

And not only an angel is sent to proclaim the joyful tidings, but a *multitude* of the heavenly host comes to sing the "Glory to God." Fitting messengers for such glorious tidings. Fitting escort for such a heaven-sent messenger. Christ *might* have come with all the pomp of an Eastern monarch. But no; he prefers to come as the child of poverty. He is King of kings and Lord of lords, and yet,

> "Cold on his cradle the dewdrops are shining,
> Low lies his head with the beasts of the stall."

The heavenly messenger might have been sent to Herod, but instead he came to a little company of shepherds on the hillsides of Judea.

Jesus was to be called "the Lion of the tribe of Judah," and the glad news of his birth was first told to Judah's sons. And they, overjoyed at the wondrous story, leave their flocks and hasten away to Bethlehem, to "see this thing which is come to pass." And when they had seen they made it known abroad. The first to say on earth "A Savior is born," was the angel of the Lord—the next a company of Judean shepherds. And as we read the story we wonder what all this great mystery means. Why should

Jesus, who was one with the Father, leave his heavenly home and come down to earth to bear the woes
of humanity? Why should he choose to leave a
throne for a manger? or exchange a royal robe and
crown for swaddling clothes?

While we are wondering we turn to John iii, 16,
and read, "For God so loved the world that he
gave his only begotten Son that whosoever believeth
in him should not perish but have everlasting life."
And then the mystery is all solved. All is made
plain in that one word, *Love!* Love to whom? To
his Son? No. For dear as was that Son, father-
love is held in subjection to his love and pity for our
lost condition, and he gives that Son so well-beloved
to save a sin-cursed world.

Christ was not only born into the world, but he
came as our sacrifice, our all-sufficient atonement.
No wonder the angel host burst forth in that joyful
anthem, "Glory to God in the highest, on earth
peace, good will to men!" And O, blessed privilege,

> "With joy the chorus *we* repeat,
> Glory to God on high!
> Good will and peace are now complete—
> Jesus was born to die!"

"For this cause came I unto this hour," said the
Savior when the terrible agony drew near.

O, when we contemplate the wonderful incarna-
tion we feel humbled. All our efforts to praise him
seem so insignificant. We bow our faces in the dust
and in our amazement and humility cry out,

> "O, eternity's too short
> To utter all his praise!"

But God in his tender pity for our weakness has given us the privilege to praise him, yea, we may call him what even the angels may not, "Our Brother!" And while the angels surround his throne in heaven, praising him for his love to man, *we too* are permitted to lift our glad voices in a hymn of praise here below. And God in his wisdom and abounding goodness has left man without excuse.

Margie Hays's Valentine.

T was only two days before St. Valentine's day, and the windows of the village bookstore were filled with a variety of bright-colored valentines, ranging all the way from the most sentimental down to the most comical and ludicrous.

The children, on their way to school, stopped and gazed with open-mouthed astonishment at the wonderful display. The misses and boys of larger growth — with just as much interest, but more dignity—walked slowly by, as they scanned with careful eyes the tempting variety, in "prices to suit purchasers," resolving to examine more closely on their way home.

A group of girls, ranging from thirteen to fifteen years of age, had knotted together in the "hall" of the school-building, and were talking over the prospect for some fun, and wondering whether they would receive any valentines themselves, and hoping for something "real nice." The tap of the bell presently called them from their gossip, and soon the recitations were going on with their usual monotonous routine. But thoughts of valentines were still uppermost in their minds, and crowded out more important thoughts; and, as a consequence, when the "class in history" was called out they felt them-

selves wholly unprepared.   The answers were mostly
confused and hurried, and while some were correct
it was more of "guess-work" than genuine knowledge.   Only one member of the class seemed to have
studied the lesson thoroughly, and that was Margie
Hays, a young girl of fifteen, who had but recently
entered the school, and who, because of her reserved
manner, evident poverty, and uniform good lessons,
was not very popular with her more favored, though
less diligent, schoolmates.   To-day the class felt that
Margie had a decided advantage over them, but tried
to brave it out.   But guessing did not succeed very
well, and when Miss Burton asked the question: "In
what year was Florida discovered, and by whom?"
the answers given were wide of the correct one, while
some acknowledged that they "did n't know."   The
question passed nearly round the class, and reached
Margie Hays, and, although she felt that the eyes of
the whole class were fixed on her with a look which
seemed to say, "Do n't you dare to answer correctly," she answered, clearly and distinctly, as if
sure she was right: "In 1512, by Ponce de
Leon."

There was a little sniff of contempt from the delin-
quent members of the class, as Margie took her place
at the head, and as they took their seats it was evident that the "new scholar" had not gained favor by
answering the question correctly.

When recess came, and they were outside the
school-room, their bottled wrath had opportunity to
vent itself in words.

Bessie Hoyt thought "she ought to be ashamed

to set herself above the rest of the class, when she had only been in the school two weeks."

While Susie Brown was sure "she wore the same dress to Sabbath-school that she wore to the public school."

"Hush!" whispered Nellie Hall; "she may hear you."

"Who cares if she does?" responded Bessie, with a toss of her head; ": but there is no danger, for she is poring over her books as if her life depended upon having every word perfectly."

"She ought to study them well, for they were a present from the school board; I heard papa say so yesterday," said Susie, with a sneer.

While some one added, in a tone of evident scorn, "Humph, a charity scholar!"

Presently Bessie's face brightened up. "O, girls," she whispered; "I've thought of something that will just take the starch out of her in a hurry."

The bevy of girls hovered nearer to Bessie, all eager to know the plan by which they could over-throw this feminine Mordecai, who refused to do hom-age to their superior position, if not talents.

"O Bessie, what is it?" they whispered in chorus.

Bessie felt the importance of her position, and answered, with dignity: "If you will promise to keep it secret, I'll tell you." All were ready to make the required promise. "Well, then," said Bessie, in a stage whisper, "we will send her a val-entine."

"Good—good! what will it be?" cried the girls, in a breath.

"The Charity Scholar," said Bessie.

The girls took up with the suggestion at once; but recess was over, and there was no time for discussion until noon.

On the way home the plan was talked over, and it was decided that the book-store had nothing suitable, so one of their number, who had a "gift" for caricature, was employed to draw up a sketch of Margie receiving her books from the school board, the faces in the sketch being enough like the originals to be recognized, and "The Charity Scholar" printed in large letters below.

On Valentine's eve Nellie Hall was commissioned to mail the sweet-looking package, which contained such an unkind caricature.

This was Nellie's first experience in sending an ill-natured valentine, and some way the affair did not seem so pleasant as in the beginning, and she walked rather slowly along the street towards the post-office.

"I wonder how I should feel if I were in Margie's place?" thought Nellie; "I 'm sure she will think us ill-natured; and may be she is n't selfish, as we think, and if she *is* poor she can 't help that."

The more she thought of the unkind picture, the more she wished she had not consented to take part in the trick. Cautiously she took the package from the pocket of her water-proof and looked at it, walking more slowly all the time, as if undecided whether to go forward or backward.

Finally she stood still, with the, envelope in one hand while she jingled some loose coin in her pocket with the other; then, as if a new thought had suddenly taken possession of her, she said, with a little gleeful laugh, "Margie shall never see this naughty picture. I 'll fix it all right, and the girls shall never know," and with this resolution Nellie started forward again. But instead of going straight on to the post office, she turned down the street leading to the book-store.

Nellie approached cautiously at first, and glanced through the glass doors to make sure that none of "the girls" were within. Having assured herself that the coast was clear, she stepped in, and, hastily making her purchase, wrote a few words on the inside, slipped it into a large white envelope, then directed it to Miss Margie Hays.

She hurried to the post-office, dropped it in the box, and hurried away, scarcely able to decide as to whether she had done a very kind or a very mean thing.

Morning came at last, and what a rush there was for the post-office as soon as breakfast was over. No matter if some did have to go four or five blocks out of the way, in order to pass it on their way to school. Each one was anxious to know if there was a "letter for me," and as the good-natured postmaster and his clerks knew most of the anxious faces, it was not necessary to give their names in full.

Mrs. Hays had sent Margie by way of the post-office that morning, to mail a letter. Margie mailed it, and inquired if there was any mail for "Mrs. Julia

Hays," but it never entered her head to ask if there was a letter for herself.

"No, there is nothing for Mrs. Hays," the clerk answered, as he looked over the bundle of letters; "but," as Margie turned away, "here is something for Miss Margie Hays, if that is one of Mrs. Hays's family."

"O, yes, it is for me; thank you," and Margie tucked the beautiful white package under her shabby cloak, and hurried on to school, for it was almost nine, and she prided herself on her punctuality and perfect lessons.

When she reached school, she had barely time to take her seat when the last stroke of the bell warned those who were not seated that Miss Burton would have a tardy mark opposite their name at the close of the day.

Margie longed to see the contents of the mysterious package, but she was obliged to wait until recess. Bessie and Susie tried to read Margie's face, as she took her seat, and for some time after their eyes would wander to her desk; but concluded that she either had not received the valentine, or else it had not had the effect which they had expected it would. Nellie felt like a poor, guilty thing, and tried to keep her eyes on the lesson before her, but her face reddened every time she caught the eyes of the plotters.

Recess came at last, but Margie did not leave her seat, but sat quietly waiting until the scholars had left the room; then she took out the package, looked at it carefully, then broke the seal.

Bessie, Susie, and Nellie, with two others who were in the secret, had stationed themselves in the hall, where they could see Margie bending over her desk, although her position prevented their seeing the valentine or getting a fair view of her face, and it must be confessed, to the credit of Bessie and Susie, that the trick did not seem half so funny now that they thought they were about to triumph over the unpopular stranger.

Only for a moment or two did Margie look at her valentine, and then down went her head upon the desk, and the watchers saw that she was sobbing violently.

Bessie and Susie, with their companions, tried to feel triumphant; but, instead, felt as if they had been guilty of a very mean act.

Nellie was puzzled, and her heart almost leaped into her throat. Could she have made a mistake, and mailed the wrong package, after all? O, what should she do!

Margie's half stifled sobs, had attracted the attention of Miss Burton, who had been busily writing at her desk. As she looked up and saw Margie with her head lying on the desk and sobbing, she suspected that some unkind or thoughtless prank had been played on the new scholar, and, laying down her pen, she went to Margie, and laid her hand on her head.

The spies cast upon each other a look of dismay. Now the teacher would see the hideous picture, and would pity Margie, and they would all be questioned about it, and may be punished.

"What is it. Margie?" Miss Burton asked, kindly, and the girl, startled out of her sobs, looked up, showing a face wet with tears.

But the teacher, with a surprised look, and without waiting for Margie to answer her question, reached out her hand and took from the desk the missive over which Margie had been sobbing; but, instead of the ugly caricature, the girls saw a beautiful valentine — more handsome than any they had received themselves. Nellie drew a breath of relief. "It *is* all right, after all," she said to herself.

The others uttered an exclamation of surprise, and, forgetful that they had been acting the part of spies, opened the door and went forward on tiptoe. As they came near, Miss Burton was saying:

"Was this what made you cry, Margie?" and Margie, brushing off her tears with the back of her hand, answered:

"I know it seems foolish; but it was such a surprise. I did n't think the girls cared for me one bit, and this is the first valentine that I have received since papa died, four years ago."

Bessie was near enough to see that at the bottom of the inside page was written, with a pencil, the words, "With good wishes, from your classmates," and, with a glance at Nellie, they knew they had been "sold."

Without waiting to see or hear any more, they retreated to the hall, Nellie with the rest. As they turned for one look before closing the door, they saw Miss Burton take Margie's face between her hands, and kiss her lovingly.

"O girls," whispered Nellie, her eyes full of tears, "don't be cross; I couldn't help it. It seemed too bad to send her that horrid thing, and so I bought this with my own money, and burned the other."

Bessie's better nature triumphed, and she said heartily: "Good for you, Nell!"

And Susie said, with a sigh of relief, "I'm glad Nell didn't mail the other; I've felt real mean about it all the time."

But the recess was ended, and there was no more time for talking, but all through the day Margie's face beamed with good will whenever she looked at her classmates, for she supposed it was a partnership gift; and the girls, glad to have the other affair off their shoulders, were only too willing to treat Margie with more cordiality than usual, and, a few days after, they compelled Nellie to let them pay their share in the bill of expense.

The acts of kindness performed for Margie in their little "shamming," had not only softened their own hearts, but Margie's, and there were soon no better friends in all the village than Margie and her classmates; and Margie never heard of "The Charity Scholar."

"Wouldn't Mother Care for Such Things?"

I SUPPOSE the excursion to L—— will be a very pleasant affair, as there will be no more tickets sold than there are seats in the coaches, and there will be a whole day for sight-seeing in the city."

The speaker, Mrs. Huston, was a young wife and mother, who had brought her little twelve-months'-old baby and some sewing to "finish off" while she spent an hour or two with her neighbor and friend, Mrs. Starr, a bright, bustling woman, with a family of four children, who were as bright and bustling, in their own particular way, as was the mother.

Mrs. Starr answered her friend's remark cheerily,

"Yes, I think so. I expect to enjoy it very much."

"Why, do *you* think of going?" asked Mrs. Huston, in apparent astonishment.

"Yes; why not?" with an amused smile, as she saw the look of surprise on Mrs. Huston's face.

"Well, I don't know why not, only I didn't suppose you would think of going on such a trip, while you have such a family on your hands," and her friend looked as if she was uncertain as to whether she had made a blunder or a hit.

17

"That is the very reason I am going.   I need the change, and so do the children," was replied, pleasantly.

"You surely will not take *them* with you!" and Mrs. Huston looked more astonished than before.

"No, indeed. I could not think of taking them out of school just now; but I expect them to get as much real benefit from the trip as I will; for I know I will be all the brighter for the change, and—"

"O, you are always bright and cheerful, any way," interrupted Mrs. Huston, with a deprecatory gesture.

"But you do not know how much of an effort it requires, sometimes, for me to be bright and cheerful;" and Mrs. Starr finished the sentence with a sigh, then added, thoughtfully, "I find I must keep pace with my children if I would retain my hold on their respect and confidence."

"I do not see how you can afford the time; you say you are already overburdened, sometimes, and then there are the children," persisted Mrs. Huston, as she fastened her thread, as if it were an unanswerable argument.

"I think the time will be well spent; and as to leaving the children for forty-eight hours, I don't know but it will do them good to miss mother for just a little while. You know the song says,

"Strange we never prize the music
Till the sweet-voiced bird is flown."

And I have concluded that my family will appreciate me just as much if I allow myself a little rest and recreation, and give them an opportunity to see what I do when I *am* here."

"But it does n't look right to leave the children in the care of a servant who feels no personal interest in them. I know *I* would n't have a minute's peace if I thought my precious Maud was left to the tender mercies of Bridget," and Mrs. Huston picked up her little one, that had been clinging by her side, and gave it a little hug that was meant as an emphasis to her words.

"In the first place, I shall not leave them to the care of the girl alone. Their father has scarcely a moment of time for them, but Aunt Mary has promised to stay here until I return, and as the children are in school nearly all day, there will not be very much care or responsibility as to their welfare resting upon Norah. Now, are you convinced?" and Mrs. Starr laughed good-humoredly at her friend's sober face.

"And yet that sounds so unlike you. Have n't you always told me that I must make up my mind to stay at home and devote myself to my family, and when they were grown, educated and out in the world, then it would·be time enough for me to think of enjoying life?"

"Yes, I acknowledge it all, and I want to beg your pardon, and I hope that you will, in a measure, consider that advice as if it had never been given— not that I would not have you and *every* mother devoted to the interests of her family, but the way to do that is not by making herself their slave. And I want to tell you how I came to change my views

about such things; for it.is, as you say, a new thing
for me to talk as I do on this subject." And the
good woman rocked herself to and fro energetically
while she pulled out basting threads with a vigor that
harmonized well with her words and tone.

"I was calling on Mrs. W. when this excursion
was first talked of, and she expressed a strong desire
to go. But the family treated the idea as absurd, in
fact, as a sort of joke, that such a thought had entered the mother's head; and even Mrs. W. herself
laughed a little, while her face reddened, apparently
at the consciousness of her own temerity in even
dreaming of such a thing. You know there is no lack
of the necessary funds, and her family would not be
seriously inconvenienced if she should be absent for
a few days; but the prevailing thought in the mind
of husband, sons, and daughters seemed to be that
'mother' had stayed so closely at home during
the past years, that she had lost the capacity for
enjoying any thing that was not connected in some
way with food or dress for the family. And yet I
know, from the hungry expression which came over
the care-worn face, that she was neither too old in
years nor too old-fashioned in sentiment and taste to
long for mental food and for the social and intellectual treat which this trip would be likely to afford
her. I managed to keep silent, but I felt rising to
my lips an indignant protest against the selfishness
that would set the wishes of the wife and mother
aside as if she were a mere child, incapable of deciding for herself. If she is old-fashioned and lacks
'style' it is because she has given up her own will

for years, denying herself luxuries, and even what you and I would consider necessities for mind and body, in order that her children might have such advantages as would fit them to move in the best society. You need n't smile and look so amused, for I was really quite indignant, and deserve great credit for not speaking out there and then.

"Since then I have been thinking it over, and this question comes to my mind, When I am fifty or sixty years old, will my husband and children coolly set me aside and say, practically, if not in words, ' You have stayed at home so long that you will not enjoy society now ; besides, you are too old-fashioned, and it is our duty to keep you from making a spectacle of yourself.' You remember that handsome bonnet I purchased last Spring, just before I took down with the lung fever? I only wore it once, and when I recovered from the fever, and was able to be out again, it was time for a Summer bonnet, and so the Spring bonnet was left in its box. Last week I took it out to see if it would not do for this Spring. Well, the material is all good and fine, but you can understand that it is entirely out of style, and would need a thorough remodeling if I wear it. I do n't want to be kept shut up until I am entirely behind the times, like that bonnet. Neither do I want to have those, for whom I have spent the best years of my life, tell me that I am so far behind the times that I can not appreciate the beautiful in art or literature. I had not thought it was possible for me to go on that excursion, but after I thought it all over, I decided to go."

"And what did your husband say?" queried Mrs. Huston.

"O, John looked surprised enough, and I had to state the matter fully and clearly the second time before he seemed to fairly comprehend that it was not a joke. I told him that it would do me good, that I was fairly tired out with the Spring work, and asked very meekly if he thought he and the children could get along for a couple of days, provided Aunt Mary would oversee Norah. He said 'Of course,' a little dolefully, and then added slyly, 'I thought you were conscientiously opposed to leaving the children until they were old enough to take care of themselves?'"

"And what could you answer?" asked her listener.

"Well, I pulled his ears just a little bit, to punish him for his impudence, and then I told him the whole story and my conclusions about the matter; and the dear, good soul said he was glad of it, in fact he had thought for a long time that I was making a slave of myself for him and the children, and that he did n't want so many pies and puddings, nor so many extras on the girl's dresses, if they were going to steal the roses from my cheeks (the flatterer, he knows *they* have been gone these five years, unless it be *yellow* ones), and the comfort from my life. I told him I considered it a privilege to be able to work for him and the children, but I wanted to keep so that I could be a companion to them, and not a mere servant. So we have turned over a new leaf. John has always had a week or two of vacation from his business every year, and sometimes twice a year, and I am to have mine from this on; and I really believe I feel better already from the mere prospect of a little change from the old routine of all work and no play."

"But you would not have mothers leave their little ones and go off on a pleasure trip every few weeks or months?"

"No. I fancy there are a good many pleasure trips which we might take in our own homes *with* our children, if we can not afford family tickets to the mountains or the city, as the case may be. For two or three dollars invested in some entertaining book of travels or history, something that will please as well as instruct, a great amount of real pleasure and profit may be obtained. Let the children go over it together, the mother adding her own knowledge of countries and people to what is in the book, and she will find herself growing nearer to her children, and they will prize her more highly because of her sympathy with them and for them; and, if she can now and then, for a few days, leave home behind and look on new scenes and new people, she will be better fitted for the task of training her children, and she will live longer and to better purpose than if she spent her life in one incessant round of toil, with the one aim, 'that the children have a good time,' which too often means a selfish enjoyment at her expense, and I am confident they will respect her just as much if they are made to feel that self-denial is as necessary and commendable for them as it is for the mother. There," tossing her work upon the table,

"that garment is done, and so is my lecture, I believe; and as I did n't charge an admission fee nor
take up a collection, I want to know if you can give
it a recommendation?" and the little woman leaned
back in her chair as if her conscience was clear and
her mind relieved at least.

"Well, perhaps you are right, but I do n't see *my*
way clear yet," and Mrs. Huston began to fold up
her work as she looked at the clock.

"I know, it is often easier to state a theory than
to put it in practice," admitted Mrs. Starr, "and my
newly fledged ideas may need considerable guiding and
training, but those are my notions about it now; but
next time you come I hope you will not let me do
all the talking," she added, half-playfully, half-apol-
ogetically, as she assisted in wrapping baby Maud
that no breath of April dampness might reach her,
and the friends said a cordial "Good afternoon," and
Mrs. Huston went home to think it over—and Mrs.
Starr turned to her kitchen to suggest an extra dish
of fruit for the tea-table.

THE children had been looking over, and commenting on, some new photographs of old friends, and as Charlie, the eldest of the group, closed the album, he turned to Mrs. Hammond, who sat near the table, mending little garments, and said:

"Mother, what is the meaning of the word 'album'? We often use it, but I do n't know whether I know its real meaning or not. Does it mean a book for pictures only?"

Mrs. Hammond smiled, as she looked up from her work, and said:

"You are not the only one who is in the habit of using words whose meaning they but half understand. Our word 'album' comes from the Latin *albus*, signifying white, and among the Romans it formerly meant a white table or register, on which any thing was to be inscribed."

"Then why do we call this a photograph album?" asked Lizzie, as she turned to the book in question.

"Because it is a blank or register where we place the faces, or pictures, of our friends; and as we look over this register, as you have been doing this evening, the sight of the familiar faces calls up many pleasant memories."

"What about those quilts upstairs?" asked Jennie; "you call them 'album quilts,' but there are no pictures on them, though I believe there is something written on each block."

"Perhaps *you* may not be able to trace out pictures on them, but to me there are many bright faces—and a few sad ones, too—that seem to rise up before me whenever I look at those plain, faded pieces. If the pictures are not on the quilts, they are indelibly inscribed on my memory."

"O, please tell us about the persons whose names are in the center of each block," chorused the children, eagerly.

"If I am to tell you about them, you must ask Mary to bring the quilts down to the sitting-room, where we can look at the names and pieces together; though you will not be likely to find them as interesting as I do," answered the mother.

The quilts were soon brought and spread out upon the table, and as they grouped about it, the children expressed their wonder in various ways:

"Why, mother, what a funny quilt!"

"Every block is an odd one!"

"No two blocks are of the same color!"

"Neither are there two faces of those whose names are written here exactly alike. Each block is pieced from the remnant of some dress or apron worn by the person whose name is in its center. This quilt, joined with pink, was presented to me by the mothers of my Sunday-school class of little folks, years ago, and is pieced from scraps of their children's aprons, dresses, and blouse-waists, and I love to think that, while these bits of calico and gingham are growing old and faded, those little boys and girls are budding and blooming into a beautiful manhood and womanhood. Here are the names of two little brothers, Frank and Willie J——; sweet little fellows, with bright eyes and eager questions. The little one was, no doubt, the means of bringing his father and mother to Christ. One night, after he had said his evening prayer, and was about to kiss his mother good-night, he looked up into her face and asked: 'Mamma, why do n't you and papa pray to God too? are you too *old* to pray?' What answer the mother made I can not say, but the question served to awaken the parents to a sense of their need of prayer. Shortly· after, they gave their hearts into the keeping of that Father in whose sight we are all but children. The little calico waist was long ago laid aside or worn out, and, if the boys are still living, I presume they have forgotten all about the circumstance, but I trust they have not grown too old to pray. This one, marked 'Dottie W——,' we used to call 'Dottie Dimple,' as a pet name; she has probably outgrown the name, but I hope she has not outgrown the sweet, innocent ways, even though the dimples may not remain. This brown-and-white, with the name F. M——, is for a little, timid, trembling child, whose very look was more like a frightened fawn than any thing else. I never saw a child of her years so far from doing wrong; in fact, I do not think I ever knew her to do a positively naughty thing during the two years that she was in my class, in the public school and in the Sabbath-school."

"O mother, I hope all these children were not as good as those you have told us about; it sounds like the children in books," interrupted Lizzie.

"No, they were not all good, and those who were called good were not *always* good; but I have only shown you the good or bright side of their characters. This pink-and-white, marked Nettie Black, was for a little pink and white girl, whose name, you see, was not White; I hope she has not grown up as an illustration of Mrs. Stowe's 'Pink and White Tyranny.' This brown-and-white gingham represents Miss Pink-and-White's brother, whose ways and complexion were in as strong contrast to his sister's as are the colors in the two blocks of patch-work."

"And here is one with 'Baby Alling' marked in the center. Was that the real name?"

"Yes, Jennie, that was all the name he could claim then. As there were three brothers and sisters, besides father and mother, to be suited with the name, it was some time before the name was finally agreed upon. But, dear little 'Baby,' he did not need an earthly name long, for he was called to his heavenly home before he had reached his fifth year."

"What about these marked C—— and G——, mother?"

"These were pieced by the fingers of two sisters who were too large to be in my class of little ones, but who were favorites of Charlie's—who was only a 'baby' then, although he was three years old. They were as frisky as two kittens, and quite as mischievous. But we have talked long enough, and there is more than one pair of eyes that want to say 'good-night,' even if their owners do not."

"Well," said Charlie, with a wistful look at the quilt, as it was refolded; "I did n't suppose there could be so much of a story in that faded, odd-looking quilt."

"O mother, there were more than a dozen names that you did not tell us about, besides the quilt with ladies' names upon," and the younger children joined with Lizzie in pleading to hear more.

"It is too late, and you would grow tired before I had gone over half the names, for I should never know when to stop, if I should once begin to talk of them. I can only say that the memories I have of those dear sisters and their families are very pleasant, and I feel grateful to the Giver of all good for the many pleasant associations that I was permitted to enjoy during our two years' stay in the little village. But you really must say 'good-night,' now, or we shall hear of some little folks having a very sleepy time over their lessons to-morrow, and perhaps get 'zero' opposite their names."

SUPPOSE you are looking forward quite anxiously to 'Commencement Day,'" said Mrs. Spencer to her niece, as she came into her room, on her return from school, one afternoon in May. Mrs. Spencer was spending a few days with her brother's family in M——, where he had settled some half dozen years previously, in order that his children might have the advantage of a college without going away from home.

"Yes; I shall be through my four years' course in about six weeks, and I shall be so glad!" and Fannie sat down in the easy-chair by an open window, giving a sigh of satisfaction over the prospect of soon being free from the requirements of school.

"You are anticipating a great deal of pleasure when school-days are over?" questioned Mrs. Spencer, pleasantly.

"Yes, indeed; it will be so pleasant. No lessons to study, nor rules to obey."

"But what do you propose to do when you come into possession of this boon of liberty from which you anticipate so much?"

"O, I have n't decided yet. I think it will be delightful to do just nothing at all for a few days.

Why, auntie, I am twenty years old, and for the past ten years it has been nothing but books all the time, from morning to night, from one year to another. As soon as one lesson was finished I had to take up another. When I get my diploma, I intend to make up for it by having a good time for a little while."

"It seems to me that you will have a good many lessons to learn even after you get your diploma; and as to obeying rules, I think you will find it as difficult to please yourself as any of your teachers and preceptors, especially if you start out with the idea of living for your own pleasure, without reference to the wishes or the happiness of others."

"Well, I don't know; but it always seemed as if it would be a pleasant thing to have one's own way."

"Very likely; but it seems to me there are other ways of enjoyment quite as commendable. How about your mother? Isn't she a little overtaxed sometimes?"

"I don't know, I am sure. I have been so busy with my studies that I have not noticed. She never complains."

"No; she is not one of the complaining sort. But it seems to me she has her hands and heart pretty well filled. I presume Miss Williams will make your graduating suit?"

"No; mamma will make it herself."

"How is that? I thought Miss Williams usually did your dress-making."

"So she does, usually; but the girls are all going to dress so nicely, and, of course, I don't want to wear a cheap thing; and the material has cost so much that mamma says she can not afford to hire it made these hard times, and so she will make it herself."

"I believe you told me your friends, the Misses M——, were coming to spend the Summer with you. If your mother feels that she can not afford to hire extra help in the house, it will make more work for her."

"Yes; I know it will, and extra expense besides. But mamma is very anxious for them to come. They are very intelligent, and she thinks it pays to entertain intelligent and refined people. I expect to gain a great benefit from their society."

"But somebody must do extra work while they stay; and if your mother feels that she can not afford to employ an extra girl, it will make the work heavier for her, will it not?"

"Yes; I should suppose so. But, auntie, why do you ask so many questions? I never knew you to be so inquisitive before." And Fannie looked into Mrs. Spencer's serious face as if she half believed she was being teased, without comprehending it.

"I did not mean to be impertinent, my dear; but I can not help thinking it would be a good plan if you could lighten your mother's burdens by helping bear them."

"But mother enjoys company as much as I do."

"No doubt of it; but possibly it may be as much on your account as for her own pleasure. You have been busy with your school-books during the past few years, and your mother has been equally busy with home-cares and duties. Suppose, when you have graduated, that you offer to form a partnership with 'mother,' and relieve her of a portion of her labor and care, giving her rest while you are gaining a knowledge of household duties, that can never be properly understood except by actual practice, and some of which will require as much 'brain' as the scientific studies you have been trying to master. And, then, would it not be a pleasant surprise for you to give her your place in the carriage occasionally, when some delightful excursion to the country is to be enjoyed, while you remain at home to care for the little ones, who are such a constant tax on her strength and patience?"

"I guess it would be a surprise!" and Miss Fannie looked as if the suggestion was a very great surprise to herself. "She will either think I am insane or that I have suddenly grown 'too good for this world.' But," more soberly, "auntie, do you really think me very selfish?"

"Not more so than most young girls of your age. Perhaps 'thoughtless' would express it in your case. But loving mothers are apt to screen their daughters as much as possible, taking all the care and responsibility upon themselves, until, finally, the daughters come to look upon their mother's careworn face as a matter of course, and if any thing is said about it, the usual reply is, 'Mother could n't be happy if she was n't hard at work.'"

"O, auntie, I am not so bad as that!" and Fannie's face reddened at the imputation.

"I do not mean that you have come to that yet,

nor that you do not love your mother very dearly;
but do not forget, dear, that your mother is just as
capable of enjoying and appreciating little, unexpected kindnesses or pleasures as you are, though
she may be forty and you only twenty years of age.
I did not intend saying these things when we began
our little talk, and you must forgive me if I have
said any thing that sounded unkind or harsh; for I
have said it for your own good, knowing that when
you have to be separated from that mother, it will
be a sweet memory if you can look back over your
home-life and say, 'I did all I could to make her life
pleasant and happy.'"

"I am not offended, auntie, dear; but I did not
know how selfish I was until you have shown me. I
am ready to turn over a new leaf, and to try to make
things easier for her; but I am afraid I am but poorly
prepared for any thing like usefulness at home."

And real tears came into her eyes as the young
girl looked back over the past year and saw where
she might have lightened her mother's cares and
labor if she had only tried.

"If you are only willing, you can soon learn to
do things that seem awkward and difficult at first;
and if you can keep your mother's heart and face
free from unnecessary care for ten years longer by
these little acts of self denial, I am sure you will not
regret it."

ND so you propose to give Esther a business education?" interrogated Mrs. Henry, in reply to a statement of her friend, Mrs. Burrell.

"Yes, a very practical one, too, I hope," was the response.

"But I do not see where she will find time for so many studies. By the time she has completed French, and takes a thorough course in music and painting, I think she will have but little time left for a course in a business college, unless she intends to devote herself to the life of an old maid."

"Old maids are not the most unhappy people in the world, and Esther might possibly do worse than to live and die one," quietly responded Mrs. Burrell. "But I do not know that our means will permit us to give her all the advantages you mention; but if any must be struck off the list, I think it will not be the business part, although she may never see the inside of a business college. There are a great many things to be learned that are not found in college curriculums. I think Esther will make a practical woman if she has the opportunity, and if I have my way she will have such instruction as will fit her for taking care of herself."

"I did not know that Esther had manifested any special talent or taste for 'business,' as you call it," replied Mrs. Henry.

"Neither has she manifested any special talent for French or music; but that is not urged as an objection to her studying these branches, and if she should happen to have a little less French and a little more practical English, I shall be just as proud of her, and I have a fancy that she will be just as happy and as much respected," answered Mrs. Burrell earnestly.

"Really you are quite progressive in your ideas. I was not aware that you entertained such advanced notions," Mrs. Henry said, half smiling at her friend's enthusiasm. "I was not surprised when I understood that you and Mr. Burrell had decided that your three boys should each learn a trade before choosing a profession, but I did not suppose you would insist that your only daughter should pursue the course of study you indicate. It seems out of place for one in her position."

"I do not consider it as out of place at present, and the time may come when it will be very much in place. The education that merely serves as polish is all well enough, but something more is needed if a woman desires to fill her place in life as a reasonable and reasoning being.

"Esther is but sixteen, and is quite proficient in her studies so far as her text-books are concerned; but I would like for her to be able to make a practical application of the knowledge acquired. To give her a little insight into every-day costs and expenditures, I have intrusted the family accounts for the year to her keeping, and she is delighted with it, although it did seem a little tiresome at first. Now, every item of expense is placed upon the book, and carefully footed up monthly and quarterly. She has discovered that it costs something to keep up the various necessities as well as the luxuries of a family of seven, and it is quite amusing sometimes to hear her talking of the family expenses, and planning how they may be reduced. The first month showed rather a large bill for Esther herself, and she came to me with rather a sober face and asked, 'Mamma, do I cost that much every month?' I told her I guessed so, and sometimes a little more. She looked more thoughtful than before, and said, 'I wonder you and papa are not provoked at my extravagance.' I tried to laugh it off, and told her she was worth all she cost us, and more too. She kissed me, and said, 'I'm glad you think so; but I'll see if I can not manage to be less expensive after this;' and she has succeeded thus far, even resisting my efforts to tempt her into a little extravagance. Each month her books are brought to her father and me, for our inspection, and she is learning some valuable lessons in the cost of living, and begins to see very good reasons for our denying her and her brothers many things that she would have considered almost indispensable a year ago. When our bills are less than usual she, seems to take pride in the fact."

"Why, my dear!" exclaimed Mrs. Henry, "I am afraid you are training Esther to be a perfect miser. The idea of that child measuring the expenses of the family. I fear she will be a stingy, penurious woman in after years."

"I hope not. I only want her to be a careful one. If she learns a little about the cost of living now, if ever she has a home of her own, her knowledge may prevent her bringing her husband to finan·cial ruin through her ignorant extravagance; for nine-tenths of the extravagance among women comes from ignorance and not real indifference as to the cost of their luxuries."

"But what put these ideas into your head so strongly of late?" inquired her friend.

"It is not a late thing, really, but my attention has been called to the subject with more than usual force by what I have seen of the inconvenience and real suffering of women through the lack of a knowledge of the every-day business affairs of life. A neighbor of mine has recently buried her husband, and aside from her grief at the loss of her companion, her helplessness, so far as business matters are concerned, is pitiful to see. With a woman's confidence in her husband's judgment, she has always left every thing, except the actual care of the house and the children, in his hands, and while she is considered an excellent housekeeper and cook, and her bread and cakes are the envy of a good many of her neighbors, she told me she could not tell the price of a pound of sugar or butter or of a hundred weight of flour. And as to property, personal or real estate, she has no idea of its value. In bewailing her ignorance of these things, she said to me, 'My husband always told me to get what I needed, and he would

settle the bill, and I need not trouble myself about his
affairs.   If he paid the bills that was all I need care
about it; women could n't understand business.   I suppose he thought it was best, but I begin to see that it
was a sad mistake.'   This woman, left with a family
of five children, herself utterly ignorant of every
business form, uncertain as to whether a single step
she took in the settlement of her husband's affairs,
was legal, felt that she was at the mercy of those
who had it in their power to deprive her and her
little ones of the remnant of property left them by
the husband and father.   And this is only one of
scores of similar cases that have come under my own
observation, and I am determined that my daughter
shall have such a knowledge of business that she will
not be left to the tender mercies of unscrupulous
sharpers.   I shall always feel thankful to my father
for the practical business lessons which he gave me.
Himself a careful man, never going beyond his
income, he often took me into his office that I might
assist him in making out his quarterly reports; and
while I was assisting him in comparing the books, he
gave me, without my being conscious of it, an insight
into practical every-day business."

"But was it not irksome to you, a young girl, to
sit for hours adding up long columns of figures which
meant nothing to you?" asked Mrs. Henry.

"I do not remember of ever tiring, for I was
proud to feel that I was helping my father, though I
can see now that the work was given me more for
my own sake than for any real help which I gave.
But those columns were not mere dry figures to me.

I knew what every unit represented, and sometimes
I took special delight in the success of men who
made purchases of small tracts of land, for my father
was agent for men who were known in those days as
Eastern land speculators.   That is, they had bought
up large tracts of land at Congress prices years before,
and then sold it 'on time' in small tracts to suit purchasers, they giving their notes, payable in one, two,
and three years, sometimes five years, while the
seller gave a bond for a deed when the notes were
paid off.   No, I did not think it dull work, for I
always enjoyed doing such work, whether it was
counting up interest on 'partial payments' or measuring a 'corn pen' and calculating its contents.   Husbands and fathers make a mistake when they try to
keep wife or daughter ignorant of their business, under
the notion that they are shielding them from care
and responsibility.   Better let them share the care
and responsibility while there is some one to assist
and explain, than to let it come upon them suddenly
and at a time of life when cares and responsibilities
are apt to be burdensome.

    " A true wife will want to know something of that
which concerns not only her husband's, but her own
and her children's, temporal welfare, and it is much
better for her to know their financial standing and so.
be able to regulate their expenses accordingly, than
to indulge in luxuries that they can ill afford until
bankruptcy ends it all, or the death of her husband
leaves her an ignorant, helpless woman, needing a
guardian as much as the babe in her arms."

    "Really, my dear, you are quite eloquent,"

laughed Mrs. Henry. "With a little practice you will make a capital lecturer on woman's rights."

"I never made a woman's right's speech in my life, and never expect to. I am only urging what seems to me a necessity, not for the woman's sake alone, but for the better protection of her children, sons as wells as daughters. And as example is said to be more potent than precept, I intend to give my own daughter the training that will enable her to take care of herself, and a husband, too, if necessary, and I confess I am a little anxious to demonstrate my theory."

19

Was It a Thanksgiving?

HE Thanksgiving sermon had ended, the collection for the benefit of the poor had been taken, the closing prayer offered, the choir had sung

"Praise waiteth for thee, O God, in Zion,"

and the congregation had united its voice with the choir in

"Praise God, from whom all blessings flow;"

the benediction had been pronounced, and the people came forth from the temple, each going their respective way—some to dine with friends and relatives; others, perhaps, to meet again on the next annual Thanksgiving, and perhaps *not*. But there was one of the congregation—or, rather, of the choir—Louise Harmon, a girl of twenty years, who seemed in no hurry to join the crowd that pressed toward the door; she stood on the steps of the orchestra, with hymnal and anthem book on her arm, while, with thoughtful face, she watched the crowd as it passed in procession before her.

Bowing occasionally, with a sort of dreamy greeting, to some acquaintance or friend, she listened to the broken fragments of conversation which came to her ears as the speakers drew near the door, their faces and words alike being lost in the mingled noise and bustle outside.

The congregation had gone, and Louise suddenly remembered that the sexton would want to close the church, and go home to his family and Thanksgiving dinner, whether that dinner was to be turkey stuffed with oysters or only a plain dinner with an extra pudding or pie gotten up in honor of the day. Drawing her wrappings more closely about her throat, and adjusting her veil so as more effectually to shut off the sharpness of the north wind, and with a hasty nod to the sexton, who stood holding the door for her to pass out, she stepped from the church into the street.

A faint smile passed over her face, and ended in a curl of the lips and a shrug of the shoulders, as she saw the street was almost empty of life, and that she must walk home alone; that, however, did not matter particularly so far as the walk, so much as the idea of being forgotten by others.

"At any rate, *mother* has not forgotten me, I am sure," she said, half aloud; and the words seemed to dispel the unpleasant thoughts, if such they were, and, with resolute step, she hastened homeward.

Mrs. Harmon was an invalid, and had remained at home because she was too feeble to walk so far, and their straitened circumstances would not permit them to keep a carriage.

When her daughter entered the room, the mother expressed surprise that she should be so late in returning.

"O, I was so busy watching the people, and listening to their comments upon the sermon and upon each other, that I almost forgot to come home; and it is lucky for me, and you too, that I am here now, instead of being locked up in that old church. But I am here, you see, and we will have our dinner, provided Ann has not gone to sleep over her beads."

Mrs. Harmon looked up in pained surprise, more at her daughter's tone than the words, and said, in gentle reproof, "Louise, dear, we must not be cross to-day."

"No, mother, I am not cross; I am only thinking."

And, stooping, she kissed the fair brow, and then, drawing back, she smoothed the silvery hair that was fading prematurely; then, looking lovingly a moment into the sweet, patient face, she left the room, to superintend the dinner, which she considered too important to be left to Ann's somewhat blundering hands.

Mrs. Harmon was a widow, dependent on her daughter's small salary for her support, and to-day her dinner would not be a very extravagant affair, only roast chicken, instead of turkey; but there were vegetables and pies—mince and pumpkin—and doughnuts, for Mrs. Harmon was a New England woman, and if the three last-mentioned articles had been wanting she would hardly have considered her dinner orthodox.

A neighbor, who was also a widow, with her two daughters, were the only guests, and the afternoon passed very quietly, though cheerfully, for Mrs. Harmon had learned the art of being contented with little, and to make others equally so.

When their guests had said their good-byes, Lou-

ise and her mother were left alone in the twilight of
their little sitting room, and drawing a stool to her
mother's side, she seated herself upon it, and resting her head on the mother's knee, while she drew
the slender hand to her, and gently pressed it to her
lips.

For some minutes the two sat in silence, Mrs.
Harmon, with her disengaged hand, quietly stroking
the soft, wavy tresses of her daughter's hair, which
had been allowed to drop from the bands that had
confined it.

There was a perfect understanding between the
two, and a bond of sympathy that drew mother and
daughter very near together.   While Mrs. Harmon's
ill health made her dependent upon her daughter for
food and raiment, Louise, in turn, leaned upon her
mother for counsel and encouragement, as well as
instruction in temporal and spiritual things.

To-night Mrs. Harmon knew, intuitively, as it
were, that her daughter's mind was disturbed with
some sort of perplexing thoughts and questions. As
to what they were she could only guess, but she felt
sure that before Louise said "good-night" she would
unburden her heart.

Presently the silence was broken with: " Mother,
why will our thoughts run just where we do not
want them to?"

" Wiser heads than yours have been puzzled over
the same problem, daughter; but why do you ask
the question? Have *your* thoughts been running wild
to-day?" and the mother stroked the pure white brow
of her child very tenderly.

"Yes, in spite of me. I was so tired last night, and I thought I would enjoy this holiday so much, and I said, 'To-morrow will be a day of real thanksgiving and rest.' This morning I asked God to give me grace to be contented with my lot, and to enable me to be thankful for all his goodness to me; and when I went to Church to-day, and joined in the singing and listened to the prayer, I thought I was thankful, and I am sure I tried to be so; but while the minister was recounting our many blessings and mercies, as a nation and as individuals, I found myself murmuring because you could not be at Church to-day and on other days; and when I saw Mrs. Worth and Mrs. Lewis in silks and costly furs, and knew their carriages were in waiting to take them to grand houses and loaded tables, I thought of you, compelled to stay at home and put up with the poor provision that I can make for your comfort. I am afraid that there was not much of the true thanksgiving spirit in my prayers after that. And then, after all was over, and I stood on the steps of the orchestra, and heard the various comments on the sermon—its substance and delivery—I could not help wondering why people who do not care for or appreciate their privileges should have favors heaped upon them, while those who would enjoy and be grateful for them should be denied constantly. To tell the truth, I am tired, and perplexed, and disappointed," and, with a little sigh, Louise turned her head and laid her cheek against the palm of her mother's hand.

Mrs. Harmon made no comment upon her daughter's confession, but sat quietly, as if waiting for it to be continued. Presently Louise asked, "Are you angry with me, mother?"

"No, dear, not angry; only a little disappointed," was answered, gently.

Louise started at the echo of her own words.

"Mother, dear, tell me what is wrong. Where was my mistake? I *wanted* this to be a real Thanksgiving, and it was not. Was it my fault?"

"Yes, my child, I think it was. But are you willing that we should go back and review the day together?"

"O yes, if it will help me out of my trouble."

"Well, then, to begin: you asked God to give you grace to enable you to be content with your lot. When we have to *ask* for grace to be content, it is because we feel the spirit of unrest disturbing us. We are not quite thankful to God for his mercies. The thankful heart is content. Do you understand, dear, what I mean?"

"Yes," in a low voice.

"You say you 'thought you were thankful, and you are sure you tried to be so.' When we are really thankful for a favor, it does not require an effort."

"But can we not be more thankful by trying?"

"My child, did you ever try to love your mother?"

Louise drew a little closer, and a tear fell on Mrs. Harmon's hand.

"O no, mother; I can not help loving you."

"And so it should be with our feelings toward our heavenly Father. If we fully appreciate the gifts which he bestows so liberally, even though he may withhold some things which we desire, yet his tender mercies and his loving kindness are so great we should find our hearts swelling with gratitude; and instead of praying for grace to be thankful or *trying to be content*, we would find ourselves inquiring, as did David, ' What shall I render unto the Lord for all his benefits toward me ?'   I do not wish to reprove or find fault with you, my daughter; but if this day, and every other day, is not one of thanksgiving and praise, it is because our selfish hearts are longing for that which our heavenly Father does not see best for us to have ; and in sighing for what we have not, we fail to be thankful for present blessings.   While it is right to ask for what we think we need, it is also good to praise him for what we already have."

Louise withdrew her hand from that of her mother, and, rising from her low seat, very quietly lit the lamp, and placed it on the table by her mother's side ; then, laying the family Bible near her hand, before taking her seat preparatory to their evening devotions, she stooped and kissed the dear motherly face, saying, in a humble yet joyous tone, while the tears gathered in her eyes: "I have learned a precious lesson.   I will never *try* to be thankful again."   And the mother returning her daughter's caress, responded in a gentle voice : "His mercy endureth forever."

O N'T give me any more work; I have
more than I can do now," remonstrates
one who is already burdened with cares
and responsibilities. And yet to these same
busy ones extra work is given—the task of
pushing forward some enterprise for the benefit
of the Church, the nation, or the world at large;
and, notwithstanding the numerous duties that
were pressing them before, they still find time
for the new work, and it is forwarded and success is achieved, while the previous duties are
not neglected. Go to a temperance convention, and take a look at the workers. You will find
that those most interested in missionary, literary, and
like enterprises are the ones who are chosen to do
the most laborious and difficult duties of the society.
In such a convention, where some were asking to be
excused because of their many cares, one prominent
worker, known to be untiring in labors for the ref-
ormation of men, and who, to use her own language,
"had to work, as well as pray, for her daily bread,"
responded, "That is just the kind of women we
want. The busier, the better. Those who are doing
nothing are not fit for this work." She was right;
and the same demand is being made everywhere.
It is not the man or woman of leisure who is in most

demand, but those who are already at work. Those
who are the busiest are the ones who are thrust out,
as it were, to do the extra work, who receive the
loudest calls to positions of responsibility. And
why? Those who are idle are not so of necessity,
but because they have not had sufficient energy or
tact to make the most of their opportunities and
privileges, and if placed in charge of some special
work would either be too stupid or too indolent to
carry it forward to success. Such persons shut themselves out from many a golden opportunity, and the
Savior's parable finds ample illustration, "From him
that hath not shall be taken away even that which he
seemeth to have."

The man who gives wisely of his temporal blessings for the good of others does not find himself
growing poorer because of his benevolence; and he
who uses God's best gifts, both of mind and heart,
for the benefit of the world, does not find these gifts
diminishing or growing weaker. On the contrary, as
the 'mind reaches out and grasps new thoughts, and,
in turn, gives them out to others, it increases its store
of knowledge and also its capacity to receive and
impart that knowledge; and the same may be said
of our desires and efforts to help others in spiritual
things. If we make use of the means and opportunities placed before us, they will be increased, and
with the opportunities will come the ability to do.
Beyond this ability to do, they cease to be opportunities.

We may take the busiest business man, the Christian man, who considers his business as belonging to

God and himself as the Lord's steward, and while that man is thronged with business, he yet finds time for special work for his Master. And we do not see that man's business suffering, nor his soul growing lean, because he is bestowing blessings, spiritual and temporal, upon those who are in need. A long list of names of prominent Christian men might be given, men who are not only successful in business, but who have attained a high standard of Christian experience, and who attribute their success in busi-ness to the fact that they withheld nothing from God, either of money or time.

. We see the mother, whose hands and heart seem crowded with home cares and loves, and she will find time to minister to the necessities of others, let those necessities be either temporal or spiritual. And she is far more likely to be ready to go out to "rescue the perishing," to care for the sick and the dying, than is her sister who sits idly at home, demanding that she shall be ministered to instead of ministering.

The pastor who is most zealous in the perform-ance of his duties to his own flock will be likely to have the most opportunities for doing good, because he will make such opportunities. He will not only observe the letter of the law, but he will take in its spirit, also, and his influence will be felt as a power on the side of right and of needed reform. Some one says: " The happiest people are those who have just a little too much to do," and we would write a new maxim: If you want an extra piece of work done, go to the one who is already burdened with duties.

THEODORE KAUFMAN and Henry Woodford were fast friends, and in some respects they were rather inclined to be "fast" young men, although they had not, as yet, allowed their love for company and what they called a "good time," to materially interfere with their business. On this particular evening they had been talking over their programme for the New-Year's calls which they expected to make together on the following day. From this they had drifted into a quiet conversation, much more sober and thoughtful in its tone than it was usual for them to engage in, and then they gradually lapsed into silence and each sat busy with his own thoughts.

Suddenly Woodford turned to his companion with, "I say, Theo, how do you suppose these calls will end?" We have a pretty long list. How about the wine those delightful ladies will offer us?"

"I suppose we can *taste* without *swilling*," and Kaufman elevated his eyebrows as if surprised at the question.

"Perhaps so; but *will* we? My remembrance of last New-Year's is not very pleasant; the winding up, at least."

"O, well, I hope we each learned a lesson, and

the last New-Year's affair need not repeat itself," Kaufman replied, impatiently, for he felt nettled that his friend should remind him of the day in which both had become quite boisterous, and returned to their rooms reeling under the effect of the numerous drinks they had taken in their round. Woodford was silenced for a few moments, and then said, with an apparent effort, looking at the wall instead of in his friend's face: "I tell you what, Theo, I must either say No, every time, and not touch wine at all, or the New-Year of one year ago will be very apt to repeat itself in *my* case."

Kaufman looked at his companion as if he thought him jesting, but a glance at the serious face, which reddened to his hair under his scrutiny, convinced him that he was in sober earnest.

"O, nonsense, Hal; you are not that far gone, I hope," half angrily.

"I *am* just that far gone. I am ashamed to own it, even to you, Theo; but there is just one of two things for me to do: I must either give up tippling entirely or go to destruction. I can't take one glass and stop there. If I take one, I'll take half a dozen, and you know the result."

"Now, see here, Hal," and Kaufman's eyes flashed angrily; "do you propose to go calling with me to-morrow and make yourself ridiculous by drinking nothing but coffee and lemonade?"

Woodford looked into his friend's face, and as he saw the contemptuous look upon it his own became a trifle paler, and his eyes fell to the floor, but he asked in a low tone, "Theo, would you rather I should make myself ridiculous by drinking only coffee and lemonade, and come home to-morrow night with a clear head and steady step, or drink wines all day and have to be helped home, as on last New-Year's?"

"Of course, I don't want you to drink enough to affect you in that way. You can just *touch* the glass to your lips. You can be polite without getting drunk."

"If politeness means tasting every glass of wine offered me, I am afraid I shall not be very sober when the day is over. I know I'm a weak fool, but if I put a glass of wine to my lips I shall *drink* it; and if I drink one glass I shall probably drink a dozen more, and you know where it will land me," and Woodford rose and began drawing on his overcoat and picking up hat and gloves to go to his lodging place. Kaufman did not offer to detain him, and it was plain that he was not pleased with his friend's sudden resolution. When ready to go Woodford turned to him and extended his hand, "I do not want you to think me stubborn or contrary, but I *must* stop while I can—I am in more danger than you think."

Kaufman started to his feet as if awakening from a dream, and grasped his friend's hand.

"I guess you are about right, and I shall do nothing more to induce you to break your resolution; but if you can refuse all through the day, you are plucky, that's all. It's a good deal more than *I* could do. Don't think hard of me for what I said," and with a hearty grasp of hands the friends separated.

The next day was a trying one to young Woodford, and more than once he was on the point of yielding to the persuasions of his lady friends, who "could not see why he should be so singular." However, he stood firm, for, knowing his danger, he determined not to be overcome. Before they had completed their round there was need of his steady nerves and cool head, for Kaufman seemed to think he must make amends for his friend's singular notion, and drank more freely than he was aware, and Woodford was obliged to take the reins and drive the spirited horse that was likely to become unmanageable in Kaufman's hands. There were yet four or five names on the list, but Woodford saw that his friend was not in a condition to make calls, and turned the horse homeward. Kaufman remonstrated a little, but he was fast becoming stupefied by the wines he had drunk, and by the time they had reached his rooms he was unable to walk without assistance, and in his case the scene of the year previous had repeated itself.

After seeing that his friend was properly cared for, Woodford turned his steps toward his own lodgings with a heart sadly perplexed. He had, it was true, been laughed at because of his sudden resolution, and some of those from whom he had expected encouragement had seemed offended. But, notwithstanding his disappointment, he felt glad that he had had the courage to resist the temptation to drink, and this feeling was strengthened when he thought of the condition in which his companion had been carried to his rooms.

Kaufman called earlier than usual at his friend's

room the next evening. When seated by the fire, he said, a little humbly,

"Hal, I suppose I made a fool of myself, yester. day; but for pity's sake, do n't say any thing about it so that my employers will get to hear of it."

"I shall certainly not mention it; but I am afraid I was not the only one who saw that you had been over polite."

"Yes; and hang it all, I should have been all right if I had had the 'grit' to say 'No,' as you did. I tell you what, Hal, I felt proud of you yesterday, even when I laughed at you."

"If you had known how much I wanted the stuff, and how near I came to taking it several times you would n't have felt quite so proud of me, and," he added with a sigh that was almost a groan, "I feel as if the battle had but just begun."

"I hope you 'll fight it out, any way, old fellow," responded Kaufman in a voice that sounded as if hope for himself had almost died out of his heart.

"To tell the truth, Theo, I have been living too fast lately, and it has been troubling me like fury," began Woodford again, as he drew his chair to the table and leaned his elbows upon it.   "And another thing, my head is not fit for business for two or three days after it has been muddled with alcohol. I feel I *must* quit it if possible, and with God's help I am going to turn over a new leaf."

"Well, success to you. I like your pluck, and wish I was in your boots; but it would be no use for *me* to try to quit."   And the young man looked

utterly helpless and despairing as he leaned his head
in his hands, as he sat opposite his friend. Woodford sat watching him for some moments, wishing he
could help him, yet feeling that he needed help himself. At last he said, with hopefulness and energy:

"Look here, chum; I believe I was to blame for
getting you into these habits, at the first, and I'm
sorry for it. We've sown our wild oats together
during the past two years, suppose we 'right-about
face,' and start out on a different line. I shall feel
as if I was ready to trip up if you are pulling the
other way all the time. Can't we help each other?"
Kaufman looked up with a sort of incredulous smile
at the suggestion that he could help any one toward
leading a better life, but he listened while his friend
went on eagerly,

"Say you'll do it, and we'll draw up a total
abstinence pledge, and sign it to-night."

"Yes, and both break it in less than a month,"
was the hopeless response.

"We'll not do any such thing," responded
Woodford, as if filled with new life. "Let's write
out the pledges right now. We can go each other's
security, and send the pledges home to our mothers
for safe-keeping. I tell you what, Theo, we'll make
two blessed women happy if we do," and Woodford
shoved back his chair and came and laid a hand on
his companion's shoulder.

"If I thought I could keep it, I wouldn't mind,"
Kaufman said, drearily.

"Keep it? Of course you will. Where's paper,
pen, and ink? Let's have them now."

It was impossible to resist Woodford's enthusiasm, and Kaufman drew back from the table that the
papers might be taken from the drawer, saying, with
a smile:

"I believe this is *your* desk, not mine, Hal; so
help yourself."

He sat watching while Woodford wrote out the
pledges. Then they signed both, and placed them
in envelopes, to be sent to their mothers in their
quiet country homes. When this was done, they
relapsed into silence; and thus they sat for some
time; and if their faces were the index to their
thoughts, they must have been very serious ones,
and not altogether pleasant.

At last Kaufman said: "Hal, if I keep that
pledge it will be a terrible struggle. I never told
you, because I was ashamed to own what a slave I
was; but I have tried three or four times during the
past year to give up drink, and in less than two
weeks I have gone back to my cups again. God
only knows how I shall succeed this time; but it is
a serious business, I can tell you; for I am not
playing. I mean all I have said."

"And so do I," responded his friend, heartily.
"It may be that I shall fail. I hope not; but "—
hesitating, as if in doubt as to how his friend would
receive his suggestion—"I 'm not one to talk cant;
but, Theo., you know where our mothers go for
strength to do right—'grace,' I believe they call it—
and you know that 's where they urge us to go.
Suppose we try it. I believe praying has kept my
mother up when nothing else would. She has had

some pretty tough places to go through, I fancy. What do you say? Shall we try it?"

Theodore Kaufman rose from his seat without a word; but his face showed that the right chord had had been struck—one which would be most likely to produce harmony in both their lives. Extending his hand, as Woodford rose and took a step toward him, they clasped hands with a firm grasp, and there was a look in their faces that betokened higher resolves and a step toward better lives. They stood thus for a moment, looking into each other's faces, and then, with a fervent though scarcely audible " God help us !" they separated, and the morrow looked more hopeful than its wont, even though they knew there was a struggle before them ; for they were strengthened by the thought that their mothers' God would be to them a tower of strength.

How Worth Hill Conquered his Enemy.

A Story for Boys.

IT was rather a gloomy, dissatisfied face that Worth Hill carried into his mother's sitting-room on the evening after the "first day" of the Fall term of the village school, and Mrs. Hill asked, a little anxiously:

"In trouble, Worth?"

"No," peevishly responded the boy.

"Not sick, I hope?" still interrogated the mother, without noticing his disrespectful tone.

"No, I'm not sick; but "— pulling, in a sort of confused way at the corner of the table-cover.

"What is the matter, then? You look as if you were distressed in some way," still insisted the mother.

"Why, mother, you see, last Spring Miss Aldrich promised me that if we were both in at the opening of the school, Will Morris and I should be seat-mates during this term, and to-day she gave Will another seat, and put Jim Brown in the seat with me; and I say it's too bad - for he's the meanest boy in all the school!" and Worth's lip quivered with disappoint-ment and scarcely restrained anger.

"If the other seats are all occupied, some one must share with him," said the mother, kindly.

"I suppose so. But I do n't see why she need

put him in *my* seat. The boys were making faces on the sly all through school hours; and as soon as we were out of doors Sam Moore called out, 'Three cheers for the new firm of Brown and Hill!' and the boys all cheered and laughed as if Sam had said something very sharp; and, mother, I just can't stand it!" and the boy went to the window to hide the tears he could not keep back.

"Perhaps Brown may not prove as disagreeable as you anticipate," suggested Mrs. Hill, encouragingly.

"O mother, I know him like a book! He is just as disagreeable as any one can be," answered Worth, his face still toward the window, and with a tone which showed that he did not intend to be cheated out of the pleasure of complaining, at least.

"Well, my son, try to make the best of it. I hope you will not have any *trouble* with Brown," was Mrs. Hill's reply, as she laid aside her sewing to look after things in the dining-room.

When tea was over, Worth had his lessons to study; and so nothing more was said about the unwelcome seat-mate.

At the close of the second day Worth's face was even more cloudy than on the previous evening. Throwing, rather than hanging, his hat on the rack, he walked straight to his mother's room, and, without waiting for the usual greeting, said abruptly:

"Can't I stay at *home* and study?"

Mrs. Hill scanned her boy's face carefully for a moment, and then asked:

"Have you quarreled with Brown already?"

"No, and not likely to; Jim do n't even look at me. But the boys tease so. Sam wanted to know if we were going to steal chickens on the shares, and if I had agreed to take half of Jim's ferulings. They made me so angry I could n't study, and I missed my lessons; and I wish I could stay at home," sobbed Worth, leaning his head on the table at his mother's side.

Mrs. Hill soothed him as best she could.

"I am busy now; but after tea we will talk this matter over. Perhaps we can think of a plan to have your seat-mate changed."

Worth's face brightened.

"O, will you? You always was the *best* mother, any way;" and he gave his mother the kiss he had forgotten, in his haste to settle his school troubles.

When the younger children were all tucked away for the night, Mrs. Hill brought out her work-basket, saying pleasantly:

"Now, while I mend these garments, tell me all about Jim Brown? What does he do that he is dis-liked so much?"

"Do? Why, every thing! I could n't tell the half of the mean tricks he plays on us;" and Worth closed his book and looked up, his eyes flashing at the remembrance of his wrongs.

"Do you boys never tease him?"

"Y-e-s, sometimes—just to get even, you know. O my! you ought to have seen him Saturday, when Dick Allen called him a pauper's son! Jim sprang at him like a tiger, and gave him a blow that sent him reeling against the fence."

Mrs. Hill looked grave.

"Is it true that his father is a pauper?"

"Yes; or it *was* true. He died in the alms-house three years ago, when Jim was ten years old. His mother takes in washing, and Jim does errands mornings and evenings. Sam Moore says they 're awful poor."

Mrs. Hill's face was very thoughtful.

"If what you say about the Brown family is true, Jim certainly has enough to make him feel uncomfortable; and this may account, in part, for his bad conduct. What have his school-mates done to make it pleasant for him at school?"

"Why, mother, he is so cross we can 't do any thing for him. He would n't let us."

"Have you ever really tried?"

"No; I'm afraid *I* have n't. You see, it does n't seem natural to try to please a fellow you do n't like."

"I suppose it is n't *natural*, exactly; but I think you had better try the law of kindness on this boy for a while. The other law seems to have had a pretty thorough trial."

Worth made no reply. His mother's plan was not exactly what he had anticipated, and he did not relish the turn the conversation had taken.

"'Heaping coals of fire' after the Scripture plan may do him good," suggested his mother.

"I do n't know as it would do him any good, he just seems to hate every one of us," said Worth, excusingly.

"Very likely," answered Mrs. Hill dryly; then she said, earnestly, "Worth, I hope *you*, at any rate, will try to do right toward this unfortunate boy; and remember that you can not win his friendship by retaliation. You must control your own temper, and ask God to help you to do as you would be done by if you were in Jim Brown's place."

His mother's words made a deep impression on Worth, and he felt as if he would like to do the right thing; but his reply was:

"I do n't believe I *can* be good to him, mother; he is so cross. If it was any body but Jim Brown, I might do it."

"If it was a better boy than Jim Brown, he would not need your kindness so much," was Mrs. Hill's quiet reply, as she turned to her work, feeling that she had said enough for the present.

Worth turned to his lessons again, and tried to make up for the time that had been spent in their talk.

The next morning, as Worth kissed his mother good-bye, she said softly:

"Do n't forget."

However, it was pretty hard not to. "forget," for Jim Brown looked daggers at him as he took his seat, and the boys made wry faces and comic gestures at him as they passed to the recitation-room.

He soon found, as we all do when watching for it, an opportunity to try the effects of kindness and self-denial.

Just before recess, Jim drew out his slate, and began fumbling in his pockets for his pencil, but failed to find it.

The rules forbade pupils leaving their seats at that

hour, and if he failed to have his lesson, he would have to remain indoors until he had mastered it.

Worth saw his perplexed look, and guessed the cause, and, for a moment, he felt inclined to rejoice over his discomfiture; but his mother's words, "do n't forget," came into his mind, and, after a momentary struggle with self, he quietly laid the extra pencil he always carried on Jim's slate.

At first the boy pretended not to see it, but in a few moments necessity overcame his pride, and he took up the pencil and began the work; but some way the examples seemed harder than usual, and, though he tried them over and over, there were two that would not come right, and when the recess bell rang the lesson was incomplete.

Worth had just finished his own arithmetic lesson, and was about to leave the room with the other boys, when a thought struck him, and he took his seat again, saying, carelessly:

"Won't they come right?"

"No," without looking up.

"Going to stay in and work at them?"

"None of your business," growled Jim, looking as if he intended to resent all efforts at teasing.

"I know it is n't," answered Worth, good-naturedly, "but I do n't care for playing ball to-day, and, if you 'll let me, I 'll look over these sums with you; I do n't know them any too well, myself."

Jim looked at his schoolmate as if he suspected some trick back of the proffered help; but he pushed the slate toward Worth with evident reluctance, and

pointed, without a word, to the examples in the
book.

By the time they were solved and Jim had been
made to comprehend them, recess was over. Jim
did not say 'thank you,' as Worth would have said
for a similar favor, but as he closed the book and
laid it with his slate, he muttered, as if to himself,
but loud enough for Worth to hear:

"I'm awful glad they're done."

It was not just the sort of reward Worth expected, but his own satisfaction at having done a
kind act made ample amends for the lack of courtesy
on the part of his companion.

He longed to tell his mother when he went home
of his victory over self, but she asked no questions,
and it would look like boasting if he should speak
of it without she inquired into matters.

But if Mrs. Hill said nothing, she was, nevertheless, watching her boy's face, and she saw, day by
day, that the clouds were gradually disappearing, and
she left him to work his way out of his troubles
without her help.

One evening, about two weeks after the affair of
the arithmetic lesson, Worth came bounding into the
sitting-room with the exclamation:

"O mother, guess what's happened!"

Mrs. Hill looked at the bright face, and said:
"Nothing bad, I guess."

"No, indeed; it's about Jim Brown."

"I suppose Miss Aldrich has taken pity on you,
and given Brown another seat," answered his mother,
watching Worth's face.

"Now, mother, I don't believe you're trying to guess," and he looked almost offended.

"Then you had better tell me, and save time," and she laid aside her work, that she might listen more attentively.

"Well," drawing up a low seat where he could rest his arms on his mother's knee, and look into her face at the same time, "I tried the 'heaping coals' plan, mother, and Jim and I have got on pretty well most of the time. To-day the teacher told him he must have a new Reader, if he wanted to stay in his class, and he came to his seat looking just as sullen as could be. Any other boy would have been glad enough to receive orders to get a new book, and his old one is all in pieces, and half of the leaves gone. I knew in a moment he was ashamed because he wasn't able to buy a new one, and was too proud to say any thing about it. I hadn't brought my Reader home since I bought my History, last week; and you know you said I might give it to some one who needed it. I took it out of the desk and wrote on the fly-leaf 'James Brown's book,' and then shoved it over in front of him, leaving it open, so he couldn't help seeing what I had written.

"You ought to have seen how queer the boy looked; he just stared at me a moment, and then took up the Reader, and turned the leaves over and over and looked at the bright, clean binding— you know it's nearly as good as new—then he laid his head down on his desk and began to cry. He sobbed so hard that the children all heard him; I tell you they opened their eyes, for Jim has always said 'nobody but girls and babies ever cry.'

"Miss Aldrich asked him what was the matter, and he just held on to the book and cried the harder; at last, he told the teacher that his mother could not afford to get him books, and he had spent all his money for a pair of boots, and he thought he would have to quit school, and he had so wanted to get an education, so he could make a living, and he thought nobody cared for him at all until I had given him the book just when he needed it.

"I felt pretty cheap to have him say such kind things of me right before all the school, but the boys did n't laugh at him one bit, but they looked as if they had half a mind to cry, too.

"Pretty soon school was dismissed, and, just as we were leaving the yard, Jim pulled my sleeve, and said:

"'Do n't hurry, Worth; I want to tell you something.'

"So I loitered along behind the other boys, and then he told me he was sorry he had ever treated me so badly, and that he always thought I just hated him, and that was why he had played tricks on me; but he says he 'll stick to me forever, if I 'll forgive him for treating me so mean."

"By a little kindness and by watching over yourself, you have changed an enemy into a friend," said Mrs. Hill, in a low tone, as Worth paused for breath.

He looked at his mother's smiling face for a moment, then his face lighted up if he had made a discovery.

"O mother, was that what you meant about planning to have my seat-mate changed?"

"Yes; are you satisfied with the new one?"

And the mother looked inquiringly into the earnest face that looked into hers.

"I guess I am! I am awful glad you told me how it was to be done, too," he added, in a tender tone, as he gathered up hat and books, that had been tossed on the table, in his eagerness to tell his story.

As the school progressed so did the friendship between Worth and his unpopular schoolmate; and the friendship seemed to have a good influence upon other pupils, as well as Jim Brown.

The leaders soon quit teasing, when they found that Worth was determined to stick to him, in spite of his rags and uncouth ways; and the feeling that some one really cared for him gradually softened his heart, making him more susceptible of good impressions, and created a strong desire to make himself worthy of the respect of others. And the final verdict of Sam Moore and Dick Allen was: "Jim is not such a bad fellow, after all."

BESSIE DEAN'S GRIEVANCE.

HE front gate at the Dean residence swung to with a vigorous clang, and the latch gave an angry click, as if in protest against the rather emphatic jerk bestowed upon said gate by Bessie Dean, as she closed it after her, and walked up the path toward the house. That something had "gone wrong" with the young lady was very evident from the manner in which she emphasized her steps; and her brother Charlie, eying her from his hammock under the shade-tree, muttered half aloud: "Whew! I wonder what ails her ladyship now! Something to pay, I 'll warrant." Her "ladyship" did not hear the complimentary remarks, and so was neither the worse nor the better because of them.

Going into the house with the same positive ring in her steps, she marched straight to the sitting-room, where she knew she would find her mother. Taking her hat in one hand, and pushing back her "bangles" with the other, she threw herself into a chair just opposite Mrs. Dean, and, without waiting for preface ôr prelude, asked impatiently: "Mother, do I look like a fool?"

Mrs. Dean had looked up in half-reproof at her daughter's unceremonious manner of entering the room, and she now looked in evident surprise at the question, wondering what it meant.

A glance at Bessie's tragi-comic expression and attitude brought a smile to the mother's face, in spite of her effort to appear displeased. At last, seeing that Bessie expected an answer, she said, while an odd twitch about her mouth betrayed the *effort* to keep a sober face:

"Not to *my* eyes, dearie. But you had better go to some one else for a decision. I am an interested party, and perhaps not capable of giving an unbiased opinion."

"At any rate, every body treats me as if they supposed me incapable of a single sensible idea," retorted Bessie, giving her hat a spiteful twist.

"Not 'every body,' daughter," protested Mrs. Dean.

"Well, then, 'most every one, especially the gentlemen. Why, mother, they all talk as if I were a baby, and had to be amused. You know I went to spend the day with Nellie Meyers. A gentleman, an old friend of Mr. Meyers, was there to dinner. Nellie says he has been nearly all over the world, and that he is a regular correspondent for two or three magazines, and we thought we would have a rare treat in hearing him talk about his travels; and so we did, while he was talking to Mr. Meyers; but if by any chance he felt called upon to say any thing to Nellie or me, it was almost sure to be something light and trifling; and if he did say any thing sensible, he would throw in some compliment, and spoil it all. It was too provoking."

"I presume the gentleman did not mean to offend. He only thought it his duty to say something pleasant."

"Yes; that is the provoking part of it. People are always saying soft and silly things, just to please us; and we are not half so well pleased as they imagine we are."

"Whom do you mean by *us?*" asked Mrs. Dean.

"Women and girls — especially girls. The gentlemen think we do n't know any thing, and treat us accordingly."

"Perhaps that may be true so far as knowledge is concerned. Some of us do n't know so *very* much." And Mrs. Dean laughed at the serious face of her daughter.

"But we do n't like to be told of it quite so plainly. Only last week, at Mrs. Harris's party, Lulu Harris gave me an introduction to Dr. S., who has nearly a dozen capital letters attached to his name, representing degrees conferred upon him in this country and in Germany. I felt a little afraid of his learning; but I thought, 'Now I will have an opportunity to find out something I want to know very much;' and I had a half-dozen questions ready, if only the way was opened to ask them. We were near the center-table, and I picked up a copy of Burns on purpose to get him to say something about Scotland, thinking I could easily lead him from there across the channel. But he would n't lead a bit. He commented on the different 'style' of the ladies, talked about the 'beautiful evening,' and asked me if I was fond of croquet and lawn tennis—just, for all the world, as Tom Jones or Charlie Wilmot would have done—and I was disappointed. He seemed to think me shallow, and felt compelled to descend to my level, if he would make himself agreeable to me."

"Bessie, I am sure you must be exaggerating a good deal," said her mother, earnestly.

"Not at all. They every one talk to us just in that fashion. Dr. S. could talk sensibly enough to father and the minister, and so could the others; but the moment they turned their conversation toward a lady, they began to smile and say 'pretty' things."

"You should not say *all*, daughter. I am sure your father seldom talks nonsense to ladies."

"No, *he* does n't; and I am just proud of him. But, if you except Uncle Henry, papa is about the only gentleman who ever talks to me as if he thought I had sense enough to appreciate sensible talk."

"Perhaps the fault is not all on the part of the gentlemen," suggested Mrs. Dean. "Do not ladies usually show more interest in light and trifling subjects than on more solid ones?"

"Yes; but half the time it is because they are afraid of being called 'blue-stocking' or 'strong-minded.' You know, mother dear, that you never allow yourself perfect liberty of speech except when you are talking to papa or uncle, or on very rare occasions, and yet *we* know you can talk sense with any of them. We girls might be more sensible if people would talk sense to us. We do n't want any stilted grandiloquence, nor any Greek or Latin, except on state occasions," laughed Bessie, getting back to her usual good-nature, "but just sensible, every-day talk.   'Pretty' talk may do occasionally, but it is n't fair for our brothers to say solid, sensible things to each other, and give us only the chaff.   We may not be overwise, but talking nonsense to us is not likely to make us any wiser."

Earning Her Own Living.

RS. WILLIS was paying a visit to her old friend and schoolmate, Mrs. Danely. The ladies had been friends in girlhood, and had made it a rule to visit each other once a year, at least, though residing in cities some distance apart. Mrs. Willis had only arrived a couple of hours before the date at which the conversation I am about to record began. Having changed her traveling dress for a fresh one, and partaken of some refreshment, the two ladies were soon busily engaged in talking over old times and home news.

"Where is Annie?" Mrs. Willis asked between one of the brief pauses in the conversation.

"She is at the office. Did I not write you that Annie is book-keeper for the firm in which her father is partner?"

"Why, Helen! You are surely joking," a look of incredulity taking the place of the surprised one which her friend's answer had called forth.

"No, Annie. I am serious about it. She has been in the position for three months, and seems to be very much pleased with the business."

"But why is she doing it? Mr. Danely is not in financial difficulty, I hope?" and Mrs. Willis looked at her friend with evident anxiety.

"No, indeed. The firm has never been more prosperous than now."

"Then why do you allow her to do such a thing?"

"She wanted the place, and the firm gave it to her, after a month's trial," responded Mrs. Danely, quietly.

"But I thought you were going to make a lady of her?"

"That is the intention still, but not one of the helpless kind, I hope."

"But what do the ladies of your 'set' say about such a step?"

"Not much now. They were very much concerned at first, and some went so far as to inquire into our bank account, but when they found *that* satisfactory, they seemed to feel a little easier; but they evidently think us either 'queer' or 'stingy.'"

"But if Annie was so anxious to be independent it seems to me there are other kinds of work much more suitable for a young lady than keeping books in a factory."

"I don't know about that. Annie seems to enjoy real business. She doesn't care particularly for music, that is, not enough to make it a special study, and at her own request she has quit taking lessons, though you know she plays and sings very well. She dislikes millinery and dressmaking, and has felt as if she was without a mission since she is out of school, so when her brother Henry was appointed superintendent of the factory, the firm had to look up a new book-keeper, and Annie asked her

father's permission to apply for the situation. We
had some little doubts about the 'propriety' of the
step, but she seemed so anxious for it that we consented to the trial if the other members of the firm
were willing. They had doubts about her ability at
first, but now, after three months, they seem perfectly satisfied."

"Some way a *factory* seems so out of place for
Annie," persisted Mrs. Willis.

"It seems more suitable for her than any thing
else, just now. If she were clerking in a store or
at work in a shop, she would have to mingle with
people whose society would not be beneficial. Where
she is now her father or brother can accompany her
home every day, and one of them is always in the
establishment, and I feel that she is much safer than
if she were with strangers."

"Well, that may be; but how could you consent
to it? I have always wanted to be proud of my
namesake, and now the idea of her being a book-
keeper in a *woolen factory* is not at all to my notion.
If you were poor and Annie was obliged to earn her
living, it would not seem so absurd; but for a man
who is worth sixty or seventy thousand dollars to set
his daughter—an only daughter at that—to earn her
own living, seems hardly fair."

"We may not always have so much money, and
it is well for Annie to know how to take care of herself, and I am sure we do not feel ourselves disgraced
by it," Mrs. Danely answered, pleasantly.

"Well, Helen," replied her friend, "I presume
it's all right; but you did n't talk like this during

our school days. Do you remember how you used
to talk about the sphere of woman?" The two
friends joined in a hearty laugh at the remembrance
of some of their school-girl talk about the dignity of
woman.

"Yes, I remember all about it; but, my dear
Annie, I have learned a good many things in the
past twenty years, and my ideas have undergone a
change. I have seen the wheel of fortune cast off
a good many who once had an abundance of wealth.
And because of their wealth they had never considered it necessary to teach their daughters any practical lessons. But poverty came, and these daughters
must go out to earn their own living. A false notion
of dignity prevented their seeking a position where
manual labor was required, and the only alternative
was to eke out a sort of half existence teaching a
private school, or trudging from house to house
teaching music to girls who take lessons because
it is the fashion, and not because they have a talent
for or love music for itself. Then, again, I have
seen women left with a family of helpless children to
support. Perfectly ignorant of business, their little
property slipped from their hands into the pockets of
unprincipled men, who are always at hand ready to
take advantage of their ignorance, and they are left
to earn a livelihood for their families by the needle or
the wash-tub."

"That is, no doubt, true," replied Mrs. Willis,
slowly; "and yet it hardly seems worth while for
you to borrow trouble as to your future or Annie's."

"I know, so far as present appearances go, nothing seems more unlikely than that we should be poor, but if such should be the case and Annie sticks to business as she does now, I will not be under the necessity of urging her to marry for fear she will be burdensome to us."

"But, Helen, you surely would n't want Annie to stay single all her life, would you?"

"By no means; I think every woman would be the happier for having a home and a family about her, but I want my daughter to choose for herself, and not feel obliged to accept the first offer, whether suitable or not, for fear she will be left to die an old maid. I would like to see the day when every American boy and girl will be compelled to learn a trade that will stand them in the hour of need; when such is the case, our list of suffering poor will be lessened very considerably."

Mrs. Willis sat silent for some moments; at length she said: "If you are right, then I am afraid I have made a mistake in training my own girls; my boys are learning their father's business, but I doubt whether the girls could be persuaded to undertake what your daughter has taken up of her own accord."

"I would not advise them to do that unless under favorable circumstances; and then there are but few like Annie in taste and disposition. But I would have them learn some business or trade, something for which they may seem to have an aptness, and that will not seem to them mere drudgery. There come Annie and her brother, now; watch her, and tell me if you think she seems less a lady than she did a year ago."

Annie gave her mother's friend a cordial greeting, and Mrs. Willis could not help being pleased with the dignified, yet earnest, warm-hearted girl.

At the close of her visit, she said to Mrs. Danely:

"I believe you are right, after all; and I only wish my Helen took hold of life and its duties as fearlessly and with as much relish as your Annie does. I do n't want to hear a word against 'business women' after this. It is perfectly wonderful what an influence she has over her brother, too; why, he defers to her opinion as if she were ten years older, instead of two years younger, than he; and she seems to understand business full as well as he — without being mannish, either."

"I am glad you are not displeased with Annie," answered Mrs. Danely. "I think the fact that their education has been so near alike has saved Henry from much evil influence; he is inclined to be wild, but she loves the same kind of books that he does, and they enjoy them together, and she has held him back and shielded him from evil, while the restraint has been a pleasure to him. Take my word for it, my dear friend, it will be better not to make too wide a difference in the education of our sons and daughters; and you will find, too, that both will be happier for having something to do besides amusing themselves or being amused. Poor men's children are not the only ones who need to be busy."

WHICH IS THE BETTER WAY?

—•◦•—

"LOOK, Aunt Mabel; isn't she sweet as can be?"

And Mrs. Hunt adjusted the sash and smoothed back the folds of the skirt, as she turned her little eight-year-old "Gertie" about, for "Aunt Mabel" to get a good view of the dress and its lovely wearer.

Mabel Hunt was Mr. Hunt's maiden sister, and some ten years older than her sister-in-law, and, though she possessed a very attractive face, coupled with gentle, winning manners, when you came to know her in her daily life, you in some way ceased to wonder as to why she had not married, and began wondering how she could possibly be spared from the place she already occupied, that of elder sister, counselor, and ever-ready helper to all who needed her aid.

In answer to her sister's call, Miss Hunt laid down her pen, and turned to look at the little figure before her.

No one could question the sweetness of the face, nor the loveliness of the figure; but, instead of answering the mother's appeal, she looked at the child for a brief moment, and then, suddenly reaching out her hands, she drew her to herself, imprinting a kiss on each rosy cheek, at the same time giving her a

22

look that had in it more of pity than of admira-
tion.

"O Aunt Mabel, *do n't* hug me so; my dress will all be rumpled, and not fit for the party."

And Gertie withdrew herself from her aunt's arms, with a little gesture of impatience, as she smoothed the folds of the dress, with a glance toward the mirror.

The mother looked inquiringly at her sister's sober face.

"Do n't you like the dress, Mabel? Is n't it stylish?"

"Yes," absently, "*very* stylish;" then as Gertie ran off to show the dress to Katie, and receive her extravagant praises, she added, "almost stylish enough for the stage, but it is not exactly such as I would choose for Gertie."

"Why, sister, I thought you liked to see children dressed nicely."

"So I do—nicely and suitably; but it hardly seems appropriate for a child of eight years to be dressed in the garb of a fashionable young lady."

"But it is all the style now to dress the children just as nearly like grown folks as possible."

"It may be the style, but I do n't admire it any more for that. Men and women thirty-six inches high may serve to amuse us, as we look at other curiosities, but they are only deformities, and untrue to nature."

"O, you dear, whimsical old maid," laughed Mrs. Hunt, giving Mabel a playful little caress, as she took her seat and sewing; "if you had a husband and three or four children about you, as I have, you would be very apt to do as I do, and try to dress your children as your friends dress theirs."

"Perhaps so; but it would not be the right thing to do, if it was to make them unnatural," responded Miss Hunt.

"Come, now, if you are going to preach, don't stop with merely announcing your text; please give us your reasons," said the sister, with a smile of evident unbelief.

"I am perfectly willing, if you really wish to know. Some one has said 'Dress a man like a gentleman, and, ten chances to one, he will act like a gentleman,' and if you dress a child like a fashionable young lady, she will be very apt to try to act like one; a little child, dressed as a child, will be a child, unless her head has been filled with nonsense by others. It isn't natural for a child to care more for her clothes than for the caresses of those she loves, and I am sure I would rather see Gertie digging wells or making mud pies, in the back yard, than flirting a fan at an evening party, tiptoeing across the room, with anxious glances toward the looking-glass, to see if her over-dress is looped gracefully."

"But, really, Mabel, I do not *want* to crowd my children forward or spoil them; I love them too dearly for that," Mrs. Hunt replied, earnestly.

"Of course, you love them, and there lies the danger. If mothers could always love 'wisely,' and not 'too well,' there would not be the danger of over-indulgence and over-praise; but it is next to impossible for a child to be flattered continually by those she loves and others with whom she associates, and not be spoiled by it, sooner or later. If she is told several times a day that she is a 'beauty' and the 'sweetest child in the world,' it will be a great won-der if she does n't come, by and by, to believe it herself, and to find this flattery a necessity to her happiness."

"Well, whatever may be said of your argument, you are certainly very candid!"

And Mrs. Hunt's tone showed that she had made a personal application of the illustration

"I hope you and I love each other too dearly to be otherwise than candid in our intercourse with one another," answered Mabel, gently. "I know it sounds 'old fogyish' for me to talk about how things were when I was young, but there are some things to-day that I can not think an improvement on the past. I dearly love a *real child*, and not a child who is trying to act the part of a young man or woman. The daughter of to-day scarcely seems to have any girlhood at all; it is simply a skip from the long clothes of the cradle to the longer ones of the trained evening dress of the fashionable lady. Instead of the ten-year-old girl eating a plain, wholesome sup-per and going to bed in time to get the sleep and rest that will help her to grow into a strong, health-ful and helpful woman—mentally and physically, such as the world needs—she must sit up until midnight, frequently eating indigestible food at unseasonable hours, while she is kept under a continuous strain of nervous excitement, and forming habits that will, in a greater or less measure, mar her whole future life."

"You ought to be on the list of the Lecture Bureau, Mabel," smiling at her sister's earnestness.

"I beg pardon for intruding my opinions upon you, but I have spent considerable of my life among the children, and, though I am only an 'old maid,' my observations in the school-room and elsewhere have confirmed me in the belief that 'society' is shortening the lives and marring the usefulness of the children, especially the daughters. We were all justly incensed at a certain spiritualist, who kept his little daughter up night after night, while he humbugged the people with his 'séances,' pretending that the child received communications from deceased friends of those who were willing to be deceived; and when the child died from sheer physical and mental exhaustion before she reached her fifth year, we all shook our heads and said, as it is usually safe to say after an event has occurred, 'Just as I expected.' The nervous and physical strain was too much for her years, and overtaxed nature gave way. But while we censure these parents for exposing the life of their child for the gains of sorcery, are not those mothers who permit their little children to turn night into day, teaching them to appear what they are not, recreant to the trust confided to them in the care of an immortal soul? It is the duty of parents and teachers to so train their children that they may be of the greatest possible benefit to the world. But if they are allowed to form habits that will undermine the health, they certainly can not be as useful as they would have been with a perfectly developed and healthy organism."

"I am afraid you air developing into a regular utilitarian, Mabel. There are some things for beauty, others for usefulness."

"No; I am not utilitarian—at least, not in its offensive sense. And as to beauty, I can not conceive of any thing more beautiful than a perfectly developed and healthy physical frame united with a well-regulated mind. If a woman is perfectly well, she will be happier herself, and will make others happier, than she could if she were suffering constant bodily pain or weakness. It is all very well to point us to those instances of intense physical suffering in which the sufferer could so far subdue self or forget herself as to pass through years of physical suffering with perfect tranquillity, and to prove a blessing to those around her; but that is the result of divine grace, and not the natural consequence; and the man or woman who has grace enough to be patient, and even cheerful, under such circumstances, would, with divine grace and a healthy body, be likely to be a great deal more cheerful and helpful. We like to shift our responsibilities to others' shoulders. Indulgent and doting mothers will allow their daughters to spend their girlhoods' brief years in one continual round of excitement, and if at the age of fifteen or twenty the overstrain cause the silver cord to break, they bow their heads in sorrow, and wonder why she 'died so early,' when the only real wonder is that the human frame could endure, even for that short time, the continual tax. There are many cases of so-called dispensations of Providence, which are but the natural consequences of a violation of the laws of health."

"But what can I do? If I do not allow my children to dress and to do as my neighbors' children do, I will be criticised and censured as over-strict;" and Mrs. Hunt looked really perplexed.

"You have a conscience of your own, I trust, sister. Because your neighbors choose to murder their daughters by a system of slow torture, I do not see that you, therefore, should do the same by your daughter. Find, or try to find, what is best for your children, and then have the courage to put your convictions into practice; and even though your friends may not approve of your course, you will receive the gratitude of your children when they shall have become old enough to appreciate your motive and judgment."

"Well, I don't know," wearily; "perhaps you are in the right. I wish I knew just what I ought to do; but where can Gertie have gone? I had forgotten about her. She will ruin that dress, and then she will have to miss the party to-night." And Mrs. Hunt hastily threw down her sewing, and went in search of the absent child, not even waiting to reply to her sister-in-law's declaration that "both events would be a blessing for the child."

"Careful and Troubled About Many Things."

MRS. ELLIOT had just heard the last little one say its evening prayer, kissed all three "good-night" for the second or third time, and had finally succeeded in quieting the restless ones, rendered unusually so by the sultry atmosphere of a July evening. Then she returned to the parlor, where her sister, Mrs. Martin, who had arrived only that afternoon, sat rocking and resting in the dim twilight. Mrs. Elliot drew a sigh of relief as she seated herself on the stool at her sister's feet, with an arm laid across that sister's knee. "There, the prattlers are in bed and asleep at last; and now for an old-time talk, Martha. I wonder how father and mother could have made such a blunder as to call *you* Martha. I am sure you never seem 'careful or troubled about many things,' nor 'cumbered with much serving,' like the rest of us. But, now, let us hope we shall have one hour together without interruption."

"I suppose if some one should need you very much, you could forego the pleasures of our little chat, could you not?" asked the sister, quietly.

"Yes; but, I fear, not very willingly; and that

suggests a topic for discussion, one that has been in my thoughts on a good many occasions, and I am anxious for the benefit of your opinion. Why is it that, at the very time my heart is 'set' on doing some particular thing, something else, that my heart was *not* 'set' on doing, comes up, and either prevents my doing it at all, or hinders me, so that it is only by combating difficulties of the most obstinate character that I succeed in accomplishing my purpose?"

"For instance?"

"Well, for instance, yesterday, just as I had succeeded in quieting the house, and had seated myself to write a short article for our county paper, in comes John, and wants to know if I can't shorten the sleeves of his dressing-gown. 'Only five minutes' work, Jennie,' as he saw me lay down my pen a little regretfully. It took me a full hour, and then baby woke and had to be cared for. Then callers and tea-time came, pretty close together, too. After tea, callers again; and then the children must be put to bed; and after that I was too tired to do any thing but rest. If I plan for a week of genuine comfort with my books—and you know I *must* read if I would instruct my children—no sooner do I think every thing is in order than I suddenly discover that Hallie is out at the knees and must have a new suit, or Lulu's wardrobe needs 'fixing up,' or my 'girl' gets it into her head to go home. 'Me mither is awful sick, shure; and would, I be kind enough to let her go home just for a week, to look afther her?' Of course I can not say 'No,' and I close my books with a disappointed sigh, tie on my kitchen apron, and proceed to assume the duties of mistress of the house and maid of all work. Now, why can't I have the privilege of a week's rest, and feast without this continued interruption?"

"I suppose it is because you have more irons in the fire than you can attend to easily, and so you have extra work and care."

"But I love to read and I love to write, and sometimes I feel as if were almost starving for lack of intellectual food; and it *is* a trial to have to deny one's self the luxury of scribbling a few scattering ideas on paper occasionally. It is said of Fannie Fern that, during a period of fourteen years, she never failed for a single week to have her article for the *Ledger* ready on time, and I don't wonder that Grace Greenwood should want her to enlighten her sisters as to how she managed things and met all her engagements. Now, my luck is about like this: I receive a card from my editor, asking if 'that story' is almost ready, when I haven't written a sentence of it. Down I sit to write it. Presently John comes in with letter which states that Mr. So-and-so and his wife will be in on the evening train and can only remain a few days."

"As this afternoon," suggested Mrs. Martin, slyly.

"Now, sister, you know that I am just as glad as can be to have you here, and I intend to keep you as long as possible, by way of proving it," remonstrated Mrs. Elliot. "But you interrupted me in my story. O, yes: I shove paper and pen into the desk, and proceed to plan a bill of fare, for I must have something nice for my company to eat, and I either write my story while other people sleep, or let some more fortunate sister send her story 'on time,' and get the pay for it while I wait."

"Would n't your friends be just as happy without so much extra effort on your part for their comfort?"

"May be so; but you know people have formed the idea in some way, that if a woman scribbles a little for the press, her house must of necessity be always turned topsy-turvy, her bread stale, and the coffee muddy, and I am determined they shall have no reason for saying that I neglect my house."

"At the risk of over-taxing yourself, ruining your health, and—and temper?" inquired Mrs. Martin.

"I hope not; but I am not the only one who feels so. Now, there is my friend, Mrs. W. She was called into the temperance work during the crusade, and has been lecturing ever since. God has wonderfully blessed her labors in saving the drunkard; but she says she must keep her children neatly dressed always, and her table must not be lacking in any way, and she must entertain strangers often, though the angels come but once in a life-time. *She* did n't say any thing about the angels, but I presume she has looked for them long and patiently; and in order to do all that she feels she must do all she can to keep up the 'reputation of the house,' she must work half the nights when she is at home to atone for her absence."

"And give her husband the privilege of hunting

up a step-mother for his children in less than ten years, in all probability."

"Perhaps so. But you haven't told me what I ought to do, nor how I am to manage so as to have things the way I want them."

"Did you ever know any who had things just as they wanted them?"

"Yes, I think so."

"Perhaps if you were to know them better you would think differently. Do you know that I, your elder sister, have always thought you had such a wonderful faculty for getting along smoothly, and writing your delightful little yarns at the same time? I didn't dream you were troubled at all, and here you are, pouring out a perfect Jeremiad about your hinderances, and I find you are just as much perplexed and worried as others."

"And that doesn't comfort me a particle. I see other women whose time is not cut up into odds and ends like mine. They seem to have some sort of system about their work, while mine is done just as it happens; very frequently it is a regular assortment of work that is not assorted at all. Just look at my sitting-room now if you choose, and examine my work-table. Bits of paper written over in part with pen and in part with pencil; spools of thread, needles, thimbles, blotting paper, rubber erasers, buttons, envelopes, scraps of embroidery, etc., all mixed in endless confusion," and Mrs. Elliot's laugh sounded as if her trouble was not at all a laughing matter.

"Sister, dear, if all this troubles you so, why don't you quit 'scribbling,' as you call it?"

"Did n't I tell you that I love it? It is the one thing that I really enjoy. It does n't amount to much either intellectually or financially, but then it is a comfort to be allowed the privilege of expressing an opinion; besides it is a relief to get it off your mind; and, like most other people, if a luxury costs a good deal, I am all the more loath to give it up."

"Well, if that is your decision, stick to it; and as 'hard things' are said to be 'good for folks,' I presume these interruptions, that are so trying to the patience, will do you good. You will bear them better by and by."

"I hope so; but it seems a slow way to learn, and not a very pleasant way either," sighed Mrs. Elliot.

"Nevertheless, you will learn, though it be but slowly; and by constantly struggling with obstacles we gain strength. If you were to have your own way, you would be likely to grow selfish."

"I *am* selfish, goodness knows! The only trouble is, I do n't have the opportunity to make it manifest."

"Granting, for argument's sake, that you are a little selfish, the fact that you are conscious of that defect in your character is a very favorable indication. The majority of our selfish people seem wholly unconscious of the fact. Keep on, doing the work that lies nearest to your hand, and if it should not be just the kind of work you would choose, do it to the best of your ability, and the time will come when you will receive the 'well done, good and faithful servant,' and the joy you will feel in the Master's approbation will fully recompense you for these little annoyances which are such a perplexity to you to-day."

Charles Mitchell's Thanksgiving.

HANKSGIVING and Prayer," repeated Charles Mitchell impatiently, as, thrusting into his pocket the daily containing the President's proclamation, he looked about to see if things were in order preparatory to going home for the night.

"There are a good many things I might pray for if I thought there was any probability of my prayers being answered; but as to thanksgiving, there is precious little reason for thankfulness on my part this year," muttered the young man half-aloud, then, as if suddenly recollecting himself, "But what would Annie say if she should hear me talking like this?" and buttoning his overcoat closely about his chest he prepared to face the sharp November sleet that seemed to pierce and chill the whole frame.

A long walk through the storm did not serve to assist his better feelings to rise above the discouragements that were perplexing his mind, and when he reached his home it was with the bitter, dissatisfied feeling in his heart that Providence had not granted him the favors and the successes he deserved. As he looked at the pale, careworn face of his wife, the thought came with increased bitterness, "Thankful for what? That Annie is wearing out her life because I can not afford to pay for proper help, I suppose."

The wife saw his preoccupied and gloomy look
during the evening meal, but she made no comment,
thinking, "It will soon pass away; he is tired, and
this dreary weather is enough to make one gloomy."

During the evening Mrs. Mitchell picked up the
daily which her husband had laid upon the table, and
her eyes fell upon the "Thanksgiving proclamation."
What memories it awakened! How her thoughts
carried her back to the old home with all its tender
associations. Father, mother, brothers, and sisters,
with smiling faces and happy hearts, gathering about
the bounteous board; the prayer and thanksgiving
formed into words by the father, or it may be the
pastor, to which each heart responded a fervent
Amen. But this was all over now, and she far away
from those who had helped to make Thanksgiving
such a blessed, joyous day. Some had already
passed over to the "other side," and though she
tried to repress them, the tears would come. When
she could trust her voice, she said:

"Charles, Thanksgiving will be here in three
weeks. How shall we celebrate it?"

"By making a feast for our fair-weather friends,
I suppose," was the husband's answer, with more
of bitterness in his tone than he was probably aware
of. The pained and startled look on his wife's face
aroused him, and he added apologetically, "We are
too poor to keep Thanksgiving this year, Annie."

"We can not keep it in the style of a few years
ago; but, Charles, I do not like it to pass unob-
served, for the children's sake, if not for our own."

"Precious little cause have we or the children

for keeping Thanksgiving," the old bitterness rising
in his heart again; "with you working yourself to
death, and the children only half-clothed."

"O, no, it is not so bad as that," Annie answered eagerly. "I do have to work hard, but I am
glad I have the strength; the children are well, and
if they can not have luxuries, they are at least comfortable, and if our home is very small and humble,
it is ours, and that is something to be thankful for.
But I can not bear to hear you talk so; it doesn't
sound at all like you, Charles," and the tears gathered in her eyes.

"I know it doesn't sound like *me*, as you say;
but I tell you, Annie, I almost doubt sometimes if
there *is* a God, or if there is one, if he cares whether
his creatures try to please him or not. There,"
as Annie made a gesture as if to interrupt him,
"don't talk to me about it. I am holding my present position by the day, and should not be surprised
any day if the firm should tell me they could not
afford to employ me any longer." And then, as if to
shut off any further conversation, he turned to his
book and tried to fix his mind on its contents. Mrs.
Mitchell slipped away to her room to hide her sorrow there; sorrow, not so much for the reverses
that had come to them through the general financial
depression, as that her husband was allowing his
financial troubles to shake his faith in the loving-
kindness of an all-wise heavenly Father. As she
looked upon her little ones, sleeping so sweetly, she
could but feel her heart go out in gratitude to God
that these had been spared her, and that he had seen

fit to allow their money to slip away from them
rather than that these precious treasures, their children, should be given up.

The following morning Mrs. Mitchell arose with
a strange ringing in her ears, and with such a sensation of dizziness that she could scarcely steady her
steps sufficiently to prepare the morning meal. I
must not give up," she said to herself. "Charles
must have his meals regularly and in order. He
misses the luxuries of other days more than I do,
and I must make it up to him if I can."

The breakfast was tempting enough to Charles
and the children, but she had no appetite for food, and
her husband was too much engrossed with his own
thoughts to notice that she did not eat, and with a
hurried good-bye he went away to his business.

Little Nellie remained from school to care for
" Baby," for the mother felt that she had not the
strength to prepare dinner and give the little prattler
the attention necessary. It was well for him that
Nellie stayed at home, for when dinner was but half
ready Mrs. Mitchell was obliged to lie down, and
when her husband returned he found her burning
with fever and talking incoherently of mother, home,
and Thanksgiving. A physician was called at once,
but the over-taxed system did not readily yield to
the influence of medicines, and in a few days the
mother and sister were called from a distant State to
watch over the dear one who had toiled beyond her
strength that her family might not miss the luxuries
of better days.

For many days she seemed to hover between life

and death, and as Thanksgiving drew near the husband recalled the conversation of the evening previous to her sudden attack; and as he thought of what that day might be to him and his little ones, he lifted his heart, crushed and bleeding, to Him whose providence he had blamed, and whose existence he had even tried to doubt, and prayed for forgiveness and help in his great need.

When the financial crash, under which so many prosperous men went down, had overwhelmed them, Mitchell's proud spirit could not bear the thought of having their straitened circumstances made known to his wife's family, and so, during the past year, Annie had not urged her mother and sister to visit her, much as her heart had hungered for their society, for Charles, without intending to be selfish, had said:

"Let us wait until times are better; I can not bear that they should see our poverty."

And Annie had crushed back the longing of her heart, and waited.

Now, when mother and sister bent over her with anxious watchfulness, she did not recognize them; and it seemed as if the poor, tired spirit would leave the clay tenement without giving them the look or word of recognition for which they were longing and praying.

Thanksgiving eve came, and the physician said: "To-night will decide her case; she *may* be spared to you and your little ones, but you had better prepare for the worst."

In an agony of suspense they watched and waited, while the words "Precious little cause have we for thankfulness," spoken so bitterly on that evening three weeks previous, kept ringing in the husband's ears. How deeply he repented those murmurings now.

"Why could I not see how good God was in giving me such a companion? and why should I have complained so long as my wife and children were spared to me?"

And with throbbing heart he watched through the early hours of the night. What change will the night bring—life or death?

Gradually the fever left her, and she became quiet from sheer prostration ; then she seemed to sink into a sleep, fitful at first, but at last she slept quietly, and the watchers could only wait and pray.

One o'clock, and still she slept. At two, the physician, who had remained in the house, came to her bedside and watched her for an hour.

How much Mitchell wanted to ask the question, "Will she live?" yet he dared not, for fear the answer would crush out all his hopes.

But as they watched, there was no mistaking the quiet, regular breathing, and the physician pronounced the crisis past, and said: "She will live."

Thanksgiving dawned, but O, so different from what they had feared on the previous day, or from what Charles Mitchell had expected three weeks before.

The precious patient was better, but very weak, and it would require days, and perhaps weeks, of careful nursing before she would be able to take her accustomed place in her family.

But all that chill November day, though the house was hushed and each one stepped with careful tread, for fear the dear one should be disturbed, yet from one heart, at least, humbled and chastened though it was, there went up a psalm of thanksgiving and praise:

"O Lord, I will praise thee: though thou wast angry with me, thine anger is turned away, and now thou comfortest me."

And to the heart of the husband these words came with a meaning they never had before.

Three weeks after, Mrs. Mitchell, leaning on the arm of her husband for support, entered their little sitting-room, for the first time since her illness.

As he placed her in the arm-chair, before the fire, Mitchell said:

"Annie, the past three weeks have been to me one continued thanksgiving to God that he has spared your life; and I have been enabled to see how much above wealth or worldly position is the precious gift of a faithful and loving companion and children; and while he spares my life, I hope I may never so far forget his mercies as to say I have nothing to be thankful for."

And on that evening, as the reunited family bowed at the family altar, husband and wife lifted their hearts in gratitude to God for those blessings which wealth and worldly favor can not buy—health and loving hearts.

BENNIE'S CHRISTMAS.

W HAT a buzz there was when, at the close of the Sabbath-school, the superintendent announced that the officers and teachers had decided to have a Christmas tree.

Outside the church door, a group of boys gathered to talk over the prospective fun and to interchange opinions.

"I think it will be jolly," said Dick Hollowbush; "that is, if I get all I have been wishing for."

"If Dick gets all he's wishing for, there will be no room on the tree for any of *our* wishes," objected a boy at Dick's elbow.

There was a general laugh at this little thrust, for Dick's habit of wishing for almost every thing he saw, and for a great many things that he had never seen, was no secret to his schoolmates.

They finally agreed that "a Christmas tree would be jollier than a concert."

But while the merry group were talking over the "good time coming," there was one who, though an interested listener, had taken no part in the conversation. As he stood leaning against the corner of the church, trying to warm himself in the sun, and at the same time be sheltered from the keen December wind, that seemed to pierce him through his threadbare clothing, it was easy to see that he, with his pale, baby face, and scanty clothing, did not belong to the same "set" with the rosy-cheeked and comfortably clad lads who were chatting so merrily.

Bennie watched the group, and his eyes grew, if possible, more wistful and hungry-looking as he listened. At last, when there was a lull in the merriment, he managed to get near a boy who stood on the outside of the group, and to ask, timidly:

" Will they make uth pay to thee it, Charlie?"

"I do n't know, I 'm sure," Charlie answered, carelessly; then he called to one of the larger boys: "Say, Ed, what 's the price of a ticket — reserved seat, you know," with a wink toward his companions.

" O, about twenty-five cents, I guess, for all over twelve, and fifteen cents for children. I 'm off the baby-list, and will have to pay full fare," and Ed straightened himself up, with all the dignity of twelve years and six months.

"I did n't ask on my own account; I do n't care for a quarter," answered Charlie, a trifle nettled, for he lacked three months of being twelve years old; "but Bennie here wanted to know if it would cost *him* any thing."

The boys laughed thoughtlessly as they caught sight of the little, pinched face, that looked so disappointed.

Fifteen cents seemed as far out of Bennie's reach as the same number of dollars would have seemed to some of the boys around him.

"I guess you 'll have to sell your coat to get the change," suggested Ed.

"Or that 'yittie thithter' he talks so much about," mimicked Charlie.

For, by the way, there was a new baby at Bennie's house, and he was very proud of it, and when one of his schoolmates had taunted him with being too poor to afford a pair of nice boots, he had answered, exultantly:

"Well, I do n't care; I gueth I got a yittie thithter, any way."

And now, when some one suggested that he sell the baby to get money for the Christmas tree, he raised his thin, piping voice indignantly:

"I would n't mind thelling my old coat, if I could go to thchool 'thout it; but I would n't thell the baby for forty Kithmuth tweeth."

And then Bennie turned his back on the crowd who could n't appreciate the bright little sunbeam in his otherwise cheerless home.

He walked slowly along the way, as if afraid to run against the sharp wind. All the way home he kept thinking how much he would like to see that tree. It had not entered his head that he would receive a present for himself; he only wanted to see how it looked.

Once inside of the place he called home, the sight of the little one recalled the suggestion of the boys that he "sell the baby."

Of course, it was only fun on their part, but Bennie did not appreciate the joke. Life was all dreadfully real to him, child though he was.

The little one, in the ragged shawl and rough cradle, was sweeter and dearer to the boy's loving heart than all the world outside. Curling himself down by the cradle, he began to talk to "Baby," to give vent to his feelings, as many older and wiser ones have done.

"No, I wouldn't thell you for forty Kithmuth tweeth! no, not for a million of 'em! but I would like to go juth *onth*, and if I had fifteen centh I *could* go, too. But, O dear, I hain't even got a nickel. And tho we 'll stay at home together," he said, with a half dissatisfied, half resigned look and tone, as he bent over and kissed the little lips that were just learning to wreathe themselves into smiles.

Bennie, however, could not quite give up the hope of seeing the Christmas tree, and as he lay that Sabbath night in his bed, thinking it all out, he remembered a verse of Scripture that he had learned some time before, in the Sabbath-school: "Ask and ye shall receive, seek and ye shall find, knock and it shall be opened unto you."

"Teacher thaid it meant if we want any thing real bad and athk Jethuth for it; he 'll make it all right and give it to uth, if it ith beth for uth, and I 'll just athk him to fikth it tho I can go; and I believe he 'll do it, cauth he thaid he would."

Bennie slipped out of bed, and, kneeling on the cold, bare floor, he offered his little prayer. There were no big words in that prayer, and perhaps some of our college graduates would have considered Bennie's grammar and rhetoric rather faulty; but his theology was sound, and there were two very important points in his prayer which even some of our most eloquent divines sometimes overlook or ignore in their prayers,

Bennie prayed right to the point. He asked God for just what he wanted and quit when he got through, and what was more important, he believed that his prayer would be answered. As he crept back shivering into bed, he drew a sigh of relief, as if a great burden had been rolled off his heart, and in a few minutes the tired boy was asleep, dreaming of a vast wilderness, on which God was showering manna that in some way changed to shiny nickels as he stooped to gather it.

On Monday morning he trudged away to school with a light heart, his precious secret kept snugly in his own breast. To all the inquiries of the boys he merely answered, "Yeth I'm going," though he could not have told where the money was to come from; and when one, more thoughtless than the rest, asked if he was "going to wear that old coat," he said he "guethed tho, I'd be pretty cold 'thout it."

Bennie *was* a little bit troubled about his ragged clothes, but he had'n't courage to pray for *new ones*; for it seemed to his simple mind like presumption to ask Jesus for money and for new clothes too.

One week had passed, and Monday morning came again, and the following Wednesday night would be Christmas eve, and Bennie began to wish he knew just when he would receive the money he had prayed for. Wednesday morning the wind blew colder than usual, and as he crossed the village commons, on his way to school, Bennie could not help wishing he could be as warmly clad as some of the boys who laughed at his threadbare coat and short pantaloons. About half-way between Bennie's home and the public school lived a dear good woman, who, with her daughter, was a veritable Dorcas to all the poor widows and neglected little ones of the village.   On this special morning Bennie was sure of a good fire in this home, and a bountiful slice of mince pie; and so, knocking gently at the side door, he was soon enjoying both.   Then he hurried on to school, promising to call on his way home in the evening.

Promptly at four o'clock (Bennie was always punctual at that house) he was again in the corner, toasting his feet by the warm fire, and enjoying an ample lunch from Mrs. Smith's pantry.   Just as he had swallowed the last mouthful a bundle was laid on his knee, and he was told to unroll it.   He had often received gifts of half-worn or out-grown clothing, from sympathizing neighbors, and as he undid the bundle he expected to find something of that sort again; but this time his expectations were more than realized, for instead of a suit of half-worn clothes, a size and a half too small or too large, he found a *new suit,* — pants and vest of substantial tweed!   For once poor Bennie seemed speechless with surprise and doubt.   Were these nice things for him?   He couldn't *remember* of ever having a real *new* suit of clothes in his life, and in a vague sort of way he had always supposed that his first dress had been given him by some one whose baby had outgrown the garment or died before it was worn out.

"Aren't they nice enough, Bennie?" asked Mrs. Smith at last, tired of waiting for him to speak.

The boy started as if from a dream.

"O yeth 'm.   Are they for me?"

"Yes, for you, if they will fit you," and the lady smiled at the anxious, questioning face.

Of course the fitting was all right. Mrs. Smith and her daughter had taken the proper precaution to find a boy who was about Bennie's size, and who served as a model, upon whom the clothes were fitted.

When he was dressed in the suit and ready to start home, Mrs. Smith's son, a young man of twenty-five years, was called in to admire the clothes and the boy.

"Well, Bennie," he said, "I suppose you will want to air that new suit at Santa Claus's entertainment," at the same time slipping three bright new nickels into the boy's vest pocket.

Was there ever a happier boy? Jesus had answered his prayer, and he had received his money and the new suit besides. The cold and snow did n't trouble him at all, for with the new clothes outside, and the happy heart within, his blood kept bounding so he had no time to cool off.

How proudly he showed his money—God's answer to his prayer—to his mother, who had given him but little, encouragement to hope for the money, for she had not his simple faith in God's promises. His old hat looked a little shabby by the side of the new suit, but Bennie consoled himself with the thought that he could take it off at the church door, and the pockets of the new coat were large enough to hide it in while in the church.

When he had proudly paid the admission fee, and taken his seat in a front pew, how he feasted his

eyes on the beauties of that wonderful tree! The
Christmas hymn was sung, and prayers offered by
the pastor, and a few appropriate ceremonies, and
then began the distribution of the gifts.

The children were attentive enough now. Even
those who had found it so difficult to keep quiet during
song and prayer, were listening with perfect attention
as the names of those who were receiving presents
were called off.

Bennie listened so anxiously that he forgot he
wore new clothes, forgot that his feet ached with
standing so long, for he was "only a boy," a "roust-
about" at that, and had been "rousted" out of his
seat to make room for a more important personage.
True, Bennie's nickels were bright and new and genuine, and his apparel goodly, at least in his own
eyes; yet he wore no rings on his hands and was not
entitled to as much attention as the son of Judge H,
who had received "a complimentary." But when
Bennie's name was called and he received a new cap,
"warm and plushy," he would not have been willing to exchange places even with the judge himself.
When the festivities were over, and he had received
a scarf, a pair of mittens, and a story-book, such as
he had longed for many times, and his pockets filled
with nuts and candies, besides a new cap, warm and
plushy, his happiness and good fortune seemed too
great to be real. What did he care though the boys
had laughed at him, and called out, "Shoot the cap,"
and other nonsense? Their jokes all glanced off
without doing him any harm. Bennie was too happy
too feel annoyed at them. His feet seemed scarcely

to touch the ground as he hurried home. God had answered his prayers, and that was enough.

"I knowed he would, 'cauth he thaid tho," and like many another of God's children · he had found that his heavenly Father had bestowed upon him more than he had dared to ask for.

Thus far through Bennie's life his "happy times" have not been scattered very thickly along his pathway; but be they many or few, it is likely that the happy Christmas given in answer to his childish petition, will be looked back to as one of the sunniest spots in his life.

A New-Year's Story.

"Labor with what zeal we will,
   Something still remains undone,
   Something uncompleted still,
   Waits the rising sun."

HE words were uttered slowly, and ended with a tragical little sigh as Margaret Hilton stood looking from the window of the little sitting-room into the gathering darkness of a Winter evening.

"Waits, and will not go away;
   Waits, and will not be gainsaid;
   By the cares of yesterday
   Each to-day is heavier made."

Another voice had taken up the poem, and quoted the lines half-soberly, half-mimicking the tone of the first speaker, and an arm was slipped lovingly about Margaret's waist as Ellen, the younger sister, asked, with tender reproachfulness:

"What duty does my conscientious sister imagine she has left undone? Did you forget to send old Sarah her pound of tea? or have the Jones children been neglected in any way?"

Margaret looks down soberly on the bright face that peers half-quizzically, half-earnestly into hers:

"Neither of these, Nell; but to-morrow begins a new year, the old one is almost gone, and I had planned to do so many things this year, but now every thing is 'uncompleted.' I have not more than half finished the course of reading I laid out, and my book has not even the first chapter written. ͺI feel as if the year had almost been wasted."

Nell's head gave an impatient little toss.

"Wasted, indeed! who ever knew *you* to waste your time? Why, you dear sister, you are a regular busybody—not in other men's matters, mind you, but in doing good to others. The nearest that you have come to any thing that looks like idleness, within my remembrance, was when I found you here quoting Longfellow to the stars. Wasting your time! I half believe you are cunning enough to be seeking a compliment," and Nell gave her sister's cheek a tap in mock anger.

"But really, sister, I have *accomplished* so little," began Margaret, wearily.

"But really, you must hush now; you are only blue from looking out of the dark room into the gathering night," interrupted the vivacious Nell. "But I came to say tea was ready. Hannah was going to ring the bell and I would n't let her, because I wanted to surprise you with a formal invitation to take my arm, and instead you have surprised *me*, with your solemn 'might have been.' But, come, Hannah will be cross," and with a merry laugh the light-hearted girl drew her more dignified sister toward the dining-room.

Margaret and Ellen Hilton kept house together, being the only unmarried members of the former household. The father and mother had both been dead some years, while an older brother and sister were married and living in a distant State. Margaret was ten years older than Ellen, and after their mother's death had been mother and sister to the little girl left an orphan at eight years of age. The homestead was theirs, and though humble in comparison with the residences of some of their wealthy neighbors, yet it was a home, and to this they could turn with a feeling of security and rest.

Margaret taught in the little public school, at a moderately fair salary, and this, with the addition of four boarders, enabled them to live comfortably, though plainly.

By strict economy Nell had been kept in school and was now hoping to "finish" in some first-class university. The boarders were away for the holidays, and this gave the sisters more liberty as well as leisure, both which they thoroughly enjoyed.

When tea was over and they were again in their little sitting-room, Margaret, seated at the table, took up some plain knitting, while Nell seated herself on an ottoman at her sister's feet.

"Now, Miss Prim, you have lectured me regularly all these years, and I would like the privilege of returning the compliment, just this once." And there was a mischievous twinkle in Nell's eyes in spite of her effort to look solemn.

Margaret smiled good-humoredly. "Certainly, my wise one; go on."

"Well, then, to begin, do you think it entirely consistent for you to be always preaching patience

and hopefulness to others and then get blue yourself
and go to gazing star-ward and quoting solemn
poetry on New-Year's eve?"

"O sister, don't!" and Margaret's eyes are filled
with tears. "I can not help feeling a little disappointed. I have accomplished almost nothing. I
wanted to help pay off the church debt, and to
increase my subscription to the benevolences of the
Church, and I have not been able to do either. And
I did want to send brother Will a few extra dollars;
what I did send him seemed so meager a sum. I
know he needs it, since his long sickness caused him
to lose his place."

"And because you can not do all you *want* to do
you will insist that you have accomplished almost
nothing. Now, let me tell you a story, just as you
used to tell me, ten years ago, when I hurt my fingers or bumped my head, or cried for what I could
not and ought not to have. Once upon a time, a
village school-ma'am, who had the charge of more
than threescore girls and boys, for ten months of
each year, four regular boarders and a cook to look
after besides, took it into her head or, heart, or both,
that she had not burdens enough to bear, so she
must make herself responsible for the comfort of two
invalid and indigent old women and a family of motherless children—no, you must keep still and listen
until my story is finished," as Margaret tried to enter
a protest against the story, the application of which
was only too apparent. "Besides all this, she must
educate a certain motherless, madcap sister, and
while doing all this she must needs grow despondent

because she could n't do a score of other things at
the same time on a salary of five hundred dollars a
year."

"Nell, you *must* stop!"

And Margaret, dropping her work, caught her
sister in her arms, laughing in spite of herself, even
though the tears were on her cheeks.

"Well, the story will stop for the present," assented Nell, as she freed herself from her sister's
arms. "But I do insist that you shall not make
yourself miserable because you can not do what no
one but yourself thinks you ought to do. Pray, do
leave a few charities for others to bestow. If I did
not hope to repay all the money you spend on me, I
would n't accept it all, but I do hope to be a help,
instead of a burden, some of these days. *You* do
good every day of your life, while *I* am only a butter-
fly, and a very homely one, at that. Those old women
look upon you as an angel of mercy, and when I
take them your gifts they *thank me* for bringing them,
but they 'bless dear Miss Margaret' for sending
them. They know whose purse pays the bills, I can
tell you that.

"You could n't give fifty dollars toward paying
off the church debt, but you managed to give our
pastor's wife a present of ten dollars. You wonder
how I found it out? Well, Mrs. Sawyer did n't keep
still about it, as you told her she must, but told me
all about it, and how much good it had done her,
and 'she was so grateful to you for your kindness.'
And I might tell a good many other things my precious sister has been doing, supposing all the time

that her poor little left hand did n't know any thing about it.

"I am real sorry about the reading and the book you wanted to write, and I hope you will have more time this coming year; but you have not been idle or neglectful, and I could n't let you close up the old year with that great burden of imaginary duties yet undone. You may begin the new year with a clear conscience, my sister Margie."

And Nell's eyes were suspiciously moist, even while her tone was full of playful banter.

Margaret kissed the upturned face, with loving caress.

"Perhaps I am too anxious; I will try not to murmur, nor spend time in useless regrets; I do not want to spoil your pleasures with my long face."

"Now, that is a little like your old sensible self, and I like it much better than your 'might have beens;' just keep in that frame of mind, and I'll give up my position of lecturer."

And Nell picked herself up, and drew a chair to the opposite side of the work-table, with a proposal to read for her sister's entertainment.

She had not read many minutes before the bell rang, and Hannah appeared with the evening mail, which a kind neighbor had brought from the office.

Margaret looked at the envelopes.

"A letter from brother Will; here, Nell, you may read it first, to pay for your lecture."

And the letter was passed over unopened. Nell broke the seal, and read aloud.

After a few words of loving greeting, the writer said:

"I can not thank you sufficiently, my dear sister, for your gift of fifty dollars — or, rather, *loan*, for I shall insist on returning it as soon as I can spare it — but it was a blessing to us, how much you can scarcely realize.

"Bills were due, and I lying helpless, wondering how they could be met, and — I am ashamed to own it — almost losing faith in Providence, when your letter, with its encouraging words and material help, came. Mary and I shed tears over both letter and check, it meant so much to us.

"I am mending slowly, and have the promise of my former position, after holidays are over. I am not strong enough to write a long letter, but we pray that the holidays may be a very happy time for you and sister Nell. Your affectionate and grateful brother   WILL."

Nell looked up with a smile.

"Is n't that better than writing a book? I 'd give a small fortune, if I had it, to have some one feel like that toward me; and, really," her old teasing spirit returning, "I have a mind to be downright jealous. I am almost forgotten, and if it were not for a chance reference I should have been left entirely out of his letter. People are always pouring blessings on your head, and yet you say you have accomplished almost nothing."

Margaret smiles through her tears.

"I am glad I have lightened one burden, and made some one happier. Do n't think me foolish, but I do want the world to be better and happier because I am in it. My heart was set on writing the book, because I felt I might help some one to a better life; I trust there is time enough yet, and I am willing to bide my time, if I can only feel sure that I am pleasing Him who reads not the outward acts alone, but the motives which prompt them."

CHARLES HAVREFIELD had just returned from college, where he had graduated with honors, and all his old friends
gathered around him to show him respect.

For four years he had been away from his
boyhood's home, only returning occasionally,
during holidays or the Summer vacations.

Now he was through his course of study,
and ready for a little recreation before entering
upon the duties of his profession — that of the
law.

He was a fine specimen of the physical man,
with the social and intellectual qualities well developed also.

When just passing out of his teens, he had been
considered "a little wild," and rumor said he had
occasionally drunk more wine than was good for him;
but he was a rich man's son, and society is not usually disposed to look very closely into the conduct
of those who have money and the social position
which money buys.

During his years in college, he had, through the
restraints thrown about him and his fear of disgrace,
succeeded in overcoming his temptation, and in keeping under control his already more than half-formed
appetite.

Judge Cowan, an old friend of the family, had given a large party in honor of his young friend, and the splendid parlors were filled with the *élite* of the town.

Of course, there must be wines. Every body in fashionable society had wines at their parties, and neither the judge nor his wife had any thought of being behind their friends in the completeness of their entertainment.

The evening was passing pleasantly, and supper was announced. Young Havrefield gave his arm to Gracie, the judge's youngest daughter, a very beautiful and lovable young lady. It had long been settled in Havrefield's mind that no lady of his acquaintance came so near filling his ideal as she. Society whispered that there would soon be a grand wedding.

At the table wines were passed, and the young man filled his companion's glass, leaving his own turned upside down.

Gracie saw the omission, and, looking up, said:

"Are you not going to take a glass of wine with me?"

Havrefield colored a little under her inquiring look, but answered:

"I have not drank a glass of wine for over two years."

"The more reason you should do so to-night," replied the young girl, laughing lightly; "my father always keeps the best, and he will feel hurt if you do not taste it. Remember this party was gotten up in your honor."

"And I am very grateful for the honor conferred on me; but please, Gracie, do not ask me to take wine."

He uttered the last part of the sentence just loud enough for her ears only.

Something in his tone made Gracie look up into his face, and in an instant her own face crimsoned.

"Surely, you are not *afraid* to take a glass of wine?"

Havrefield's face changed from red to pale. He hesitated a moment, and then said, slowly:

"I would rather not touch wine to-night."

"O certainly, I shall not urge you. If you are so weak that you can not take one glass of wine, I will excuse you. But I supposed you were stronger than that," and Gracie's tone was cold and her face haughty.

For a moment the hot blood rushed to his face, and then receding left it paler than before. In that moment his mind was made up. He would show Gracie that he was as strong as others. Turning up his glass he held it toward his companion, saying in a low tone, "Will you pour the wine, please?"

Gracie complied, smiling triumphantly.

"I *knew* you could not refuse *me*."

Ten minutes after Judge Cowan turned to him, saying pleasantly: "Will you have a glass of wine with me, Mr. Havrefield?"

He was about to reply, excusing himself, when he remembered Gracie's words, and for fear of offending by a refusal, he took the proffered glass. He had intended only to touch it to his lips, but the first glass had awakened the old appetite, and he drained the last drop.

Two glasses were sufficient to set his brain in a whirl, and when two or three old friends insisted on his taking a glass for Auld Lang Syne, he could not refuse, and before the evening was over he was so much intoxicated that a friend found it necessary to take him home, in order to prevent an unpleasant scene.

He awoke the next morning with a sense of guilt and shame resting upon him. He had not only an aching head, but an aching *heart* also. He wondered what Judge Cowan would think of him. What would Gracie say?

"I must see her, and ask her pardon for this," he said to himself, humbly.

In the afternoon he called at the judge's residence, and with an anxious heart asked for Gracie. She soon made her appearance, but instead of her usual cordial greeting, she bowed coldly and took her seat on the opposite side of the room. His quick eye saw the change, but he was too thoroughly humiliated and miserable to blame her. He waited a moment for her to begin the conversation, but she seemed not to be in a talkative mood, and the silence was oppressive.

"Gracie," he said at last, with an evident effort to steady his voice, "I came to offer you an apology for my conduct on last night. I am very sorry for what happened, and"—

Gracie interrupted him: "Apologies are useless, Mr. Havrefield. If you have no more respect for me than to become intoxicated in my presence, apologies would be thrown away."

"But, Gracie, please hear me. I did not intend it. I thought I could do as the rest did, and not feel it more than they; but I am not used to wine, and it overcame me." The young lady shrugged her shoulders impatiently.

"I may as well say it now and put an end to this. I want no apologies, but hope you will consider our engagement at an end. I can not afford to marry a man who will disgrace me and mine."

Her voice was cold and hard, and her words drove every particle of color from her lover's face. He started to his feet, and then sank back again in his chair with a look of astonishment.

"O Gracie, you can not mean that," he fairly gasped.

"I certainly do. I can not think of marrying a man who is as weak as you showed yourself to be last night. My *father* has drank wine for forty years, and no one ever saw him intoxicated," she said proudly.

Havrefield sat for some moments like one stunned.

"This is your final answer, is it?" he said, rising and standing before her, a look of mingled anger and agony on his face.

Gracie bowed coldly. "It is, Mr. Havrefield."

He still stood before her, his handsome face twitching with restrained anger. Half an hour before he would have knelt in his humility at her feet. At last he said slowly, and with a fearful emphasis: "If *you* cast me off I am ruined. I did not intend to touch the wine on last evening. It had been two years since a drop of alcoholic liquor of any kind had passed my lips, and *no one but you could have induced me to touch the cursed stuff.* *You* urged me to drink, even insinuating that I was *afraid* to drink a glass of wine. I *was* afraid! I wish in God's name I had been *man* enough to have left it alone! But if I go to ruin, perhaps it will comfort you to remember that it was *your persuasions* that tempted me, and your hand that poured the glass of wine that awakened the fiend Appetite. Judge Cowan no doubt will cast me off, and his daughter breaks her plighted faith, not because I drink wine, but because I can not drink as much as her father without getting drunk."

He turned and left the room without waiting for a reply. Taking his hat from the table in the hall, he passed out of the door and down the walk. He had gone in with sorrow and humiliation in his heart; he came out full of anger and despair. The one hope of his life was taken away.

"I may as well go to the devil at once; no one will care," he muttered with clinched teeth.

When the sound of his footsteps had died away, Gracie Cowan went slowly to her room. All the joy had gone out of her life in the last few hours. Throwing herself on her bed she wept long and bitterly. Love, anger, and wounded pride were struggling for the mastery in her heart. Unfortunately pride and anger gained the victory over love, and while conscience told her she was to blame in tempting him, and love dictated calling him back, and to give him one more chance to recover his lost ground, pride held her back, even though her heart ached at the separation.

They seldom met after their angry parting, and it was only through her friends that she heard he was gradually going down to certain ruin. Her father on one occasion ventured to express his satisfaction that she had been wise enough to break their engagement before it was too late, but it was no comfort to her, for his parting words—"*No one but you could have tempted me to touch it*"—rang in her ears whenever she thought of him; and although she would not acknowledge it, even to herself, yet she could not help feeling that she was to blame for his ruin.

Havrefield made a few feeble efforts to reform, but the appetite had hold of him, temptations were thick about him, and, cast off by the one who first tempted and who might have reclaimed him, he soon sank to the level of the common drunkard. He, who with his splendid talents and education, might have been the first in his profession, went down a ruined man; ruined, too, by one whom he loved as his life, and who loved him in return, yet with a mistaken idea of true manhood she had lured him to his own destruction.

SAVING THE BOYS.

I SAY, Ben, is n't Miss Woodbury a brick! She must know how boys feel such days as this, and that 's the reason she let us off at recess to-day," said Edward Holmes, a boy of fifteen, as he and his seat-mate passed out of the school-yard.

"Miss Woodbury is always kind, but I guess she would n't be pleased if she heard you calling her a brick. You know she hates slang," said his companion.

"O, well, hang it all, a boy can 't always be watching his grammar. I did n't mean any harm, and I do n't believe she 'd care a bit. Any way, I am going to pay her back by being extra good, Monday."

"Why not all the week?" asked Ben, quietly.

"O, you 're always taking a fellow up so. I do n't believe I could be good a whole week, any time, much less such hot days as these. My! won't I be glad when vacation comes!" and the boy threw up his hat and caught it, by way of giving vent to his feelings.

"Ed. Holmes! wait; I want to tell you something," called another boy, just coming out of the yard gate.

Edward stepped to one side and waited until the boy came up. "What 's wanted, Frank?"

"Why, I want you to come over to our meadow and play ball. We'll have jolly fun. I have asked a half-dozen of our 'particular friends,' as mother says. Will you come?"

"Yes, I guess so; that is, if mother don't care, and she doesn't often object, if I'm in good company."

"Well, hurry home then and see about it, and come over soon."

And Frank Moore jumped over the fence, and went across the lot toward home.

Eddie Holmes ran home, deposited his books in the hall, and went into the sitting-room to find his mother, but she was not there. He looked into the parlor, but it was darkened, and he started for the kitchen to ask Mary about her. Mary supposed she had gone to walk with the children.

"O, bother, I want to go to Frank Moore's for a game of ball."

"You had better ask your father, then," suggested Mary.

"I don't want to; he'll only scold. I guess I'll have to, though, if I get to go;" and away he went to find his father.

Running into the office, he began:

"Father, may I go and play ball at"—

"Go back and close that door," said his father, without looking up from his ledger. "Strange you can't learn to come in without making such a racket!"

Eddie closed the door, and then said:

"May I go, father? Frank Moore wants me to come over and play ball."

"No; you had better stay at home until you can learn to behave properly;" and Mr. Holmes went on with his writing without looking up.

Eddie turned and walked slowly out of the office and back home. There was no running or throwing up his hat now; but he walked slowly along, never looking up, when a boy on the opposite side of the street called out:

"What's the matter, Ned? Going to a funeral?"

Inside the house, he flung himself on the lounge, and gave way to his disappointed feelings. He felt that his request was reasonable; and if it had not been, he was hurt more at the manner of his refusal than at the refusal itself.

"I wish I was a man," he muttered. "I guess I'd have a little fun then without being scolded about it."

Then as he thought of the good time the boys were having, he felt the hot tears coming, and hid his face in the pillow. Presently he got up and went to the parlor. Every thing seemed so silent and lonesome, and the afternoon was so different from what he had expected.

His mother came home soon and noticed the cloud on the face of her usually lively boy, and asked the cause. Then came the story of his disappointment and his father's reproof.

"But, Eddie, you know you ought to be more careful; you know how much your father dislikes a noise about his room, and you have been reproved so often for your carelessness."

"Well," muttered the boy, "he won't always have a chance to scold. When I'm a man I'll go where"—

"Eddie!" and Mrs. Holmes's voice was full of
pain. "You do n't know what you are saying."

"Well, mother, I can 't help it; it is n't right,
and you know it, too;" and he brushed off the
angry tears, which would come, in spite of his efforts
to keep them back.

Mr. Holmes took no notice of his boy's clouded
face at tea time; but as he came home at nine o'clock
from the store, he heard voices inside the yard, under
the shadow of the trees.

"Better say you 'll come. We never play for
money, and you need n't take part unless you want to."

Mr. Holmes stopped and listened, breathlessly,
for he had recognized the voice. Sam. Huffman,
one of the worst boys the town could afford, was
trying to coax his boy into one of their dens, and he
grasped his cane as if he would strike down the
tempter. Presently Eddie's voice answered:

"Not to-night, Sam."

"To-morrow night, then?"

"I guess so. I would not go at all, Sam, only—
well, I get snubbed on every hand at home. Father
scolds, and mother looks solemn, and the house is
awful lonesome. Mag and Lou are too refined to
enjoy my company, and so I 've either got to set and
mope, or hunt company away from home. Will
says it was just so when he was here; but my! do n't
he have gay times now! He says he would n't stay
here for any thing, and as soon as I 'm old enough I
mean to go, too; then I guess I won't get scolded
every time I break one of the rules of etiquette," and
there was a sneer in the boy's voice.

"Good for you!" responded his companion, with
a laugh.   "Hope you'll be man enough to cut your
leading strings shortly."

"Hush," said Eddie softly.   "I'll go to-morrow
night if you'll meet me here.   I do n't feel right
about it, though.   I believe mother's fretting about
Will's doings, and that makes her look so blue lately.
May be I'd better not come this time."

"Bah! tied to mammy's apron-string," sneered
Huffman.

For a moment Eddie hesitated, but the fear of
ridicule overcame his scruples, and so he promised to
be on time, and they separated.

Mr. Holmes shrank back under the shadow of the
trees as Huffman leaped over the fence and disappeared down the ally.   His first impulse was to call
his son into the house and punish him for keeping
such company.   But the boy's reference to himself
checked him.   Was it true, as Eddie said, that he
scolded about *every thing?*   He did n't mean to be
unkind, but his conscience told him that there was at
least a grain of truth in the boy's words.   He had also
received a revelation respecting his eldest boy.   "Can
it be possible that it is *my* fault that William is so
wild?" he asked himself, with a sigh, as he thought
of his son's reckless ways.   At last he went slowly up
the walk leading to the house.   When he entered the
sitting-room, Eddie was sitting by the table reading
a book as quietly as if he had not been holding a
clandestine meeting with the rough of the village.
The father sat down very quietly and took out his
evening paper.   Maggie, the eldest daughter, was in

the parlor practicing a piece of new music; Louisa, the younger daughter, was curled upon the lounge, reading a novel, while the mother sat mending some of the rents made by the little ones through the day. Altogether it was a very silent company. Presently Eddie said he was sleepy, and shut up his book, bid them good-night, and went to his room.

For some time the father sat thinking of what he could do to save his boy. At last he decided to ask the advice of his wife and daughters, and turning to Louisa said, in a troubled voice:

"Lou, lay by your book for a while, and tell Maggie to come here; I want to talk with you."

Mrs. Holmes looked up, startled at the husky sound of her husband's voice. "Is there something wrong with your business?" she asked timidly.

"No, I am afraid it is worse than that," he answered bitterly.

When they were all seated around the table Mr. Holmes told them of the conversation which he had overheard, not even keeping back his son's comments on his own temper. When he had finished, Lou, who was only three years older than Eddie, was crying quietly.

"O papa, am I to blame?" she asked tearfully. "I guess we are *all* to blame in part; but what are we going to do? This meeting must not take place if we can prevent it."

Finally it was decided that, as the father had some business in the city, he should go in the morning and take Lou and Edward with him and spend the Sabbath. Eddie had begged to go shortly before, but his father had told him he "could n't be bothered with a boy."

In the morning when they were at breakfast the father announced his intention of spending Sabbath in the city, and suggested that two of the family accompany him. Maggie shook her head; she was "too busy." Lou declared she was always ready to go.

"Well," said Mr. Holmes, "that is only one. Edward, do n't you want to go?"

"May I?" he asked doubtfully. The boy had already half repented his promise to Sam Huffman.

"Yes, you may go, if you like; it will make up for your disappointment yesterday afternoon," said his father, kindly. The tones more than the words, touched the boy, and he fidgeted uneasily in his chair. At last he turned away his head and coughed to hide his feelings.

"Yes, sir; I would like very much to go, if I will not be in the way."

They went to the city, and for once Mr. Holmes exerted himself to please and entertain his boy, and was himself surprised to find how much pleasure he found in the effort. Edward returned home delighted with his visit. and the sisters, who had been frightened at what their father had overheard, set themselves to work to make home more pleasant for their brother, while the father and mother decided that it was better to punish him with innocent amusement at home than that he should seek for amusement in sinful company.

Nothing more was heard of the meeting with

Sam Huffman; but one evening in the Autumn, when Mr. Holmes had taken the girls to a concert and Edward was alone with his mother, he told her how near he had come to going away with Sam, never to come back.

"I wouldn't have thought of going," he said; "but there seemed a place for every one but me, and I felt that I was in the way, and only a bother. But I guess I was mistaken about it; father lets me help him sometimes now, and he's real patient with me, too, though I am afraid, mother, I shall never learn to close doors after me or walk softly across a room," he said, smiling up in his mother's face.

Mrs. Holmes stooped and kissed the forehead of the big boy at her feet, and said gently:

"You are never in our way, my son."

But she never told him how his father had over-heard the conversation between him and Sam, nor how hard they had all worked to keep him out of such company. After a little pause, Eddie said:

"Mother, I wish Will would come home."

The mother sighed. "I am afraid your brother would not like the restraints of home."

And there the subject dropped for the time. But one day Mr. Holmes's head clerk told him he had been offered a partnership in a respectable firm, and had accepted it, and in a month or so would go into business for himself. Then Edward asked his father to write and offer Will the place.

"He is too reckless for so responsible a position, and he wouldn't accept it from *me* any way," objected the father.

"Try him, please. Let me take the letter to him," pleaded the boy. Finally Mr. Holmes consented, and Edward went to the city with the letter.

"Yes," sneered Will, when he had read the letter, "he wants me there so he can watch me and lecture me as he used to."

"No, Will, you're mistaken. Father isn't one bit like he used to be. He and I have real good times together now, and the girls are jolly, I tell you. Just as fashionable as ever, but they try to make a fellow have a good time at home. Mother looks pale and sad, but I guess its grieving about you. Of course, she wants you home," he added, hastily, as he saw Will's face flush at the implied rebuke. "Come, Will, say you'll accept."

"Give me a week to think about it," pleaded Will.

"No, sir! I won't give you an hour. We all want you home, and the girls will hug you 'most to death when you get there."

"Some danger," muttered Will; "too much afraid of soiling their finery to allow me to come within a rod of them."

"No, they're not; I tell you they're not one bit like they used to be. Besides, I want a big brother to counsel with," urged Edward.

"I wonder they're not afraid I'll ruin *your* morals if I come home," said Will, defiantly.

"Hush, Will," said the boy, with a pained look; "I tell you we all want you home. Say yes, for it is nearly train time."

"Well, yes, then; how soon must I come?"

"Right away, if you can; father said you would want some instruction from Brown before he goes out."

"Well, I 'll be down in a week, then," answered the brother, slowly; and then, with a smile, "Ned, you 're a splendid pleader; father will spoil a first-class lawyer, if he makes a merchant of you."

And so they parted.

In a week Will was back in the old home, feeling restrained and awkward, but glad to be there, notwithstanding. The next morning, Mr. Holmes told his son he would like to see him in the library, for a little while, and Will thought: "Now for an old-time lecture." But he was mistaken; not a word of reproach—only an explanation of the responsibility of the position he was about to take, and what he should expect of him; and then the father said kindly:

"When you were younger, William, I am afraid I did n't quite understand you and sympathize with you, as I might have done; but I did n't intend to be hard on you. I hope you will feel now that my greatest desire is to see you prosperous and happy. I am getting old, and need your company and help. In my old days, I hope to give up my business to you and Edward, if you will take it."

"Can you trust me, father? I have not lived as steadily as I ought;" and Will spoke with heightening color.

"But you will do better now, will you not?"

"Yes, father; indeed I will, if you will only trust me and forgive me," answered the young man, his eyes fixed on the floor.

"I have something to be forgiven for, too," answered the father, with his eyes full of tears, as he rose and placed his hand on the bowed head of his son. "I have been hasty and impatient with you very often; God help me to be more patient with my children in the future."

"Do n't, father, do n't," sobbed the young man; "I can 't bear it; I do n't deserve your confidence, but I will try to do better now."

In a few days William Holmes went to work in his father's store, with a firm determination to give up his old habits. By the assistance of his father's sympathy and his mother's prayers, aided by the cheerful home influence which his sisters threw round him, he did finally gain the victory over self, and in after years, when William and Edward were steady business men, taking the burden from their father's shoulders, neither parents nor sisters regretted their efforts to "save the boys."

SAVED AS BY FIRE.

In Three Chapters.

CHAPTER I.

THE face that looked up from the hospital bed was not *all* bad, although the marks of sin were plainly visible; and even while you looked into the face the eyelids would droop as if to ward off your scrutiny—as if afraid you would read there the mistakes and misdeeds of the past. The hospital nurse was passing, and, pausing for a moment as he came to the bed, he straightened the covering, arranged the pillow a little more comfortably, and smoothed back, with a hand as gentle as a woman's, the patient's hair, that had grown to unusual length and which gave a stronger emphasis to the already haggard expression of his face.

"Thank you: you are very kind," he said gratefully, then added, "Every body is kind to me here, but I believe I am a little homesick to-day."

"Then why not take my advice and write to the home folks? My word, you'll feel the better for it," answered the nurse with an encouraging smile.

"O, it's not worth while. They've forgotten me long ago, I presume," with an effort at indifference in his tone and manner.

"Home folks don't forget a fellow as easily as

you think, young man. . Any way, better write, and remind them of your existence," and with this injunction the kind-hearted nurse passed on to the next patient.

During the past few weeks the nurse had repeatedly urged this young patient to write to his sister, and ask to be taken into her home. But pride and shame, together with a sort of independence of character, had prevented him thus far from asking such a favor from one whose advice he had rejected years before, and so he had hesitated even while his heart hungered for his sister's presence.

For months he had been an inmate of the hospital, and for a time his life had hung in the balance. At last, however, the physicians said he would live, but gave him no encouragement to hope ever to walk again.

When the verdict of the physicians was made known to him he had uttered an audible groan and turned away his face to hide the expression of the pain the announcement had caused him.

"Better *dead* than helpless," he muttered hopelessly. "Why did n't you let me die when I was so near it?" he had asked, bitterly, when the nurse, seeing his despondency, had tried to cheer him a little.

"You were ready to die, I suppose," the man had answered, eyeing him quietly.

"No, not exactly, but as nearly ready as I am likely to be," and he turned away as if to shut out the thoughts that would crowd up.

For days he had lain brooding over the prospect before him. "Nothing but the hospital or the alms-house " he would say with a gesture of loathing and with a shudder as he thought of his future. To a young man who had builded so many castles in the air in former years the prospect was certainly not a pleasing one.

"But it is as good as I deserve. I might have known my sin would find me out, and I was taught better." And as his memory reverted to his early training, he could but acknowledge to himself that if he had heeded those instructions he would have escaped this terrible affliction and humiliation.

On the morning on which my story begins, Allen Howard was, as he said, " homesick." There had come over him such a longing for friends as he had not experienced since the day when, but a boy, he had gone out from the home roof full of hope to make his way in the world. Full of good intentions and with high anticipations of the future, he had gone out expecting "to see something of the world," but with the determination to avoid its vices, even though anxious for a share in what he called its harmless pleasures.

But the enemy of souls, ever on the track of homeless ones, had gained victory after victory over the inexperienced and unguarded boy; trifling victories apparently, yet full of importance, as they held the destiny of his future years. Appetite for strong drink, with all its attendant vices, crept about him, and before he was aware of his danger he was so completely in the toils that not only was he one of the fast young men whose companion he was, but also a transgressor of the law.

Evil companions who cared for him only because he was agreeable, and because they saw that his pliable nature would make him a convenient tool for their purposes, had led him on step by step, until the teachings of his mother and the counsel of a sister were alike neglected and forgotten.

But now he had time to think of the past, and in his hours of lonely suffering all the teachings of that mother, the loving words, the kindly reproofs and faithful warning came to him like voices from the grave, awakening all his better feelings, feelings that had been lulled to sleep for months and years; and with these awakenings came an unutterable longing for home and loved ones. He had found friends among nurses and physicians, more than he had dared to hope for under the circumstances; but their kindly care and words only served to increase his longing for home friends and faces,—for the sister who had soothed his boyish trouble and shared his childhood sports.

The father had died when his boy was but two years old, and the mother had gone to her reward when he was but twelve, her prayers for her boy's salvation yet unanswered. But He who treasures up the prayers and tears of his children had not forgotten the petitions of that mother, and now, on a bed of affliction, Howard's thoughts were being drawn toward God as memory recalled the loving counsels which had been unheeded at the time, and which he had almost forgotten. All his better nature was aroused, and at night when he could not sleep for pain, he would lie wondering if the sister he had not

seen for ten years had forgotten *him* as he had her
words of warnings, wondering if she would like to see
him again.   Two years had passed since he had written her, and she, of course, was ignorant of his where-
abouts; and his first thought, when he found himself in the hands of the law, had been to conceal his
real name, so that she need not know nor share his
shame; and only to his nurse, and on the pledge of
silence, had he made known his real name.

Sometimes he would almost decide to write to his
sister, and tell her all; then would come the thought:
"How *can* I?   Will not she and her husband despise me when they know how low I have fallen?
No, I 'll bear it alone," he would say with com-
pressed though quivering lips, ashamed almost of his
own weakness.   And for a while he would stifle the
longings of his heart rather than be a burden or a
disgrace to his friends.   But try as he might, home
faces and home voices would come to him in a way
he could not resist.   The blessed Christ was drawing him closer to himself by means of these home
ties.

Finally, one day after a severe struggle with con-
tending thoughts, he took up the pen and paper,
which the nurse had placed by his bed, determined
to write and ask his sister to take him home, though
he could not yet bring himself to tell her the story
of his past life.   With trembling hand he wrote:

"DEAR SISTER HELEN: It has been a long time
since I have written to or heard from you.   I have
been sick for months, and am still an invalid.   The

doctors say there is but little hope that I will ever walk again. It seems terribly hard, *only twenty-three years old, and a cripple for life.* I want to see your face and hear your voice again, O, so much. But my past life has not been such as you would approve of; but I can not tell you all now, though I feel as if I ought. Sister, will you be as kind to me now as you were when I was but a boy? Will you take me on trust, and be patient with me for a little while? *Sometime* I will tell you all about myself, if you will only not ask me now. I need your help more than ever before, and yet I dislike to ask it of you, knowing that I do not deserve it; but you were always so kind that I dared run the risk. Write and tell me your decision.　　　　Your brother,

"ALLEN."

Wearily folding the letter he placed it in its envelope and laid it on the table by his bed. In less than half an hour he had repented having written it, and twice he took it up with the intention of destroying it, but something held him back till at last, weary in body and mind, he fell asleep. When he awoke an hour later the letter had disappeared.

His faithful nurse had seen the struggle, and fearing he would change his mind, had dropped it in the hospital letter-box. When Howard found that his letter was gone, he lay thinking over what he had written and wishing he could recall it. But it was too late. The missive was on its way, and he fell to wondering as to what sort of a reception would be given it.

One moment he seemed to see his sister, as she was in her girlhood—fresh and rosy-cheeked, full of life, yet with a sort of motherly care, watching over and advising him. She was but seven years his senior, and yet she had always assumed the prerogative of guarding and controlling his actions, so far as she could—now checking his headlong fun, and now joining with all her heart in some innocent amusement, or helping him in his studies—and as he remembered how proud she used to seem when he had a good lesson or did some noble act, the tears filled his eyes and fell upon his pillow.

"O, I can never tell her! she will despise me!" he would sob, half-aloud. "I hope she will not get the letter; I would rather die here among strangers than have her know all about my life." And then, indignant at himself, as he thought of his wasted years, he would mutter: "What a fool I have been!"

In due time, the letter reached its destination, and Mrs. Hildreth, while shocked and grieved at the news it brought her, was a true sister, full of love for the brother whom she had not seen since he had left home, when but a boy just entering upon his teens.

He was a man now, in years; sinful he might be, but still her brother, whom a dying mother had committed to her care. He had long since gone beyond her care, but now an opportunity was offered by which she could once more regain something of the influence of earlier years, and it only needed her husband's consent before she could respond to the pleading letter, and invite the wanderer home. This consent was readily obtained, and she at once wrote to the homeless one that he need be homeless no longer.

Three weeks had passed, and Howard had almost come to the conclusion that his letter had been lost or that his plea had been rejected. As this feeling began to take possession of him, he realized how much his heart had been set upon seeing his sister, and how strong the hope had been that she would send for him to come home, and the thought that he was cast off by his only sister was as painful as it was humiliating.

But a letter came at last, bearing not the post-mark of his native town, but of a village in the south-west. His sister and her family had removed during the years of his silence, and he had not learned of the fact.

It was with hands trembling with anxiety that he broke the seal, and looked at the signature to assure himself as to the writer.

Yes, it was from Helen.

A loving letter, inviting him to her home and heart; a brief sketch of her husband and children — none of whom he had seen — but not a word of reproof for the wanderer, either direct or implied. A sisterly letter, full of hopefulness and comforting words; a few sentences reminding him of the Savior's yearning love for the wandering ones, and then a second invitation to come home.

"The *old* home is in the hands of strangers, and we are in the West; but you will not mind that, if you are able for the journey. My house is neither large nor costly, but there is room enough in it for my sick brother, and Mr. Hildreth joins me in saying, come as soon as you can. If it were possible to leave home, one of us would come to you; but Mr. Hildreth's presence is needed in his business, and my children need *me*, but we shall expect you soon."

How often did Allen read over that letter—the invitation to come home. At last he laid it, wet with his tears, under his pillow, and fell to counting the days which must pass before he could see the writer.

CHAPTER II.

AT last the physician decided that he was strong enough to undertake the journey, and, bidding goodbye to those who had been so kind to him during the past weary months, he started—an invalid, to be sure, but stronger than he had dared to hope.

As he neared his journey's end, he was conscious of a sensation of dread creeping into his heart. How could he meet all the inquiries about his past life? Some one would be certain to probe him with questions, and how could he answer?

He almost felt as if it would be better to be back in the hospital, dreary as it had seemed at times, than to have to meet all the questionings and the suspicious looks which he felt would be cast upon him.

He had not written of his starting, and when the village hack drew up before his sister's door, they were scarcely expecting him.

Slowly and with the help of the driver and another passenger, he descended from the hack, and was met at the door of the unpretentious dwelling by a matronly woman, who did not need to be told that this was the long-lost brother.

A tearful, though cordial, greeting — not many words, both hearts were too full for words — and in a few minutes Allen Howard was lying in his sister's sitting-room, weary and worn, with his long journey, with tears, which he tried vainly to hide, stealing down his pale face, and yet with a feeling of comfort and restfulness such as he had not known during the long months of his affliction.

After a few words, Mrs. Hildreth, with wise thoughtfulness, left him alone, to rest and sleep until tea was ready.

Then his brother-in-law came in, and said, with cheery tones:

"And this is Allen, I suppose. Glad you have reached us safely, my boy. We shall soon have you strong again, I hope."

The greeting, so unexpectedly cordial, was more than the poor prodigal could bear, and he could only return his brother's cordial grasp with a feeble effort, and then turn away his face, to hide his emotion.

As the family gathered about the table, and Allen was placed in a seat opposite his sister, and the children, four in number, were introduced to "Uncle Allen," the invalid felt that his home coming had not been so unpleasant as he had feared.

The first evening passed off quietly, and the days grew into weeks and no explanation of the past had been asked or given; yet the young man felt that it would be a relief if he could pour out all the miserable story in his sister's ears, and receive the comfort and counsel which he felt she could give.

Their beautiful home-life seemed a constant reminder of how far he was separated from them, and, while Mrs. Hildreth would have felt grieved if she had known his thoughts, yet he could not help feeling that he, with all his dark past clinging to him, had no right to be there.

They were all so thoughtful of his comfort, and the one topic which he had so dreaded was so carefully avoided, that he began to feel they deserved his confidence, although, with instinctive shame, he shrank from giving it.

Even Mr. Hildreth, whom he had so dreaded to meet, had taken to him very kindly; and, in truth, they had, to use his own expression, "taken him on trust."

Once, a few weeks after his coming into their home, when his sister had been doing some little, thoughtful kindness for him, he had said:

"Helen, it seems hardly fair to refuse to give you my confidence, when you are so kind and patient, and, above all, trust me so; but I hate so to think of the past, and it is so pleasant to feel that you trust me. O, if I could only blot out the past ten years, and begin again!"

Mrs. Hildreth looked at him with a quiet, pitying smile.

"If my brother can only trust all the past mistakes of his life to his Savior, I shall be satisfied, even though he does not see proper to tell *me* all about it. I am in no hurry, Allen."

"But you shall know some day, sister," with a wistful look in the pale face.

Mrs. Hildreth, seeing his distressed look, placed her hand over his lips, as if she would treat the matter very lightly. "One would think you had been a dreadful boy to hear you talk. Let us hear no more about it until I give you permission. I am not going to have my patient worrying about trifles."

But Howard was not satisfied. The more he looked back over his past life the more he felt condemned. He was trying to get into the life which he was assured his sister and her husband were living, but the way seemed dark, and every step uncertain and new. In his wanderings he had tried to forget God, and now, when he would get into the right path, his way seemed hedged up. He longed to make a full confession, to tell his sister just what he had been, and then to lean upon her for counsel and help. But the consciousness that he should probably lose their esteem deterred him from day to day, and yet instead of peace coming to his anxious heart, the burden only grew heavier. He was still an invalid, and though there was some improvement, he had but little hope of ever being restored to his former strength. Longing for sympathy and counsel, such as he knew he could only receive when his story was known, he resolved at last to risk all and unburden his heart to his sister, who had so kindly taken him into her home and heart.

One evening, as he sat in his arm-chair, in the shadow of the room where Mrs. Hildreth was also sitting, with her mending-basket by her side, he said:

"Helen, leave your work for a little while and sit here by me. I want to talk with you."

She readily complied with his request and drew her chair to his side, the flickering light of the fire and the shaded lamp only partially lighting up their faces.

"Well, what is it?" Mrs. Hildreth asked, after waiting for several minutes, and Allen had made no sign of beginning to talk.

"Are the children in bed?" he asked, in a low tone.

"Yes, and asleep. Do you want them?"

"No; but I do n't want them to hear what I have to say to-night. I must tell you the story I have kept back so long."

"But, Allen, you need not," interposed his sister, as she saw his agitation.

"Yes, I *need*. I shall never feel quite right until you know. It 's an ugly story, but I shall be no worse after I tell you than I was before. Do n't interrupt me, and do n't run away from me; but I expect you 'll hate me when you know how bad I have been."

And then, in a voice which he forced to be steady, he told of the years since he had gone out from the home roof. How he had been led, step by step, into bad company and bad habits, and how he had tried to forget God and his mother's counsel, and had gone on from bad to worse until, under the influence of drink, he had committed a crime from the penalty of which he had only escaped because a wound, received in his arrest, had rendered him a cripple, and the judge had considered his punishment sufficient.

He repeated the whole shameful story in a low voice, as if he was afraid the very walls would hear and repeat his secret. When he finished, his sister was sitting with her face buried in her hands, weeping bitterly. Allen shook with intense agitation, while the perspiration stood in great drops upon his forehead. It was over now. She knew all the terrible secret which he had so dreaded to tell, and now came the reaction. He wished he had not told her, and if it had been possible he would have recalled every word.

There was a silence for some moments, broken only by his sister's sobs. At last, unable to endure the suspense, he said, pleadingly:

"Helen."

His voice seemed to arouse her, and she put out her hand with a pitiful gesture.

"O Allen, how could you? O, our poor mother." And then she gave .way to fresh sobs of grief and wounded family pride.

They had never been a very wealthy family, but they had been an honorable one, for whose record they had never had reason to blush. But now this terrible story seemed to crush her to the earth. She had expected to hear of some wild pranks, but nothing so bad as this, and the thought that her brother was a criminal was more than she could calmly endure, under the first sense of shame and disgrace.

Allen had leaned forward in his chair, supporting himself on his crutch, and reached out his hand as if to take hers; but when she spoke his mother's name, he drew back as if he had received a blow.

"Do n't, Helen, do n't speak of her in that way. I know I have disgraced her and you; but do n't hate me, though God knows I hate myself for my weakness. But it was an awful temptation."

Then seeing she did not answer nor raise her head, he said, desperately:

"If *you* turn against me. I had better have died at the first."

The pleading, half-scared tone aroused Mrs. Hildreth, and with an effort she checked her sobs. Kneeling by the side of her prodigal but thoroughly repentant brother, she laid her face, still wet with tears, upon his shoulder.

"No, no; I do n't hate you, and I shall not turn against you; but O Allen, it seems like an awful dream. I can not realize that *my brother* could do such a thing. I am glad our mother is not here to suffer, too."

"O sister. I have suffered so much because of it. It may be if mother had lived it would not have happened; but you did your part, and no one can blame you for my sin. But you do n't know what it is to be without friends or money, home or employment," pleaded Allen, his breath coming thick and fast, as if he would suffocate. "If I were not so helpless, I might go away where you would not be mortified by my presence; but"—

"Hush;" and Mrs. Hildreth started at the strangeness of his tone; and as she interrupted him she looked into his face, and was shocked at the look of intense suffering visible there.

"Hush, Allen, your place is here with me," she said, with sudden calmness, rising and smoothing back his hair from his forehead. "You have sinned, but you have suffered enough already. I will not add to it."

For some moments she sat by his side without a word. Her mind was busy over the problem of leading this poor sinful, sin-sick soul back to the arms of the tender Shepherd.

Presently Allen said:

"You don't quite hate me then, Helen?"

"No; but I am so sorry, my poor brother. You must ask God's forgiveness; your sin is against him, not me."

"But I have lived so far away from him that I do not deserve to be forgiven," was the hopeless reply.

"It is not a question as to what you *deserve*, but what you *need*, and your willingness to take what God offers."

Allen reached out his hand, and, taking his sister's in his, he laid it against his face, with a caressing motion.

"I don't know as I can make you understand how I feel; you have always been so good that you can't feel as I do, who have never done any thing right, scarcely. Some way, it looks mean to ask God to forgive me, now that I am where I can't help myself. If I could only do something to prove that I am sincere!"

"He knows all about you. It is because you can not do any thing that he offers you pardon.

You have nothing to pay with, and so it must be a free gift, if you are saved; but *his* words are better than mine," and Mrs. Hildreth, drawing the lamp nearer to her, took up her Bible, to read a few passages of Scripture especially suited to her brother's case. Allen looked at the book, and said regretfully:

"If I had read that book more, and heeded its teachings, I need not be as I am to-night."

"Don't spend time in useless regrets. You have sinned, but you are sorry. God knows it; now look from yourself to his mercy."

Thus, patiently and lovingly, did this Christian woman point her brother to Christ. Here and there she read such passages as were especially suited to his need. And he, in utter humiliation, was ready to be taught; he was the child again, submitting to the wiser and stronger hand of his sister, and he drank in her words as if he were famishing.

At last, he looked up into her face, and noticing how pale and worn she looked, laid his hand over the page, saying:

"There, sister, do not read any more; you are tired out. I have been so selfish not to remember that you were weary, but I was so hungry for your words. Don't let the children know of this; I couldn't bear for them to have a doubt of me," and then, as he heard Mr. Hildreth's step, returning from the office: "There is John; *you* must tell him, *I* can't. It may be he will not want me here when he knows the worst."

And the lips quivered, though he tried to speak bravely.

His face flushed as his brother spoke to him, inquiring after his welfare, and Mrs. Hildreth, seeing how weary he was, insisted on his retiring for the night.

CHAPTER III.

In their own room, Mrs. Hildreth told her husband the story of her brother's fall, and also of his evident repentance, adding, timidly:

"Allen half expects you to send him away when you know what he has done."

"Helen!" Mr. Hildreth's tone was full of pained surprise. "I hope I have not forgotten that it is not my own goodness that has saved me from like sins. I should be a strange disciple of Christ if I should thus offend one of his little ones."

"You are not angry with him, then?"

"No, certainly not; it is a bad piece of business, and no mistake, but we'll not make it any worse, if we can help it."

Mrs. Hildreth's nerves had been overstrained by the excitement of the evening, and, now that her task was done, and there was no longer a necessity for a calm demeanor, she gave way to her feelings, and sobbed on her husband's shoulder, as if her heart would break.

Her tears did her good, however, and with patient kindness and true Christian gentleness did her husband soothe and comfort her, until her sobs ceased and she could lie down quietly to rest.

To say that the story had caused him pain and astonishment, would scarcely do justice to Mr. Hil-

28

dreth's real state of mind. He had suspected wrong-doing of some kind; yet, like the sister, he had not supposed that it was as bad as had been revealed. He was a proud man, and very jealous of the honor of his own children, and he had hoped they would be spared any thing like real disgrace or shame; and now it was upon them, in a way he could not remedy nor resist.

His good sense and Christian spirit, however, enabled him to decide that it was best to give his brother all the help he could, and as he seemed to be really sorry for the past, he should have a fair chance to amend, and, so far as it was possible, make a new start.

As for Howard, his confession had lifted a bur-den from his heart; the dread that his sister should know the past had hung over him like a sword of vengeance, marring every moment of his otherwise peaceful life. Now that she knew, and was not only willing to forgive, but ready to instruct and guide him, his heart was lighter; and, while he dared not hope that her husband would be equally ready to forgive and forget, yet he hoped for forbearance, at least.

It was with a flushed cheek that he looked up to return Mr. Hildreth's greeting, on the following morning, as he sat in his arm-chair by the fire, when he entered the room, and his eyes quickly fell to the floor, as if afraid to meet his brother's gaze.

Mr. Hildreth saw the look, and, quickly guessing its cause, came forward, and, placing a hand on either of Howard's shoulders, looked down into the face that would not look into his, saying, with fatherly kindness:

"My boy, this has been a sad affair, all the way through; but it is in the past now. Do n't worry over it too much. I am glad you decided to trust us at last; I felt certain you would some time, and now, perhaps, we can help you."

Poor Allen! He could have endured reproof, and even harsh words he could have braced himself against; but this hearty, unreserved forgiveness was wholly unexpected, and he wept like a child.

Grasping his brother's hand in both of his, he sobbed:

"O John, you are too kind; I did n't expect this!"

"What did you expect, then? That I would turn against you, because I did n't happen to be tempted as you were? I trust I am a Christian."

"I *know* it—I *know* it! and you have been kind to me all along. If I had had your help during these years, I believe I should n't have gone so far wrong as I did."

"Well, come now, we 've said enough about this." And Mr. Hildreth laid his hand upon Allen's head, as if he were a child, instead of a man: "You are not to fret yourself sick again; we understand each other, and there is no use in calling up the past; we 'll just shut it out from this on."

"But you would n't have me forget it all, would you?" asked Allen, looking up at last, with grateful eyes.

"No danger of that; but we 'll try to help you

to a new life—much better than the old one, we hope. You 've trusted to us, and you shall never be sorry for that part, at any rate.''

Allen tried to murmur his thanks for all these kind words, very humbly, and with a voice full of emotion.

After a few moments, he said:

''I shall always be a burden to you; that's another of my punishments, I suppose. If I could only do something to earn a living, instead of depending on you and Helen!''

Mr. Hildreth looked at his brother, without replying, for a moment, and then turned his eyes toward the fire, as if in deep thought. Presently he said:

''You must not allow that to trouble you; when *we* feel that you are a burden, it will be soon enough for you to begin fretting. Of course, you will be more contented if you could be employed; I have considerable trouble sometimes to get a competent person to do my copying; I would as soon pay you as any one, when you are able to do it.''

''O, I am sure I could be of some service if you will only give me the chance, and I can not bear to be entirely dependent.''

''I wonder I did not think of it before,'' said Mr. Hildreth, kindly. ''As soon as you feel that you are able I will bring some home, and you can do it here. It will be more agreeable probably.''

''I think I could do a little to-day, if you are willing to try me,'' and Howard's face lighted up at the thought of going to work.

"Very well, that settles it. I will bring some down at noon; but remember you must go slowly at first, until you become a little stronger; we can't have you overdoing yourself; when I find you at that I shall withdraw my patronage."

And so it was settled that, so far as his strength would permit, Allen should act as copyist for his brother, and by this means he was made to feel that he was not entirely a burden.

The past was dropped. Never by word or sign did Mr. or Mrs. Hildreth refer to it, and when, by and by, he was enabled by faith to come into the new life of a believer in Christ, he could better understand the spirit of love that had made them so gentle with the wanderer.

Time rolled on, and Allen had come to enjoy his home and his sister's family. The discipline he had received had done him good, and six years of experience and pure living had removed most of the marks of sin from his face. One thing which puzzled his sister was his apparent contentment with his lot.

One day, when one of his little nieces was engaged in a childish romp, she asked, with evident regret:

"O Uncle Allen, don't you wish you could walk?"

He looked up at his sister with a queer smile on his face, and then at the little questioner, with a shake of the head: "I don't know, little one. I guess I am better off as I am."

When the child had left the room, he said: "You look as if you doubted my sincerity, Helen."

"No, I don't doubt you; but I don't think I understand you very well."

"Suppose this had not come to me, and I had succeeded in my plans, then I should, very likely, have gone on in crime until I had become a hardened criminal. God knew what was best for me, and placed me where I had time to think."

"But you are stronger now, and if you were physically well, you would be strong enough morally to resist temptation."

"I don't know; perhaps so, perhaps not. I should be afraid to risk it. I may be a coward, but I feel so safe here in your quiet, Christian home, that I doubt whether I should care to face the world again, even if I could. John has taken away one of my trials by giving me work. I am not entirely useless, and if God sees fit to keep me here the rest of my days, I am content. It has been an awful discipline, but some way I can not help being grateful for it. I am a cripple, but he has saved my soul, even though saved as by fire."

Years have passed, and Allen Howard, leaning on God's promises, is growing nearer and nearer to a perfect Christian manhood. His chastening has made him humble and his helplessness has taught him faith, not only in God, but in man. Though he went astray, the Shepherd sought him and brought him back; though he sinned, he repented, and was forgiven, and can say, "It is good for me that I have been afflicted, for now have I kept thy law.".